Reason & Riots

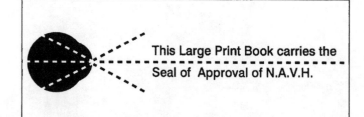

This Large Print Book carries the
Seal of Approval of N.A.V.H.

HOMESTEAD SERIES
BOOK THREE

Reason & Riots

Stephen Bly

Thorndike Press • Waterville, Maine

Published in 2006 by arrangement with Crossway Books, a division of Good News Publishers.

Thorndike Press® Large Print Christian Historical Fiction.

The tree indicium is a trademark of Thorndike Press.

The text of this Large Print edition is unabridged. Other aspects of the book may vary from the original edition.

Set in 16 pt. Plantin by Myrna S. Raven.

Printed in the United States on permanent paper.

Library of Congress Cataloging-in-Publication Data

Bly, Stephen A., 1944–
  Reason & riots / by Stephen Bly.
    p. cm. — (Homestead series ; bk. 3)
    ISBN 0-7862-8685-7 (lg. print : hc : alk. paper)
    1. Rural families — Fiction. 2. Nebraska — Fiction.
  3. Large type books. 4. Domestic fiction. I. Title.
  II. Title: Reason and riots. III. Series: Bly, Stephen A.,
  1944– Homestead series ; bk. 3.
  PS3552.L93R425 2006
  813′.54—dc22   2006010242

*For
Lindsay Ailor,
my pal
and a true
cowboy
girl*

Wherein they think it strange

that ye run not with them

to the same excess of riot . . .

1 PETER 4:4 (KJV)

One

"Sudsy ain't comin' to school no more, Miss Jolie." Cabin Johnstone flopped down in the last row of benches at the back of the one-room sod schoolhouse just as Bullet Wells rang the huge brass bell that hung above the front porch. Cabin's head collapsed on his arms, which were folded on the table in front of him. His words were barely audible. "His mama said he got run over by a train yesterday evenin' and died at sunrise."

"What?" Jolie Bowers coughed out the word as if it were a hunk of grizzled, unchewed meat.

"Sudsy's dead. He got crushed in the train yard in Scottsbluff, but I don't want to talk about it," Cabin replied.

Estelle Bowers clamped her hand over her mouth.

May and June Vockney began to sob.

Patsy Meeker whispered the Lord's Prayer.

Portie Tidwell bit his pencil in two.

Jolie clutched the white lace bodice of her gold percale dress and fought to breathe. *No, no . . . this can't be hap-*

pening. What am I supposed to do?

Biting his lip, Gibson Bowers stomped out of the classroom, mumbling, "I need a recess."

Jolie brushed tears from her smooth, pale cheeks. *Little brother is right.* "Class, I believe we all need a recess."

Bullet Wells scratched his head with both hands, leaving cowlicks like horns in his bushy brown hair. "We just got here."

"This news about Sudsy is quite shocking." Jolie pressed her fingertips against her temples. "We all need some fresh air. Let's go out and sit on the steps."

"Do we need our coats, Miss Jolie?" Patsy Meeker asked.

"I believe the wind died down. It should be fine."

After some moments of confusion, with several students taking trips to the privy, the twenty-one students gathered on the front steps of the western Nebraska one-room schoolhouse.

Cabin Johnstone leaned his head on Jolie's shoulder and cried without making a sound. She hugged the twelve-year-old and rocked him back and forth. On her left side, Peteluma Meeker, the youngest student at six years old, laid her head in Jolie's lap.

Greg Wells tossed a rock toward the foundation of the new school construction. "Miss Jolie, what happens when we die?" he asked.

"I'll tell you all what I know. That might a good question to ask your parents or your preacher. But the Bible says that Jesus is preparing a place in heaven for all who belong to Him, and He will come back for them and take them home."

"Does everyone go to heaven, Miss Jolie?" Mary Vockney asked.

"No, they don't, Mary. A person needs to invite Jesus into his life."

Lippy Brown chewed on his fingernail. "Do you think Sudsy is in heaven?"

"I didn't know Sudsy very well yet. He was only here for four weeks. But he seemed like a very happy, inquisitive boy. We can trust the Lord to be fair," Jolie assured him.

April Vockney ran her fingers through her long blonde hair. "What do you think it feels like to die?"

Jolie looked away and brushed the tears from the corners of her eyes with her fingertips. "I would think it feels scary, since we are sometimes afraid of the unknown. Perhaps lonely too. We have to leave loved ones behind."

"Mama wasn't scared," Landen Yarrow murmured.

"Oh, sweetie, I forgot." She reached out and hugged the eight-year-old. "You were with your mama when she died, weren't you?"

Tears streamed down the boy's scrubbed-clean pink cheeks. His chin and shoulders slumped. "Mama had me hold her hand. She said, 'Good-bye, dear Landen. Grow strong and faithful and brave. I'll be waiting for you.' Then the wrinkles on her forehead disappeared, and she reached toward the ceiling and said, 'Yes . . . I'm coming.' Then she went to sleep, and I couldn't wake her up."

Jolie grabbed her linen handkerchief from the sleeve of her dress. *Lord, I'm too young to have this responsibility. I'm barely eighteen. I don't know what to say. I don't know what to do. Please help me.*

Portie Tidwell yanked up the back of his duckings, which on any other day would have caused the girls to giggle. "Miss Jolie, why did this have to happen?"

"And why did it have to happen to Sudsy?" Cabin Johnstone added.

"We live in a world where accidents, disease, and disasters happen."

"Like floods and tornadoes?" Prissy asked.

"Yes, and train accidents," Jolie said.

"My Uncle LeBaron got shot by the neighbor lady, but it weren't no accident," Portie volunteered.

Jolie's voice softened. "Perhaps only the Lord knows why things happen to certain people."

"What're we going to do now, Miss Jolie?" Theo Wells asked. "I don't feel much like studying." He paced in front of the steps. The top button on his long-sleeved white shirt was unfastened.

"I certainly don't feel like teaching. Let's take a fieldtrip. Lawson, you and Gibs bring the team around. I'm lucky to have Stranger and Pilgrim with me today. They can pull all of us in one wagon."

"Where will we go?" Mary Vockney asked.

"We'll go exploring. Everyone get your jackets and lunches. We'll bring the lap blankets too," Jolie instructed.

"What're we going to explore?" Portie asked.

"The bluffs to the north," Jolie replied. "Captain Richardson says he finds arrowheads and Indian pottery up there all the time. We need fresh air and sunlight today.

We'll drive up to the Double-0 Ranch."

"Are we goin' to spend the night?" Bullet Wells asked.

Jolie stood up. *Now that, Lord, would be a frightening experience.* "No, we'll return by the usual time school is over."

"What about our spelling test?" Pammie Meeker queried. "I want to take our spelling test."

Mary Vockney rolled her eyes. "You would."

"No spelling test today," Jolie announced. "Recess is over."

Cabin Johnstone took her hand as they all meandered back into the classroom. "Sudsy was good at recess," he murmured.

Jolie patted the top of his sticky hand. "Yes, you're right. He just might have been the best we had at recess."

"You look tired, darling." Lissa Bowers brushed the auburn bangs back on her daughter's forehead.

"Mama, I didn't know what to say or do. I was so stunned by the news about Sudsy. Then when Landen told us about his mother dying, all I could think of was how I wanted to come home, crawl in my bed, and cry. That's why I took them on an outing. I think I'm too young to be a teacher."

Lissa, her long braid reaching the small of her back, stood eight inches shorter than her daughter. The two women hiked hand in hand from the barn to the sod house. "Jolie Lorita, none of us is ready for such news. I would have done the same."

"I'm afraid I wasn't much help to them, Mama. I think I cried as much as anyone, except maybe Prissy Meeker."

"You were with them. Sometimes that's all it takes. It was real for you too. They know you cared for Sudsy, and you care for them."

"I'm glad it's Friday, Mama. I need some time to think about how to handle this."

The two stopped at the edge of the garden and stared south toward the corn-field, and beyond it to the North Platte River.

"We'll start to pick the corn next week," Lissa Bowers announced. "Daddy said Mr. Armour might be interested in buying it. The railroad wants to ship on the 15th."

"Mama, you did it. You grew corn where they said it couldn't be grown."

"It was Daddy and Lawson's irrigation levees that did it. There has to be some benefit in having half your homestead lower than the river most of the year."

"Mama, you've been working day and night in that cornfield."

"I like to work hard and keep busy, Jolie — you know that. I never learned how to sit still."

Jolie slipped her fingers into her mother's callused hand. "Not even in school?"

"Remember, I had my own governess teaching me until I was twelve. So I didn't really have school like everyone else," Lissa said.

"Did you really chase her off with a bull-whip?" Jolie asked.

Lissa hugged her daughter. "Yes, but that was because she whipped my horse for no other reason than that she accidentally stepped in his poop. I was an embarrassment to my poor parents, I'm sure. Perhaps I still am."

"Mama, that's absurd."

Lissa Bowers pulled her long braid around and twirled it in her hand. "I understand young Mr. Wells almost got left on Sage Flats."

"He said he caught his foot in a rabbit hole and couldn't get loose, but I think he was wanting us all to come look for him."

"So you just drove off without him?"

"Actually, Mama, if you want the truth,

we didn't know he was gone. I had April Vockney count heads. She said we had everyone. I think she counted Lawson twice."

Mrs. Bowers's small mouth opened in a wide grin. "It's a wonder she ever gets past him."

"Anyway, we had started down Nine Mile Canyon when Prissy Meeker hollered that there was an Indian with his shirt off on the top of the cliff, and he was waving at us."

"It was Bullet?" Lissa asked.

"Yes. He was covered with dirt from head to toe. I think he buried himself in the dirt and planned to hop up and scare us."

They stopped by the large river rock and concrete foundation that stretched across the dirt front yard.

"Look," Lissa whispered. "Little sis is playing house again."

In the southwest corner of the foundation, Essie sat on a nail keg next to a calf and a fawn. There was a blue bandanna around the calf's neck. The fawn had on his neck a long, dirty red ribbon that Essie held like a leash. A huge granite boulder served as a table.

"What're you doing?" Jolie called out.

"Francis, Max, and me are pretending we're having tea in my room."

"Your room will be upstairs," Jolie reminded her.

"Yes, but Daddy said my room is straight above this. We're just pretending. Max doesn't even like tea. Frances will drink it if I put sugar in it."

"You need to come in soon and help Jolie Lorita with supper," Lissa said.

"Yes, Mama. I was just trying to get up enough nerve to tell them about Sudsy. Max doesn't like to talk about such things. How can I describe heaven to an orphan fawn?"

"Tell him it's like Montana in May," Jolie suggested.

"Oh, yes!" Essie squealed. "When the wind isn't blowing, and the sky is so deep and blue it almost sucks you right off your feet and into the clouds."

"Yes, that's one way to describe it," Lissa said. "You should write that one down in your book."

"Yes. . . . Perhaps I'll use it in *Estelle Bowers: The Early Years*."

"Send Francis and Max back to the barn and come help big sis." Mrs. Bowers turned to Jolie. "Our house will never progress until we dynamite that boulder. It seems to be a barrier to progress."

"Daddy said he'd try to remember the dynamite this time," Jolie replied.

Mrs. Bowers hiked to the east side of the sod house and stared north, shielding her eyes with her hand.

"Mama, Daddy will be home soon," Jolie encouraged her.

Lissa turned back and wiped her hands on her camel brown skirt. "I know, Jolie, but I'm missing him."

Jolie took her mother's arm. "You said he didn't leave until right before noon. He's only been gone four or five hours."

A coy smile broke across Mrs. Bowers's face. "I know I'm pathetic, but I miss him, Jolie."

"Oh, that kind of 'miss him.'" She tugged her mother's hand. "Come on, Miss Pritchett. I don't know what there is with those Bowers boys. They have girls swooning over them all day."

"Are you comparing me with April Vockney?" Mrs. Bowers smiled.

"There are some similarities," Jolie replied.

"I knew I liked that girl," Lissa added as she followed her eldest into the sod house.

A scrap of green canvas covered the table where Gibs sat.

"What is that smell?" Jolie called out.

"It's Dr. Bull's Miracle Medicine," Gibs answered. "Leppy Verdue left half a bottle of it out in the barn. I found it in the haystack."

"Are you sick?" Lissa asked her youngest son.

"Mama, I'm usin' it to clean the rust off my Henry rifle. Someday I'll be able to tote it around when I'm chasin' down outlaws."

Lissa Bowers shook her head and glanced at Jolie. "Gibson Hunter Bowers has been chasing bad men since he was two. It's in his bones, I suppose."

"I'll need to get supper started. Gibs, can you clean off the table and go help your brother with the animals?" Jolie asked.

Gibs held up the bronze receiver to the lantern light. "Do you see his *H* on the receiver? Tanner says that means Mr. B. Tyler Henry inspected it himself. Can you imagine? I'm holdin' a Henry that Mr. Henry himself once held."

"Put Mr. Henry back in the corner," Mrs. Bowers insisted. "You've messed up big sister's table long enough."

Gibs buttoned the sleeves of his shirt and jammed a cork in the amber bottle. "I was just tryin' to keep busy, Mama, so I don't have to think about Sudsy."

She rubbed his shoulders and combed his shaggy, thick brown hair with her fingers. "I know, honey, I know," she murmured. "It's okay. I wasn't complaining. But it's time for supper."

When the wagon rumbled into the yard, Essie was the first out the door. Lissa Bowers was only a step behind her.

"Daddy! Did you hear about Sudsy?" Essie hollered.

Lawson grabbed the rigging on the team. "You want me to put the horses away?"

Matthew Bowers swung down off the wagon. His tie was loose, and the top button on his white shirt was unfastened. His brown suit and vest were layered with rusty-yellow Nebraska dust. "Yes, I heard about poor Sudsy, little sis. Now let me unload some things before big brother drives off."

"I think you better hug someone before you do anything else." Jolie pushed him toward her mother.

"Oh?" He grinned. When he hugged his wife, he picked her up, and they spun around in a circle. "Did you miss me, Melissa Pritchett Bowers?"

"Yes, I did, Matthew Allis Bowers."

"I missed you too," Essie whined.

"My, I've only been gone a few hours, and everyone misses me." He grabbed Essie, hugged her, and kissed her cheek. Then he turned to his youngest son. "Did you miss me too?"

"Not that much," Gibs replied. "Did you get the dynamite?"

"Dynamite, caps, and fuse. But I had to pay cash. Fleister's will not sell dynamite on credit," Matthew Bowers said.

"Did you have any cash?" Jolie asked.

He tugged his watch from his vest pocket.

"You sold your silver watch chain?" Jolie exclaimed.

"Lawson braided me a very fine watch fob out of horse hair, and I wanted to use it."

"Matthew!" Lissa Bowers protested.

He hugged her and kissed her on the lips. "Did you ever hear anyone say 'Matthew' quite like your mama? Now, darlin', I want to have the foundation on the house done by Christmas, and I can never get it done with that granite boulder in the southwest corner."

"It makes a nice tea table," Essie chimed in. "Providing you don't set anything on it."

"You took a long time buying dynamite," Lissa pointed out.

"There's a little crate of groceries in the back. Gibs, tote that in for your sister." Mr. Bowers reached into his coat pocket. "I picked up the mail as long as I was there."

"Did we have mail?" Jolie asked.

He sorted through the bundle of letters and papers. "Yes, that seems to happen when we don't pick it up for a couple of weeks at a time. Here's one for Jolie."

"Me?" She scurried to her father's side.

He stared at the fat envelope. "From Abby's Fancy Dress Shoppe in Deadwood."

"Oh!" Jolie snatched the letter. "Samples of material for my wedding dress. Bailey Wagner said this shop is the best in the Black Hills."

"You mean, Bailey Cain," Lissa Bowers corrected.

Jolie fingered the ivory cameo necklace that hung high on her neck. "Yes. . . . Why don't I remember that?"

"The day is fast approaching when we'll have to learn to call you Jolie Lorita Wells," her mother added.

"Not until June 14," Matthew Bowers insisted. "She's still a Bowers."

"I'll always be a Bowers, Daddy," Jolie assured him.

"I know . . . I know," he sighed. "Some days I can't believe how many years have gone by."

"What else is in the mail?" Gibs called out.

"A U.S. Marshal's bulletin came for Deputy Gibson Hunter Bowers."

"He did it! Sheriff Riley said he would sign me up to get the bulletin!" Gibs grabbed the rolled newspaper and scampered to the front porch.

"Did I get my seed catalog?" Lawson asked.

"As a matter of fact, they mailed you two seed catalogs," Mr. Bowers declared.

"Two?" Lawson asked.

"Yes, one is mailed to Lawson Bowers, and the other is mailed to Mr. & Mrs. Lawson P. Bowers."

"Wh-what?" he stammered.

Essie covered her giggles with her hand.

"I do believe Miss April is quite insistent," Mr. Bowers remarked.

"I need to talk to that girl," Lissa Bowers mumbled.

"And here's one for you, Mrs. Bowers. It's from Michigan."

"From Mother?" she asked.

He handed her the neatly addressed brown envelope. "I suppose they will be asking us to come there for Christmas again."

"Didn't I get anything, Daddy?" Essie pleaded.

"Perhaps." He grinned.

"Really?" Essie squealed.

"What do I get if I give you something?" he teased.

"I'll give you a great big smooch," Essie promised.

He reached in his other suit coat pocket and pulled out a small letter. "That's the best offer I've had all day."

"Hmmm Ummm." Lissa smiled.

"Okay," he laughed, "the second-best offer I've had today." Essie threw her arms around his neck and smashed her lips into his. "Oh, my, someone has been giving you kissing lessons!"

"Daddy! I've just been watching Mama and Jolie. They're very good kissers, you know."

"I think it runs in the family," he said. "Look at this. You do have a letter!"

"Daddy, you were teasing me," Essie laughed. "Look, Jolie. It's from Leppy. And it came from Rawlins, Wyoming."

"Mother, look at this one." Jolie held up

a sample swatch of material from the big brown envelope. "It's called Angel's Cream. Isn't it lovely?"

Lissa Bowers glanced up from her letter. "It isn't white enough. You want something brighter." She glanced back down at her letter. "My cousin Marvin has been elected to Congress! And Uncle MacCleod always said Marvin was a slacker."

"Congress might be the right place for a slacker," Mr. Bowers mumbled. "When I heard about Sudsy, I went by Mrs. Fuentes's boarding house to check on Mrs. Mitchell. I heard she had stayed in town. But they told me she left the house and headed for the train yard, toting a Winchester shotgun."

"A shotgun?" Gibs mumbled. "I heard them ten-gauges kick like a nervous horse in a swarm of bees. Say . . . look at this. The marshal's office has a warning for the Nebraska panhandle to be on the lookout for Mysterious Dave Mather. He really is around here. I wish I had a new buttstock for my Henry, although I reckon it would shoot just as good with this cracked one."

"Did you know they developed a new strain of corn just for western Nebraska?" Lawson called out. "They say it grows to be eight feet tall. That's two feet taller than ours, Daddy. My, wouldn't that be a fine shinley? Maybe we can try that next year."

"We have a mighty fine crop of corn, son. But it wouldn't hurt to try something even better."

"Daddy, can I borrow your folding knife?" Essie asked. "I can't open my letter. My Leppy sealed it very tight. I suppose he didn't want anyone to peek."

"Sure, baby, hand it here," Mr. Bowers offered.

Lissa Bowers studied her letter. "Mother says she's given up on us coming home to Michigan."

"Oh, look at this one, Mama!" Jolie held up a sample. "Pure Cloud White."

Lissa flipped her long auburn braid over her shoulder. "That's the one, Jolie Lorita." She went back to the letter in her hand.

"Mysterious Dave Mather robbed a train near Laramie City!" Gibs exclaimed. "He stole over $3,000! I need to go look for him tomorrow."

Lawson thumbed through the catalog. "Did you know they have tomatoes as big as grapefruits? If you had a tomato like that, you could feed a whole family with just one."

"Especially if one of them didn't like tomatoes. Hurry, Daddy." Essie grabbed for the letter. "What's a grapefruit anyway? I thought grapes were small."

"It's like a big orange — only it's yellow and very sour," Jolie explained. "Abby Fortune says the wedding dress will be thirty dollars, but she will sell one to a friend of Bailey's for twenty-five dollars. Mama, I can't afford a twenty-five-dollar dress!"

"Oh, no. That won't work!" Lissa Bowers moaned.

"I know, Mama. I can make my own much cheaper than that," Jolie declared. "But it's fun to dream about. There's no reason to spend an exorbitant amount on a dress to be worn for only an hour or two."

"No, Jolie, that's not it. I was moaning over the letter, not your dress." Lissa handed the letter to her husband. "Read the last line, Matthew."

"Talk about a fine shinley!" Essie waved her letter straight out in front of her. "Gibs, I'll need to borrow your gun."

"They're coming here for Christmas?" Matthew Bowers gasped.

"Who's coming here?" Jolie asked.

"What do you want my gun for?" Gibs asked.

"Grandma and Grandpa Pritchett," Mr. Bowers replied.

"I have to go to Rawlins, Wyoming," Essie announced.

"Here?" Jolie gasped. "You mean, stay with us in a two-room sod house?"

"Why are you goin' to Rawlins?" Gibs asked his sister.

"Leppy's in jail, and I need to break him out," Essie declared.

"Mama, we don't have room for Grandma and Grandpa. . . . I mean . . . they're used to a big house and servants and everything," Jolie said. "I can't get this place Grandma-Pritchett clean."

"In jail?" Gibs strolled over to his younger sister and peeked over her shoulder. "What did he do this time?"

Lissa Bowers hugged her chest and rocked back on her heels. "Mother and Father said we aren't coming there; so they'll just have to come here."

"That's blackmail," Jolie declared.

"No," Essie blurted out. "It's murder. They're goin' to hang him on December 20!"

Gibs scraped the last of the scalloped potatoes from the green pottery bowl as Jolie poured her mother, her father, and herself more ink-black coffee.

"There's got to be some third alternative," Matthew Bowers sighed. "We can't afford to go to Michigan. We can't afford to buy any more cement for the foundation of the house until we sell the corn. We can barely afford to pay for groceries."

"The corn crop looks very good," Lissa reminded him. "They told us we couldn't grow corn out here, and we did it. Next year we'll have a canal and will be able to irrigate the entire place."

"But we have big bills waiting for the corn money — the grocery store, the hardware store, Mr. Mendez at the furniture store. We can't use the crop money for a trip to Michigan," Mr. Bowers insisted.

Jolie stopped behind her father and laid her hand on his shoulder. "Daddy, I have some saved and —"

Mr. Bowers placed his huge hand on hers. "Darlin' Jolie, I'm a failure because I can't take my wife east to see her family. I'm a failure because we're living in a two-room dirt house, unsuitable for them to come visit. I will not compound those failures by appropriating my daughter's wedding money."

"But, Daddy, you know —"

"Yes, I do know how generous you are." He brushed down his thick mustache with his fingertips. "But my daughter's successes should not make up for my failures. I cannot use your money."

"Matthew Bowers, would you please stop talking about failure?" Lissa scolded. "You have neither failed the Lord nor your family."

"I most certainly have failed all of you. In California, Nevada, Arizona, New Mexico, Montana, and now in Nebraska."

"Let's take a survey," Lissa suggested. "Jolie Lorita, has your daddy failed you?"

"Never, Mama. Never once in my life."

"Melissa, you don't have to do this," Mr. Bowers protested.

"Hush, it's not your turn," she insisted. "Lawson Pritchett?"

"I never met a father anywhere we have ever lived that came close to loving his children as much as Daddy loves us. April said if I turn out half as good as Daddy, she'll be a happy woman."

"Oh, she did? Hmmm, that girl's good taste overcomes her indiscretion." Lissa turned to her youngest son, who was wiping his plate with a hunk of sourdough bread. "How about you, Gibson Hunter?"

"Daddy makes every day excitin'," Gibs blurted out. "He always has wonderful new ideas for us to ponder. He does make other fathers seem boring, but that's their problem, not his."

Lissa Bowers peered across at her youngest. "Estelle Cinnia?"

"What?" she answered.

"Is your daddy a failure?"

"Oh, no, Mama! He's the best daddy in the world. Sometimes when he hugs me at night, I think that's what heaven must feel like."

"I know exactly what you mean." Lissa grinned. "Now, Mr. Matthew Bowers, you have for all these years provided me with everything a woman's heart needs. You have given me love, security, attention, wonderful children, excitement, and smooches that cause my heart to flap like a butterfly and —"

"Mama!" Jolie interrupted. "Don't embarrass us."

"So there will be no talk of failure," Lissa declared. "That's nonsense. But I believe you're right about something. We'll have to think of a third alternative for Mother and Father."

"Why don't we tell them we're so busy building our house that this is not a good season. We could invite them to my wedding. Maybe the house will be finished by then," Jolie suggested.

"What if it isn't?" Mr. Bowers asked.

"We might not have the funds to complete it the first year."

Jolie tapped her fingers on the table. "The wedding is in Scottsbluff. They can stay at the hotel in town. But it wouldn't be right to have them stay in town if they come at Christmas."

"Perhaps Jolie's right," Lissa Bowers said. "I'll tell them to wait until next summer."

"No. No," Matthew Bowers murmured. "Melissa, your mother's right. You need to see them at Christmas. Life is too short to wait."

"But how? You said —"

"I said there has to be some other way. I don't want to discuss it anymore."

"Daddy, could I check with Mr. Culburtt about what tickets would cost for all of us to go to Michigan? I know we can't afford it, but I'm curious about what it would cost."

"Jolie, look at me," he demanded.

"Yes, Daddy?"

"You can check on the ticket price, but it will break my heart and destroy me if you use one penny of your wedding money for train tickets. Please don't do that to me."

Jolie lowered her eyes to her plate. "I won't, Daddy."

"You can use your wedding money for my train ticket," Essie declared.

"To Michigan?" Jolie asked.

"No, to Rawlins. I have to go bust Leppy out of jail."

"Jolie does not need to buy you a train ticket to Rawlins," Lissa Bowers declared.

"I have to do something," Essie pleaded.

"Let's see if Sheriff Riley can find out what Leppy's status is," Matthew Bowers suggested. "We need to know more about the situation."

"But he needs me. He wrote to me. He didn't write to you, Daddy, or to Jolie. He wrote to Miss Estelle Bowers. It's right there on the envelope."

"What Leppy needs is Jesus in his heart and justice to take place," Lissa said.

"And Estelle Bowers to come get him out of prison. Mama, as soon as you heard about Daddy in jail in Lincoln, you got on a train and hurried over there," Essie reminded her.

"And if I had waited one more day, he would have been home. I didn't need to make the trip. December 20 is more than a month away. We can wait and think this through a little. We have some time," Mrs. Bowers maintained.

"Unless he gets lynched," Gibs blurted out.

Essie burst into tears and ran to the backroom.

"Gibs!" Jolie scolded.

Matthew Bowers trimmed the wick and turned up the kerosene lantern as Jolie and Lissa finished the dishes. When Mrs. Bowers dried the last plate, she stacked them on the shelf and sighed.

"What's the matter, Mama?"

"Jolie, how I will miss you. Looking at those cloth samples tonight reminded me how quickly the months will pass. The potatoes tonight were as good as in any fine restaurant in a hotel."

"That was a recipe in *Harper's*. I just followed the instructions. Anyone can do that."

"You're wrong, Jolie Lorita. You took that magazine to bed three weeks ago and read yourself to sleep surveying its recipes. Then you went to town, took your schoolteacher's pay, and bought the ingredients. I would imagine last Sunday afternoon you planned your menus for the week, and I expect that you followed every one of them exactly."

Jolie folded the tea towel across the

drying bar next to the cookstove. "I'm quite predictable, aren't I?"

"Sweet Jolie, you're a marvelous home-maker. I don't think Tanner Wells has any idea what he's getting."

"I'm sure he doesn't," Jolie laughed. "I'm not even sure what I'm giving. Mama, what if I'm not a good wife?"

Mrs. Bowers circled her daughter's thin waist. "Darling, you have the heart for it. That's all that counts. . . . You'll have some things to learn, but a whole lot less than most girls. Let's not talk about June 14. My heart has to work up to it slowly."

"Ladies, come relax for a few minutes," Matthew Bowers invited. "I want you to look at the veranda I drew on the house plans. The balcony serves as an awning over the porch below. Do you think the front of the house will look too much like a hotel?"

Lissa slipped in beside her husband on the bench. She held his arm. "It *is* a hotel. It's a rare night that we don't have company."

"That will change when Jolie's gone," Matthew Bowers stated.

Lissa Bowers began to unbraid her long auburn hair. "Yes, I was wondering how many traveling cowboys Tanner will let her tend to in the backroom of the gun shop."

"Mama!" Jolie protested. "We won't be having company there. But that place is only temporary. As soon as I get a schoolteaching job in Scottsbluff, we'll find ourselves a house."

"You can't raise children and teach school," Mrs. Bowers pointed out.

"I'll teach just for two years," Jolie declared. "We have it all figured right down to the penny."

"We?" Lissa challenged.

Jolie smiled. "I have it figured right down to the penny."

"That I can believe," Mrs. Bowers affirmed. "Have you figured out how you're going to keep from having children for those two years?"

"Mother!"

"You didn't answer me."

"Yes, we do, and I don't want to talk about it." Jolie pointed down at the drawing on the table. "Daddy, I love the balcony. You and Mama can sit up there in the evening and see all the way to Chimney Rock."

Lissa leaned her head on her husband's shoulder. "It sounds so wonderfully peaceful."

"Oh . . . I think it's time for me to go to bed," Jolie interjected.

"It's okay, Jolie," Mr. Bowers said. "You don't need to run and hide."

"Hmmm huh." Lissa cleared her throat.

"Oh." He glanced at his wife. "Perhaps you do."

"Actually," Lissa said with a grin, "I need to step out and check on the horses. They seem restless, and I don't want some varmint to spook them."

"I'll go check on them, Mama," Jolie volunteered.

"Nonsense, I can do that," Mrs. Bowers insisted.

"Hmmm huh." Mr. Bowers smiled.

Lissa Bowers poked her husband in the ribs. "Oh, perhaps that would be good."

Jolie grinned and grabbed up the lantern. "You two won't be needing this, will you?"

"We don't want you to trip out there in the dark," Mrs. Bowers said.

Jolie tugged her old brown sweater off the wooden peg by the door and pulled it on. Then she pushed out into the quiet Nebraska night. The lantern cast shadows across the cement footings for the new house. *It seems strange, Lord, that Mama and Daddy will have that new house someday, and I won't ever get to live in it. Daddy's been promising it for so long. I pray that they will have decades of enjoy-*

ment. Someday . . . someday in 1910 or in 1920 people will look at that big, beautiful house and say to their children, "That's the Bowerses' place, you know."

May Mama and Daddy find rest in this place. They've worked so hard for so many years. You have promised us Your rest, Lord. May this be their rest.

Jolie hiked over to the barn with its three walls. She stopped by the circular corral made of interlocking hand-hewn railroad ties. "Now there's a sight. A pig, a calf, and a fawn sleeping in a pile. I don't think they know they're different. Essie treats them like her children."

Pullman, the sorrel horse, and Leppy, the bay, stood sleeping in the rock corral. Pilgrim milled back and forth by the back gate, and Stranger studied Pilgrim.

"What's the matter with you big boys? Is something out there making you nervous?" she murmured.

Jolie hiked toward the garden. *There's not much left in Mama's garden. I don't think raccoons will be out there. I hope it's not a skunk.* She plucked up a broken shovel handle that had been tossed against the stone wall of the corral.

"Skunky, if you're out here . . . it's

time to run away."

The shadows from the lantern danced against the distant cornfield. Jolie studied the quarter-acre garden plot. *There's nothing left but the pumpkins. In the dark they look like boulders. There's Cousin Benny. I've never met the real Cousin Benny, but Mama says he has a head like a pumpkin.*

But I don't remember two pumpkins.

Holding the lantern higher, she inched closer.

Cousin Benny is busted open! There's something out here!

She raised the shovel handle, then heard a step behind her, and spun around with the lantern in her left hand. A very short man with a thick orange beard was only two feet behind her.

"Don't tell —"

His words had barely left his lips when the shovel handle crashed into the side of his head. He dropped to the dirt. Much of the beard was stuck to the shovel handle.

"Pumpkin?" she gasped. "His face is smeared with pumpkin!"

She stood over the little man, who struggled to his hands and knees.

"Don't hit me again, Miss Jolie," pleaded.

Two

When Stranger and Pilgrim reached Telegraph Road, they lengthened their stride. Jolie threw her weight back against the lead lines to slow them down. Essie clutched the iron rail of the wagon seat. Gibs's slouch hat was pushed so low his ears pointed out. His Winchester Model 90 lay across his lap.

"I should stop at the Wellses' and check on Bullet," Jolie said. Her green wool coat collar was turned up; yet the fall air still chilled her neck.

"No," Essie insisted. "We need to get to town to find out from the sheriff about my Leppy."

"I can't believe I hit him like that. I feel terrible," Jolie added.

Gibs aimed his pump .22 rifle at phantom wild game as they rattled along. "When Daddy took him back last night, Mr. Wells thought you did the right thing."

"Yes, but he's in my class. On Monday he'll have quite a bruise, and I'm to blame." Jolie felt her auburn bangs flap in the breeze. Her hat tugged against the green ribbon tied under her chin. "I

41

should never have picked up that shovel handle."

"Chester said he was running away from home," Essie remarked, "but coming to our garden isn't very far from home."

"Eating raw pumpkin doesn't sound too smart either," Gibs added.

"I worry about him more than any of my other students. And yet he's as smart as almost anyone. It's as if he was created without any common sense."

"Bullet isn't boring," Gibs said.

"Oh, yes!" Jolie exclaimed. "That's very true."

"He isn't afraid either," Essie added. "He wanted to bet anyone in class a nickel that he could jump off the school roof and not break any bones."

"He jumped off the school roof?" Jolie gasped.

Essie rolled her lower lip up until it almost touched her nose. "Nope. No one would bet him. He said he wouldn't do it for free."

"He's not afraid and not boring. I'll have to encourage him that way the next time I sit him in the corner and lecture him."

"Jolie, is common sense something we learn, or is it something we're born with?" Gibs asked.

"That's a very astute question, Gibson Hunter Bowers. I'll have to ask the Lord about that. Certainly there's a wisdom that comes with age."

"Isn't that Mrs. Fleister's buggy up there?" Gibs pointed to the west.

"At least, wisdom *should* come with age." Jolie studied the carriage as they approached. "I'll stop, of course."

"But I need to get to town," Essie complained, "and find out about my Leppy."

"And I want to talk to Sheriff Riley about Mysterious Dave Mather," Gibs added.

"There's no excuse not to stop and see that everything is all right."

Jolie threw herself back and yanked the lines tight. The two big horses slowed.

"There's someone with her," Gibs observed. "Why are they both sitting in the backseat? Who's driving the buggy?"

With one hand, Jolie attempted to adjust her hat. "That must be Mrs. Fleister's niece."

Essie tugged her waist-length brown hair around so that it flowed down the front of her dress. "I thought her niece had yellow hair."

Jolie studied both women as they approached. *Lord, help me to be gracious and not impatient with Mrs. Fleister.* "This is a different niece."

"How many nieces does she have?" Essie quizzed.

"As many as it takes to get Strath Yarrow married," Jolie answered.

"Wow, she's purdy!" Gibs muttered.

"Mrs. Fleister?" Essie giggled.

Gibs loosened his hat and pushed it back. "No. Her niece."

Essie shielded her mouth as they rolled closer to the buggy. "She's a little old for you, Gibson Hunter Bowers."

"No older than Leppy is for you," he countered.

"That's different." Essie clenched her teeth as she talked. "It's not the same for boys and girls."

"Mrs. Fleister, is there something wrong?" Jolie called out even before the big farm wagon rolled to a stop.

"Oh, Jolie, dear." She turned to the young woman with long, wavy raven hair. "You see, Candace, I told you homesteaders are from solid stock. They won't let you down." Then she turned back to Jolie, Essie, and Gibs. "We seem to be stranded, dear."

"Where's your driver?" Essie called out.

"It's simply inexcusable. He just walked

44

off the job. I will fire him, of course," Mrs. Fleister proclaimed.

Jolie stared down Telegraph Road in the direction of Scottsbluff. "Walked off and left you here?"

"Yes. It was quite rude of him."

The younger woman took Mrs. Fleister's arm. "Actually, Aunt Mildred called him the scourge of the North Platte River Valley and an insipid excuse for manhood. That's when he walked off."

"Lawrence quit you?" Essie asked.

"Oh my, no," the young lady laughed. "Lawrence quit last week. This was Cedric."

Mrs. Fleister dismissed the matter with a flip of the wrist. "He was a Cornishman, you know."

Gibs stood straight up and pulled off his hat. His thick brown hair sprayed out everywhere. "Mrs. Fleister, I don't believe I've been properly introduced to your lovely niece."

Jolie's mouth dropped open.

Essie began to giggle.

"Yes, how frightfully slack of me. This is my niece from South Bend, Indiana — Miss Candace Clevenger. Candace, these are three of the Bowers children. Estelle, Lawson, and, of course, our dear Jolie, whom I have often mentioned."

"Actually I'm Gibson. My older brother is Lawson. Ever'one calls me Gibs."

The dark-haired woman smiled, revealing straight, white teeth. "Gibs, it's quite a treat to be introduced to such a charming and handsome young man. When Aunt Mildred said we were driving out to meet a young man, I had no idea he would be so chivalrous."

"Oh, my," Mildred Fleister stammered. "That's not the one I was going to introduce you to. We're going to see Mr. Strath Yarrow."

"Nebraska must be filled with strong, attractive men," Candace murmured. She turned to the others in the wagon. "I'm guessing that no one except my aunt calls you Estelle. I saw you flinch when she said that."

"They call me Essie. Sometimes Jolie calls me Estelle, especially when I'm spyin' on her and Tanner. She's going to marry Tanner June 14."

"Jolie Bowers, I just know we'll be good friends. I have yet to meet a person in Scottsbluff who hasn't told me about you," Candace said.

"Oh, dear. I'm not sure I want to know what they've been saying."

Candace clapped her hands. "It has all been wonderful. They extol your talent and virtue, elevating you to near sainthood. And I mean that in a very good sense."

"You've been listening to some gracious people, Candace. I'm just a schoolteacher. Who told you all that?"

"Let's see . . . the bank guard . . ."

"Chug?" Essie giggled.

"I thought his name was Charles."

Essie nodded. "That's him."

"And a couple of men at the grocery store," Candace added.

"Luke and Raymond," Jolie said. "They're gracious friends."

"Then there was a rather sturdy lady at the butcher shop."

"Nadella Ripon?"

"She simply said that Jolie Bowers was perhaps the most handsome woman God ever created and that if she were a man, she would marry you herself."

"Oh, dear . . . Nadella does have a very colorful way of expressing herself." Jolie glanced at the long-legged black horse that stood idle in front of the black leather buggy. "Mrs. Fleister, may I offer you and Candace a lift back to town?"

"Oh, thank you, dear, but I'm afraid I never ride in farm wagons."

Candace rolled her eyes at her aunt's comments.

"What can we do for you then?" Jolie asked.

Mrs. Fleister pointed at the empty buggy seat in front of her. "Perhaps you could drive this surrey out to the Yarrow place for us. Your brother could drive the farm wagon along behind."

"I've got to get to Scottsbluff in a hurry," Essie blurted out. "It's a matter of life and death."

Mrs. Fleister's eyes widened. "Oh, dear, I trust it's not your father."

"No, it's my Leppy," Essie said. "He's going to be hung on the 20th of December, and I've got to go to Wyoming and bust him out of jail."

Mildred Fleister laughed, then patted her niece's knee. "You see what a marvelous teacher Jolie is? The children all have such creative imaginations."

"Mrs. Fleister, we really do have to get to town," Jolie explained. "I must check on Mrs. Mitchell. You heard about poor Sudsy Mitchell."

"Oh, it's so horrid I can't even think about it. And now Mrs. Mitchell is in jail for shooting Edward Culburtt," Mrs. Fleister said.

"What? She shot Mr. Culburtt?" Jolie gasped. "I can't believe that. He was such a nice man. I — I . . ."

"Oh, he's not dead. But he won't be sitting at his desk for a while. Isn't that a fine shinley?" Mrs. Fleister said. "She blamed him for Devon's death."

"Sudsy's name was Devon?" Essie asked.

"Actually I could drive the team," Candace admitted, "but Aunt Mildred insists that it's undignified."

Jolie glanced down at the lead lines in her hands.

"Yes, except for Melissa Bowers and her daughters," Mrs. Fleister hurried to say. "It's expected that they will drive and drive fast. They are every woman's hidden delight. But I'm afraid the rest of us must be chained to convention."

"Perhaps young Mr. Bowers could —," Candace began.

"Gibs needs to talk to the sheriff about Mysterious Dave Mather," Essie blurted out.

"That can wait," Gibs replied. "I'd be honored to drive your rig, Miss Clevenger."

"Oh, really?" Jolie remarked.

"It's the neighborly thing to do. I could find you and Essie back in town this afternoon," he offered. "That is, if we head that way."

"There you have it. The gallant Mr. Gibson Hunter Bowers will drive your buggy." Jolie grinned. "He'll even provide protection with his rifle. He's a very fine shot."

"Once we reach Mr. Yarrow's, I'm sure he will want to drive us back to town personally," Mrs. Fleister said.

"Strath and Landen aren't home," Gibs announced.

Mrs. Fleister's shoulders fell. "They aren't?"

"They had to help a friend north of the river move some furniture," he reported.

Mildred Fleister wrung her gloved hands. "Oh, dear."

"But I could drive you out to look at their house," Gibs said. "It's ready-wall that they shipped out from Chicago. It only took Strath and two men ten days to put it up. All their furniture isn't in yet, but it surely is a sight to behold. He has two bathtubs — can you believe that? I never heard of anyone having two bathtubs."

"It's a shame Mr. Yarrow isn't home," Mrs. Fleister murmured.

"Oh, me and Strath is pals," Gibs added as he climbed down and headed for the buggy. "He's teachin' me how to shoot over my shoulder, using nothing but a little mirror. Why, Leppy Verdue says Strath is the best shot he's ever seen, and Leppy's seen some of the best. He was down in Arizona one time and got arrested by none other than Stuart Brannon himself; so you know Leppy's seen fast guns. Yep, I can give you ladies a tour of the Yarrow house."

"Your brother seems very enthusiastic," Miss Clevenger said.

Jolie raised her auburn eyebrows. "Yes, he does."

"We will accept the hospitality, young Mr. Bowers. Do you know how to go down this road without getting all that dust in our faces?" Mrs. Fleister quizzed as Gibs took up the brown leather lead lines.

"Yes, ma'am. . . . Hang on to your hats!"

With a snap of the lines and a sudden jolt, the buggy lunged east.

"Ohhh!" the women gasped.

"Was that a shout for joy or terror?" Jolie asked.

"Probably a little of each." Essie grinned. "I've never in my life seen Gibs act like that."

Jolie drove the big farm wagon back onto the road and then let Stranger and Pilgrim

51

stretch their legs as they sprinted toward Scottsbluff. "I think little brother is growing up. He was surely smitten by Miss Clevenger."

Essie licked some jam off the back of her hand. "I think he made a fool of himself."

"Hmmm." Jolie held the lines taut and bounced in the wagon seat. "Spoken by a young lady who's going to break a man out of jail?"

Essie raised her round button nose. "That's different. It's like comparing grapefruit and lemons."

"You mean apples and oranges?"

"Yeah, that too."

The sun was still on an eastern angle when they rattled into Scottsbluff. The yellow-red dust followed on their heels like a dog chasing a cat. When they reached the Panhandle Bank and Trust, Jolie slowed the team.

"Can we go talk to the sheriff first thing?" Essie asked.

Jolie grinned as two cowboys scampered across the street to avoid the hooves of Stranger and Pilgrim. "Yes, but after that I need to take these swatches by and show Tanner."

"I thought he wasn't supposed to see the

dress until you walk down the aisle."

"That's true," Jolie replied. "But this isn't a dress. It's a four-inch square of cloth."

"Are you going to kiss him?" Essie quizzed.

"Of course I'm going to kiss him."

"Is he going to give me a nickel if I go to the store and dawdle?"

Jolie laughed. "He just might."

"I'm good at dawdling. Not as good as Mudball, but it's hard to out-dawdle a pig."

"Yes, I believe you're right about that."

Essie pointed down the street. "There's a crowd in front of the jail."

"I trust there isn't any trouble."

"They don't look very happy. It's mostly women."

Jolie threw her weight back and slowed the team. "So I see. Let's park over here and walk across the street."

Essie hopped off the wagon to the boardwalk. "When we first got Stranger and Pilgrim, you or Mama had to hold the lines every time we stopped, remember?"

"These big boys have learned a lot." Jolie climbed down from the wagon and tied off the lines to the wagon brake.

"I think Pilgrim is smarter than

Stranger," Essie announced as she stroked the big brown horse's nose. "But no one knows it because he doesn't brag like Stranger."

When they reached the covered boardwalk just east of the crowd, a large woman in a long black serge dress met them. "I'm certainly glad to see you, Jolie Bowers. Perhaps you can talk some sense in this matter."

Jolie felt tiny next to the big woman. "Mrs. Sitmore, what's the problem here? What do these women want?"

"Justice, of course. We want justice. I trust you're on our side."

"I always want what is fair in the eyes of the Lord," Jolie murmured, "but I don't know what's going on."

"Oh, dear, haven't you heard?" Mrs. Sitmore asked.

"I heard about Sudsy Mitchell. I'm his teacher. It's a horrible tragedy. I cried about it."

Mrs. Sitmore spun her unopened green parasol over her shoulder. "Yes, well, now it's time to be worried about Dusty Mitchell."

"What happened to Mrs. Mitchell?"

"She got arrested. I'm not sure what got into Sheriff Riley."

Essie stood on her tiptoes and tried to peer over the crowd of women. "Did she really shoot Mr. Culburtt?"

"Yes, but he didn't die."

"Then what happened?" Essie asked.

"The sheriff arrested poor Mrs. Mitchell. Now, I ask you, is that anything to do to a grieving mother?"

Jolie pulled off her coat and held it across her arm. "When people shoot someone, they often get arrested."

"But a woman in grief like that? It's a wonder every railroad man in a hundred miles didn't get shot. I think they came out fairly easy. It could have been worse," Mrs. Sitmore lectured.

"Maybe that's why she was arrested." Jolie studied the women who were shouting at the closed door of the sheriff's office. *Lord, why does a riotous mob lose all wisdom? In ones and twos, these women would never act this way.*

"Miss Jolie, you're a friend of the sheriff. You must do something!"

Jolie Bowers took her sister's hand and inched through the crowd. "Let us through, and we'll go talk to Sheriff Riley."

Mrs. Sitmore gripped her shoulder so hard Jolie flinched. "But the sheriff isn't here. He's hired a new deputy. Riley rode

north huntin' for that nice-looking scoundrel, Mysterious Dave Mather."

"Scoundrel?" Essie blurted out. "He's a
robber and a killer."

"Yes, but he has kind eyes. Eyes tell you
a lot about a man."

"Mrs. Sitmore," Jolie fumed, "that's the
most ludicrous statement I've —"

"Nadella!" Mrs. Sitmore hollered.
"Nadella, Miss Jolie is here. Everything
will be all right."

Nadella Ripon hugged Jolie so tight she
had to fight for a breath. "Honey, I knew
you'd come. I kept saying to the girls that
we need to be vigilant until Miss Jolie gets
here."

"I don't understand," Jolie probed.
"What is it you ladies are demanding?"

"That Dusty Mitchell be released on bail
to await the judge's hearing, like any other
person. She has been denied bail, and
Culburtt isn't even dead."

Jolie stepped back from the woman, who
smelled of vanilla and sweat. "Nadella, can
you guarantee that Mrs. Mitchell won't
shoot any other railroad men?"

The woman's laugh gurgled up from
deep in her large frame. "I can't even guarantee that I won't shoot any more railroad
men."

Pearl Anderson stepped up next to Nadella. "Poor Sudsy was purtnear pinched in two when those railroad cars caught him."

"I think I'm going to be sick," Essie groaned.

"Railroad accidents can happen," Jolie said. "There were warning signs posted all over the train yard the last time I was down there."

"It was the railroad dogs that chased poor Sudsy," Pearl reported.

Essie held her hand over her mouth. "You mean, someone saw it all?"

"Dusty Mitchell told me that she had an eyewitness tell her everything," Nadella insisted.

"If you let me through the crowd, I'll go in and talk to the deputy. Who is he?" Jolie asked.

"Celia DeLaney's fella," Nadella replied.

Essie's eyes widened. "Maxwell Dix? He's a deputy?"

"Yes."

Jolie waved her arms and called out, "I'm afraid you ladies will have to move at least ten feet back from the door, or he will never let me in."

No one budged.

"Nadella?" Jolie prodded.

"Move it," Nadella hollered, "or I'll toss you out in the street."

The entire crowd of women shuffled away from the front of the office.

Jolie knocked on the door. "Max? It's me, Jolie Bowers. May I come in?"

"Who's comin' in with you?" The usual hint of laughter in his voice was missing.

"Essie."

The door swung open, and a tall, thin blond-haired man with a black wide-brimmed hat motioned to them. Jolie and Essie slipped inside, and the door was locked behind them.

"You didn't see the sheriff ride up, did you?" he asked. He held a Winchester 1873 saddle-ring carbine in his hand.

"You cut your hair!" Essie blurted out.

"No, I didn't see the sheriff," Jolie replied. "I was told he went out after Dave Mather."

Max glanced down at Essie. "Yeah, the sheriff said if I wanted this deputy job, I'd need a haircut."

"I liked it long," Essie maintained.

"So did I, but Miss Celia cut it. She likes it like this. I reckon that's what matters." He stared out the small four-paned window at the crowd. "Now I'm wonderin' if it was a mistake."

"Celia DeLaney . . . or this job?" Jolie pressed.

"This job." He smiled. "Miss Celia is wonderful. I've never met anyone quite like her."

He glanced out the window again. "Look at that crowd of women. I had to draw a gun just to get them away from the door, Miss Jolie. I never drawed a gun on a lady in my life. At least, not a respectable one."

"Where are you keeping Mrs. Mitchell?" Jolie questioned.

Maxwell Dix pointed to a thick wooden door at the back of the office. "In the back cell."

Jolie laid her coat across an oak captain's chair. "Do you have any other prisoners in here?"

Dix ran his fingers through his short blond hair. "No, the sheriff turned the others loose just so he'd have accommodations for her."

"Max, what happened? I mean, we know Sudsy was killed, and Mrs. Mitchell shot Mr. Culburtt. What else happened?"

"She's saying that they had dangerous dogs unleashed at the train yard, and they came after the boy as he was walking along the tracks. He ran across the yard to save himself and was caught by the train cars as they were making up a train."

"She has a witness to that effect, I heard," Jolie said.

"Claims to, but said she would only tell the judge, not the sheriff."

"What seems to be the problem?" Jolie probed.

"The sheriff won't set regular bail. He says she tried to kill Culburtt and, when arrested, threatened to keep tryin' until a railroad man is dead. When Miss Ripon and the ladies came to visit her, she told a different story and claimed she was denied the fifty dollars bail usually set in a shooting case. She told the ladies she only wanted to threaten Culburtt, but she got nervous, and the gun went off."

Essie pressed her nose against the window pane and stared out at the street. "So the ladies want her out of jail?"

"Yeah, and the sheriff's gone," Dix said. "Miss Jolie, I've only been a deputy for three days. All I had to do was guard a lady, and look at this! Maybe I ain't suited to be a deputy."

"Where is the judge?" Jolie pressed.

"On his way home from Lincoln, so I hear tell."

"What do you need?" she asked.

Dix stepped over next to her. "I need a different job."

"I think you're the right one for this job. You're a handsome man with a pleasing personality and yet brave and fearless in trouble."

"Yeah, that's what Miss Celia tells me. But I ain't never faced a pack of hostile women."

"Would it help if I can get them to disperse?" Jolie asked.

"That would be wonderful. Then Miss Celia could bring me some lunch. She's afraid to come near this crowd."

"I'll see what I can do. Can I talk to Mrs. Mitchell?" Jolie asked.

"She might scream and holler," he warned. "That's all she does when I go back there."

"I'll take a chance."

"You don't want me to come with you, do you?" Essie asked.

"Why don't you stay out here and see what you can find out from Max about your Leppy?"

"I was hoping you'd say that."

When Jolie opened the rough wooden door and scooted past the iron cell doors, she smelled tobacco smoke, fried meat, and sweat. She held her breath until she reached the last cell. A short, stocky woman, wearing a gray wool blanket like a shawl, huddled in the corner of the dark cell.

"Miss Jolie? You came to see me?"

"Mrs. Mitchell, I'm so sorry about Sudsy. I so enjoyed having him in my class. I have cried for two days since I heard of his death."

There was no expression on the leathery face of the woman with bobbed-off black and gray hair. She stared at the wall. "My boy's gone. What will I do?"

"Mrs. Mitchell, Sudsy mentioned his older brothers. Are they around anywhere?"

"They left."

"When did they leave?" Jolie quizzed.

"One was fourteen and one was sixteen."

"They just left home?"

"They left me and Sudsy."

"When was that, Mrs. Mitchell?"

"Five years ago. It was just me and him. Now what am I goin' to do?"

"Mrs. Mitchell, I know the Lord will give you strength."

"What was He doin' when my boy died?"

"Shedding a tear, no doubt. He loves us, you know."

"What am I goin' to do?"

She keeps repeating that phrase like a chant. Jolie paced in front of the cell. Her boot heels tapped out a rhythm to her thoughts. "The first thing you need to do is get some legal advice. Mr. Yarrow is a lawyer friend of mine. Perhaps he could give you some counsel if you'd like. You did shoot Mr. Culburtt, right?"

"Was that his name?" Mrs. Mitchell mumbled.

"Didn't you know whom you were shooting?"

"He was the boss. He's the one to blame."

"Mrs. Mitchell, if a crime was committed, you should go to Sheriff Riley. You can't just go out and shoot people."

"I'm all alone. Do you know how frightening it is to be all alone?"

"No, I probably don't. May I have Mr. Yarrow come by and visit. He might have some advice for you."

"Why won't they let me pay bail and get out of here?"

"I think they're afraid you might try to shoot someone else. Will you shoot someone else, Mrs. Mitchell?"

The woman stared emotionless at the stone wall of the jail.

"Mrs. Mitchell?"

Her eyes dropped to her folded hands on the plain gray dress covering her lap. She murmured something.

Jolie pressed her face against the cold steel bars of the jail cell door. "I couldn't hear you, Mrs. Mitchell."

The forty-five-year-old woman glanced up with pleading brown eyes. "I don't know if I'd shoot someone else. Sometimes, Miss Jolie, I do things that I never thought I'd do. I don't know what gets into me."

"Mrs. Mitchell, I know you're mad at God because of Sudsy's death. And I don't have an answer for that. But the Lord is the only one who can give any of us real peace. While you're in here, let Him speak to your heart. You can find His peace even in a storm like this."

The woman got up and came over to the cell door. She reached between the bars and held Jolie's hand. "I've got to get out of here. I've got to have freedom, Miss Jolie. I'll die if I have to stay in here. You've got to get me out of here."

"Mrs. Mitchell . . ." Jolie tried to pull her hand back. "That hurts my hand."

"You've got to help," Mrs. Mitchell growled. The woman's pleading eyes

64

turned angry. "Get me out of here!" The voice was a deep growl.

Jolie yanked her hand away and stepped back from the bars. "Mrs. Mitchell, you told me you have no one. You worry about your future. For a day or two you have meals provided and a warm bunk to sleep in. Get some rest and contemplate what should happen next. You shot Mr. Culburtt. We must bear the consequences of our actions."

"If I can't shoot 'em, I'll sue 'em," Mrs. Mitchell threatened. "Send your lawyer friend around."

"I'll ask him to stop by. But, remember, the important thing is that justice is done."

"Hah! I don't care about justice. I care about me. What am I going to do?"

"Mrs. Mitchell, I think you're distraught. You're saying things that don't make sense. I'll come back another time if you'd like to talk."

Dusty Mitchell began to sob.

"Mrs. Mitchell?"

"Who's goin' to bury my boy?"

"Would you like for me to have my pastor, Rev. Leyland, stop by and visit about that? I'm sure he can take care of the arrangements."

"No!" the woman blurted out. "He

didn't know my Sudsy."

"No, but he's a very kind, gracious, spiritual man."

"You do it, Miss Jolie."

"Me?"

"You knew Sudsy. You take care of the funeral arrangements."

"But . . . but . . ."

"You won't turn me down, will you?" she sobbed.

Jolie took a deep breath and held it for a moment. "No, I won't turn you down. I'll look into the arrangements for Sudsy."

The woman wiped her eyes on the sleeves of her dress. "You're the only one I can count on in this whole town."

"Mrs. Mitchell, you're new here. There are many fine people in this region, and they'll help you if need be. Did you know that there are about three dozen women out in front of the jail, asking for your release. They have not abandoned you."

"Lot of good it does."

"Mrs. Mitchell, you've been in our community only a few weeks. You have kept to yourself, lost a son, and shot a nice man. Under those circumstances, you have very commendable community support. Good day."

Mrs. Mitchell's eyes narrowed to a dark

gleam. "Tell them I'm hungry for shell-fish."

Jolie spun around. "What did you say?"

"If them ladies want to do somethin' for me, tell them I'm hungry for shellfish. I'm from Louisiana, and I miss my shellfish and my gumbo."

"I will certainly tell them that," Jolie assured her.

When Jolie reached the front office, Essie and Maxwell Dix were studying maps of Wyoming.

"They said my Leppy killed a fourteen-year-old boy as he was sitting on the privy," Essie blurted out.

"Leppy wouldn't do that," Jolie gasped.

Dix studied a telegram on his desk. "There's a coal miners' strike goin' on over in Carbon County. Leppy and some others hired on to protect a fancy train from back east carrying mine owners and lawyers. There was a big riot down at the train yard, and someone tossed a stick of dyna-mite under a train car."

Jolie held her hands to her cheeks. "Oh, dear."

"Leppy dispersed the crowd with a couple of shots in the air, yanked out the fuse, and the blasting cap exploded, doing no more harm than a firecracker. He took off runnin' after the agitator down a dark alley. He said he heard a couple shots; so he yanked out his gun, but he never did find anyone."

"But why do they want to hang him?" Jolie asked.

"The next mornin' someone found the boy shot dead in the alley outhouse, and Leppy got arrested. They had a trial the next day, and of course only miners and locals served on the jury."

Jolie took a deep breath. "The next day? Is that legal?"

"Who's to say? The point is, the jury convicted him of murder and sentenced him to hang. The mine owners have left and returned to Laramie City, leavin' Leppy in a coal camp awaiting hanging. It don't look good, Miss Jolie."

"But . . . that's circumstantial evidence. Other people probably went down that alley, including the dynamite thrower. They can't convict on that," Jolie protested.

"I reckon they already did."

"I've got to bust him out so he can prove himself innocent," Essie explained. "Max said I can borrow his shotgun."

"You what? What is this with everyone wanting to shoot everyone? You will not take a shotgun."

A coy smile crept across Essie's face. "Then we're going?"

"As soon as we can, we'll go visit Leppy."

"How about right now?"

"Not right now."

"But why?"

"Estelle, it's a two-day trip to get there. I have a job, and you have school."

"We have to do something."

"Yes, I'm praying about that."

"I hope the Lord answers soon," Essie mumbled.

"How's Mrs. Mitchell?" Maxwell asked.

Jolie glanced back at the door that led to the cells. "She's confused. Remorseful one moment, full of vengeance the next. I think she's distraught and liable to do or say anything. You're right that she needs to be kept in here for her own sake. Sometimes her voice is very coarse. Almost foreign."

"I noticed that. How about you tellin' them fine lady citizens out there that it's your opinion that Mrs. Mitchell should stay in jail?"

"I'll see what I can do," Jolie offered.

"Maybe you could walk with Miss Celia as she brings me some lunch."

"You think she would walk through a riotous crowd with me?" Jolie asked.

"I reckon Miss Celia would walk with you into Hades if you asked her to. She knows the devil don't have a chance once Miss Jolie makes up her mind," Dix grinned.

"I'd go with Jolie anywhere too," Essie piped up.

"That's good, little darlin', 'cause if you aim to hike into a coal miners' riot, Hades might be easier."

Bright sunlight greeted Jolie and Essie as they stepped back out into the street. Jolie shaded her eyes even though she stood under the awning.

Nadella Ripon approached her. "Are they letting her out, or do we have to whip them by ourselves?"

Jolie stared at Nadella's two hundred plus pounds. *My word, I do believe she could do it too.* "Mrs. Mitchell looks forward to having an opportunity to explain herself to the judge. Right now she is peaceful. She is safe, warm, and comfortable."

"Did they lock her up with the men?" Minnie Clover asked.

"No, they dismissed the men. She has the facility to herself. But she did ask that you help her with one thing."

"What is that?" Nadella asked.

"She's hungry for shellfish."

"Shellfish? You mean mussels, clams, and the like?" Mrs. Sitmore asked.

"Yes, I believe so," Jolie replied.

"This is the Nebraska frontier. Where do we get something like that?" Pearl Anderson muttered.

"I knew that if anyone in town could find such fare, it would be Nadella Ripon and members of the League."

"She's right, girls," Nadella blustered. "We can go door to door asking if anyone has shellfish if there is none at the stores."

"What about our protest here? I hate to abandon our advancements," Pearl Anderson declared.

"I have a plan," Jolie suggested. "Gather close." She put one arm around Essie on her left and started to put her other around Nadella but gave up trying to circle the woman. "Why don't you take shifts? Two could sit right there on the bench in case the sheriff or judge shows up, and then they can plead their case. Take two-hour shifts. The others could find the shellfish and take care of their own families. The deputy can't make a decision without clearing it with the sheriff; so it's not fair to demand something he can't produce."

"That's what my Leonard used to tell me, rest his soul," Nadella murmured.

"I think that's a very good idea," Mary Tarnes agreed.

"Yes, well, my feet are killing me," Nadella admitted. "Mary, you and Minnie take the first shift. Pearl and I will be back in two hours."

Jolie and Essie stood on the boardwalk until the women dispersed, with Mary and Minnie settled in on the bench.

"You did it, Jolie. You stopped a riot," Essie boasted.

"It wasn't really a riot. Just some concerned citizens, that's all."

"What's the difference between a riot and a bunch of concerned citizens?"

"A riot leads to illegal actions."

"I need to get to Rawlins, Wyoming, and lead a riot," Essie declared.

"Not right now. I want to make some arrangements for poor Sudsy's funeral."

"You mean, go see the undertaker even before you go see your sweetie?"

"No, we'll go see Tanner first. Let's get the team before they remember their naughty ways and run off."

They had just stepped down into the dusty street when a dilapidated, topless two-seated surrey rattled up and stopped.

"Would you two fine ladies like a ride out to view scenic Scott's Bluff?"

"That ain't two fine ladies, Bob. That's Miss Jolie and little darlin'."

"I know who it is, Bill. I was just makin' small talk."

"Hi, boys," Jolie grinned. "Is this your buggy?"

"Yes, Miss Jolie," Bob reported. "It was a secret gift."

"Not only that," Bill added, "but we cain't tell you who gave it to us."

"We formed a buggy company."

"How is the Condor Brothers' Buggy Rental goin'?"

"It couldn't be better," Bill beamed.

"It would be better if we had a payin' customer," Bob contradicted him.

"Business is slow?" Jolie asked.

"No, ma'am. We offer the fastest trip to Scott's Bluff available," Bill proclaimed.

Essie held her nose and rolled her eyes.

Jolie studied the sunken eyes in Bill Condor's thin face. "You boys smell like . . . eh, a campfire. Do you know what I mean?"

"Yes, ma'am, we cook over one ever' day," Bob reported.

"People who ride on trains are not

campfire folks. They're the type that eat in the fancy restaurants with lilacs on the table."

"Lilacs is tasty when a man's hungry," Bill declared.

"Here's my point," Jolie continued. "If you want to attract those people in your buggy business, you'll need a hot bath, a shave, clean clothes, and some tonic water."

"Miss Jolie, we need all of that just to give them a ride out to Scott's Bluff?" Bob moaned.

"I'm afraid so."

"Maybe we should go into the freightin' business," Bob mumbled. "Freightin' don't require you to take a bath and shave."

"But we don't have a freight wagon, Bob."

"I know that, Bill, but we're fast. Maybe we could have the fastest freight service in town."

"Bill and Bob's Fast Freight." Bill grinned.

"Bob and Bill's, you mean," Bob insisted.

"What do you think, Miss Jolie?" Bill pressed.

"I think Condor Brothers' Conveyance would be nice," she offered.

"That's a big word, Miss Jolie," Bob said.

"Yes. It would make you sound much more distinguished."

Bill Condor sat up and fastened the top button on his dirty white shirt. "Then Conveyance it is!"

Three

The bell above the door at the Platte Valley Armory rang once, and the wide-shouldered man at the back bench spun around with a grin. His dark brown hair flopped down across his forehead, meeting thick, dramatic eyebrows.

He wiped his hands on a towel. "Jolie and little sis. This is goin' to be a great day. What brings the beautiful Bowers girls to town?"

Essie ran to the back of the combination display room and shop, her heavy lace-up shoes clunking across the bare wooden floor like a reluctant teenage boy's at his first dance. "Hi, Tanner, did you hear about my Leppy? He's in jail, and me and your sweetie are goin' to Rawlins, Wyoming, and bust him out. Have you got a lever-action shotgun I can borrow, or do you think a 10-gauge has too much recoil for a girl my size? Gibs said it would kick me into Kansas, but I'm sturdier than I look." She stared down into a long wooden box. "Wow, look at that! A whole crate of Winchester 1873 saddle-ring carbines. I've never seen a whole box of them. You have such a nice store, Tanner. Why, I could just stay right here all morning," Essie gushed.

Jolie stepped up to him and slipped her arms around his waist. He held her shoulders. "Hi, darlin'." He grinned.

She kissed his cheek. "Good morning, Mr. Wells. You look busy today."

"Saturdays are always this way. They come to town Saturday mornin' and want their gun fixed before dark." He brushed a soft kiss on her lips. She released him and stepped back. "Now what's all this about Leppy? You two are goin' to do what?"

Jolie plucked up the shop towel and began to dust the tops of the small cardboard cartridge boxes. "We understand that Leppy Verdue has been convicted of murder and is to be hung December 20."

"Are you really going to Rawlins?" he asked.

"Yes, but I just don't know when or how." Jolie took Tanner's hand and began to wipe the gun oil off the back of it.

"Are you dusting me up now, Miss Jolie? You know," he smiled, "I am capable of cleaning my own hands."

Jolie bit her lip. "Sorry." She shoved the towel into his jeans pocket.

"At least she doesn't comb your hair using her spit," Essie noted.

"Estelle. Don't you have something better to do than gawk?" Jolie snapped.

"I don't think so. Tanner's store is a sight to behold." Essie cleared her throat. "I reckon I could just look at these things for hours. Tanner has everything except hard candy."

"Candy?" Tanner said.

"I sure do like hard candy. They have a butterscotch one that's like divine nectar shared with mere mortals."

Tanner started to laugh. "She's been reading a lot again, I see. What are you really talking about, Estelle Cinnia?"

"He can be quite dense at times, Jolie."

"So I've noticed." She took his arm and waltzed him to the front of the store. "But he does scrub up nice. You know, in a rustic, gunsmith sort of way."

"I feel like a hog bein' led by the ring in his nose. Ever'one knows what's happenin' except the hog."

"I think Essie is hinting for a bribe," Jolie suggested.

"Oh . . ." Tanner spun back around. "Say, li'l sis, here's a nickel. How about you meanderin' down to Saddler's Grocery store?"

"Give me two nickels, and I'll be gone twice as long."

"Estelle!" Jolie huffed.

"I was teasing," Essie said. "Sort of."

Tanner led Jolie over in front of Essie. "You don't have to leave at all, little sis."

Essie looked at Jolie's eyes. "I don't?"

Tanner spun Jolie around and kissed her on the lips.

"Oh my," Jolie gasped.

"I'm leaving." Essie giggled and skipped toward the front door. Then she turned. "That was a good kiss, Tanner. You're almost as good as Daddy."

"Thank you, Essie. How about Jolie? Was she as good as your mother?"

Essie smirked. "No one can kiss like Mama." She slammed the door behind her.

Jolie hugged Tanner and laid her head on his strong shoulder. "I love you, Tanner Wells."

"And I love you, Miss Jolie Bowers." He stepped back out of her grip. "Hey, I have an idea. Why don't you and me get married?"

"Right now?" she smiled.

"You set the date."

"I already did, and you know it. Don't you try to get out of that big church wedding. Mrs. Fleister has our reception

79

supper already planned."

"But that's seven and a half months away."

"Are you getting impatient, Mr. Wells?"

"Yes, ma'am, I surely am."

"A little impatience is good for your maturity, Mr. Wells. I'm sure you'll survive," she beamed. "I have a swath of cloth to show you. I'm thinking of making my dress out of . . ."

Loud banging from the backroom caused her to stop and stare at the door that separated the store from the living quarters in the back.

"What was that?"

"Oh, nothing," Tanner replied. "Show me the cloth."

She reached for her handbag. "Well, Mother and I think . . ."

Further banging erupted from the back. "That most certainly is something." She stepped toward the back door. "What is . . ."

He stepped in front of her and blocked her way.

"Show me the cloth," he insisted.

She tried to prod him to the side. "Tanner Wells, what are you . . ."

He didn't budge. "Darlin' . . . it's a surprise."

"What's a surprise?"

"I'm building you something, and it's a surprise."

"You most certainly are not building me anything. You're out here. But someone is hammering in your room."

"Darlin', really, I want to surprise you. Chet Washburn is a good carpenter and wanted to buy a new gun to hunt with; so I'm trading him some work. I'm havin' him build you a surprise."

"What is it?" Jolie demanded.

"Now, darlin', how can I surprise you if I tell you?"

"A surprise?"

He nodded. "I think you're goin' to like it."

She took a deep breath and sighed aloud. *Lord, why is it I don't like surprises? Mama says it's because I can't be in control of surprises. Maybe she's right.* "When do I get to see this surprise?"

"As soon as it is completed."

"And just when do you expect that to be?" she pressed.

"Sometime before the 14th of June."

"What? But that's seven and a half months away," she moaned.

"A little impatience is good for your maturity, Miss Jolie. I'm sure you'll survive," he beamed.

"Isn't that a fine shinley?" she mumbled.

"And I don't want you sneakin' back there and taking a peek."

"But I clean your room once a week," she insisted.

"No more."

"But — but . . . you can't expect me to . . ."

"Yes, I do. Do you promise not to peek?"

"This is not fair, Tanner Wells."

"Do I get to see that dress when it's made?"

"Of course not. But that's an established tradition."

"I'm establishin' a new one." He grinned. "Please, Jolie, it's important to me."

She stomped back to the front of the store. "I suppose we're at an impasse. What will we do after we're married and we arrive at an impasse?"

"I suggest we smooch."

"Hah," she protested. "You think that's a solution to most every problem."

"How does your mother settle problems with your father?" he challenged.

"My mother? That's not a fair comparison."

"Why?"

"Because my mother can't keep from kissing Daddy. It's in her bones."

"You mean her daughter didn't inherit any of that?"

Jolie rolled her gray-green eyes. "Okay . . . Tanner Wells. I'll wait until you can surprise me, and if I get extremely impatient, I'll just have to grab you and kiss you. I trust I don't get impatient at a church social or in your parents' front room," she laughed. "Then you like this swatch?"

"Darlin', anything you wear is wonderful to me."

"Tanner, you're so easy to please."

There was a serious cascade of hammer crashes from the backroom. She glanced at him. "I really don't get to see?"

"Nope. But I'll show you something very interesting. Look at this." He pointed to the Winchesters in the wooden crate.

"You're changing the subject, Mr. Wells?"

"Yes, but it's a mystery that needs your help in solving," he declared.

"Oh?"

"Last Monday I had a person come in and sell me these carbines, new and still in the crate."

Jolie tugged the rag out of his jeans pocket and stooped to dust off the crated guns. "This is a gun shop. What's the mystery in that?"

"Yes, but very seldom does an individual have a crate of guns. Usually only armories or hardware stores buy them by the crate."

"I would imagine the big ranches buy them by the crate," Jolie suggested.

"Not often, since they only add one or two men at a time, not a whole crew."

"So who sold them to you?" She tucked the rag back into his pocket.

Tanner tried to brush his thick hair behind his ear. "Sudsy's mama."

"Mrs. Mitchell?" Jolie folded her arms and stared at the crate of guns. "Where did she get a crate of Winchesters?"

"Here's the story she gave me. She was very convincing. She said her late husband and she were on their way to Idaho to open up a store. They had a wagon full of supplies. But when they reached Custer City, South Dakota, he became sick and died there."

"I knew she was a widow," Jolie declared.

"She said she had to sell off the things for income but had kept the guns to the last because her husband had been so proud of them. Anyway, she wanted to sell the entire crate full for fifty dollars."

"Five dollars each for a new rifle?"

"Yes, and I turned her down."

"You did?" Jolie asked.

"I bought them for eight dollars each. If I buy them from the factory in New Haven, I have to pay eleven dollars when I buy them by the case. I thought it only fair. They are brand-new."

"So what's the mystery?"

"She made it sound like her husband had been dead for years."

"That's my understanding," Jolie said. "I know her older boys left her about five years ago, and Mr. Mitchell was out of the picture then."

Tanner picked up one of the guns. "Then I have a problem."

"What's that?"

He turned the gun over and pointed to the lower tang. "According to their serial numbers, these guns were manufactured last year."

"What?"

"Each Winchester is stamped with a serial number, see? This one is 352957, which means it was manufactured last year. If her husband died years ago, he couldn't have purchased these."

"What are you saying, Tanner?"

"She doesn't look like the type that would steal them. But I don't have an explanation that satisfies. I was goin' to ask her again next time I saw her. But with Sudsy's loss and her shooting Mr. Culburtt, I didn't want to press it. I think I'll write to the Winchester factory in New Haven and see if they have a record of who these were originally sold to."

"Hmmm." Jolie stared down at the crate. "That *is* a mystery."

The hammering in the backroom continued.

"I'm surrounded by mysteries," she murmured. "I don't suppose you've changed your mind about telling me what's going on back there?"

"No."

"In that case . . ." She sashayed to the front door. "In that case, I shall go and arrange a funeral."

"A funeral?" he jibed.

"Not for you, Mr. Wells . . . though the thought may have crossed my mind. I promised poor Mrs. Mitchell I would make arrangements for Sudsy. I have no idea what I should do, but I'll check with Rev. Leyland."

"Would you like for me to close up shop and go with you?" he offered.

"You said you were swamped with Saturday repairs." She looked at his eyes. "You would, wouldn't you?"

"Yep."

"Seven and a half months is a long, long time, Mr. Wells. You stay here."

"Are you leavin' without a smooch?" he teased.

"You are as pathetic as my mother." She marched back over to him and brushed a soft kiss across his lips.

It was shortened by the hammering from the backroom.

"I'm leaving before I go screaming into the backroom."

He walked her to the door. His strong, callused fingers locked into hers.

Rev. Leyland was not at home, but she left word with the minister's wife and then proceeded to hike east along Main Street. A fat black-and-white cat that looked like it weighed thirty pounds rested on the bench in front of Saddler's Grocery. Next to it sat Essie with a jaw so swollen that some would have thought she had a bad case of mumps.

"My, who is your friend?" Jolie called out.

"Are you talking to me or the cat," Essie mumbled.

"You. Just how many pieces of butterscotch do you have in your mouth?"

"Sssshicks."

"Six? But you only had five cents."

"Sssshicks for a nickel."

"And you couldn't eat them one at a time?"

"I didn't want to get my hand schticky." Essie wiped the back of her hand across her mouth.

"Yes, I can see that." Jolie reached down and scratched the top of the big cat's head. "And who is this?"

"That's DirtDoug."

"DirtDoug?" Jolie grinned. "Who does he belong to?"

"Cats don't belong to anyone. But he lives in the alley behind the meat market."

"Yes, I should have guessed that. I'm goin' to see Mr. Mendez. Do you want to come?"

Essie wiped butterscotch drool off her chin with her fingertips. "No, I think it best if I stay here."

"You might be right." Jolie started to walk away, then turned back. "I don't know why under those circumstances you continue to sit there. I would think you'd be embarrassed."

Essie sat up. "Oh, I'm not embarrassed. DirtDoug is a nice cat."

"I was talking to the cat." Jolie grinned.

Essie stuck out a very butterscotched tongue.

The Colorado Furniture Emporium stretched along half of the block, but it had only a single entrance. When Jolie reached the front door, Mr. Ephraim Mendez opened it for her.

"Miss Bowers, nothing happened to your mattresses, I trust." He stepped out on the sidewalk and glanced down the street.

"No, Mr. Mendez, they are very nice. And, no, my mother didn't come to town with me."

He stepped back inside and stared at a brown leather chair with red oak trim. "And what can I do for you?"

"Mr. Mendez, I need your help. Perhaps you know that Mrs. Mitchell is in jail, and she asked me to take care of the burial arrangements for her son." Jolie paused and bit her lip. "I'm sorry, Mr. Mendez. Sudsy was one of my students, and I'm not dealing with this very well. Anyway, I agreed to plan things, but I have no idea what to do. Rev. Leyland was out of town; so I wondered if you would help me little."

Mr. Mendez seemed to be talking to the chair. "Would you like to see him?"

"Rev. Leyland?"

"No, young Devon Mitchell."

Jolie's mouth dropped open. "He's here?"

Ephraim Mendez's chin was so narrow it looked as if something was missing. "I'm the only one on this side of the river who sells caskets. So I end up being the undertaker as well. Would you like to check on him?"

"Oh, no . . . eh," Jolie's breathing became labored, "that won't be necessary."

"Good choice. I have him in a casket already, just waiting for word from the family."

Jolie glanced around the huge display room of the furniture store. "You picked out a casket?"

"I had Chet Washburn build a pine casket yesterday. It was too gruesome to leave the poor boy rolled in a blanket. But I need to get him buried by sundown today."

Jolie pulled off her straw hat and fanned herself. "Today?"

"Miss Bowers, I'm a furniture salesman, not an embalmer. I'll be happy to surrender the body to whoever wants to take charge. But I must get the body buried today. I'm trying to discreetly say the body will begin to, eh . . ."

"I understand, Mr. Mendez, but what about the cemetery?"

"The county will provide a plot if the family cannot afford one. But the regular gravedigger is, well, drunk and passed out at the Oriental. So I'm beside myself to know what to do."

"If there is a funeral this afternoon, it doesn't give much time for a proper service."

"Perhaps he could be buried today with some graveside words, and then you could hold the funeral service next week."

Jolie retied her hat. "Yes, perhaps so. Thank you, Mr. Mendez. What is the cost of the casket?"

"My wife and I donated the wood. Mister Washburn should be paid three dollars for his effort. But I can take care of that if there are no funds."

"Mr. Mendez, I'll pay Mr. Washburn. And I'll see if I can find someone to dig the grave. I'll bury Sudsy before I leave town today."

"Thank you, Miss Bowers. I would rather not touch the casket today, it being our Sabbath. I trust that doesn't create a problem."

"We all have our religious traditions, Mr. Mendez. I respect yours."

He stared at an elk antler kerosene lantern that hung overhead. "I know you do, Miss Bowers. Your family is a credit to Christianity, and, believe me, I have not often said that."

He walked with her back out to the sidewalk.

Jolie paused at the doorway and shook his hand. "Mr. Mendez, what kind of things does Mr. Washburn build, besides caskets?"

"Oh, he's a very fine craftsman. He built my wife quite a lovely wardrobe closet — that is, if one doesn't buy ready-mades."

Jolie tugged her hat down in front as she stepped out into the dirt street. *Yes, a wardrobe closet! My Tanner is having a wardrobe closet built for me because there are no closets in the backroom. He's a sweetie.*

The old surrey pulled up to her as she reached the center of the dirt street.

"We're a freight company now, but we still ain't got no customers, Miss Jolie," Bob Condor said.

"Give it a little more time," she urged.

"You got any freight that needs hauling?" Bob asked.

"She ain't got nothin' but her coat and her purse," Bill noted.

"I can see that, Bill. But she might have some freight at the depot or something."

"She's got a wagon twice this big," Bill continued. "She don't need no one to haul her freight."

"Boys, would you like a job? It'll take you about two hours, and I'll pay you one dollar each."

"A cash dollar?" Bob asked.

"Yes."

"In coins or greenbacks," Bill asked.

"They're worth the same," Bob declared.

"I don't trust them greenbacks. I want coins," Bill insisted.

"Then I'll pay you in coins," she promised.

Bob glanced up and down the street. "Do you need us to shoot someone?"

"No, of course not."

"That's good." Bill grinned. "We ain't got no bullets."

"I told you not to tell anyone that," Bob growled.

"Miss Jolie ain't goin' to call us out," Bill argued.

"Boys, I need you to dig a grave for me."

Bill pulled off his hat and scratched his head. "For you? Are you feelin' puny, Miss Jolie?"

"No, the grave is not for me but for the

young Mitchell boy who died at the train yard yesterday. I'm in charge of his arrangements."

Bob reached under his torn shirt and scratched his armpit. "You just want a hole in the ground?"

"Six feet long, three feet wide, and six feet deep. Can you do that?"

"Where 'bouts?" Bill asked.

The drift of wind shifted a little, and the odor from the Condor brothers reminded Jolie of a hog farm. "In the cemetery on the north side of town. I'll meet you there after lunch and mark it off for you."

"Just dig a hole?" Bill repeated.

She stepped closer to their buggy as a fringed surrey trotted past her. She fought off the urge to hold her nose. "And cover up the casket after the burial is over."

"And you're goin' to pay us one dollar each?" Bob quizzed.

"Yes."

"Shoot, Miss Jolie, we've done it before for less money than that," Bill boasted.

"We ain't neither," Bob protested.

"Yes, we have — many a time," Bill said.

"We have never put the body in," Bob fumed.

"Oh, we get to put the body in?" Bill rubbed the back of his oily hair. "Now isn't that a fine shinley? Usually we take them out. We dug out twelve that one night for them doctors in Lincoln."

Jolie felt her neck tighten. *I don't want to hear this, Lord.* "I'll meet you at the cemetery at 1:00 p.m."

"Do we bring the spades and picks, or do you?" Bob asked.

"I'd appreciate it if you did that."

"This day turned out purdy good, Bob. And you said we ain't had a good day since we found those mice in the oats."

Jolie turned and hurried away.

The Nebraska Hotel was only fifty feet wide, but it stretched back to the alley and contained twelve deluxe rooms upstairs. The restaurant below was considered the finest in western Nebraska. At least that's what all the railroad brochures declared.

It was owned by the railroad.

And the finest second-story room overlooked main street with a view of Scott's Bluff in the distance. It was occupied by the district railroad superintendent, Edward Culburtt, but it was Cutter Davenport who sat with a shotgun across his lap outside the door.

Davenport tipped his hat. "Miss Jolie."

"I came to call on Mr. Culburtt."

"He's been expecting you."

"He has?"

"Yep. He said, 'Wake me up when the Bowerses come callin'.' I'll check with him." Davenport rose from the plain oak chair, carbine still in hand.

"Mr. Davenport, how did it happen that Mrs. Mitchell could march right in and shoot Mr. Culburtt with a shotgun without anyone stopping her?"

"Because he wanted to talk to her. The boy's death grieved him sorely. We just didn't think she had any intention of using the shotgun."

When he returned to the hall, he ushered her in and remained at the doorway. Jolie went to the bedside of the gray-haired man. He lay on his side with the sheet pulled up to his chin. His face looked whiter than the sheets.

"Mr. Culburtt, how are you?"

"Miss Jolie, please sit down. I had hoped to see you today."

She pulled up a green-velvet-covered cherry wood side chair. "I'm so shocked and sorry about your injury."

"Davenport," Mr. Culburtt called out, "please keep your vigil outside and close the door." When the door clicked shut, Culburtt turned back to her. "Miss Jolie, where do I begin?" He closed his eyes. "I'm a railroad man. That's all I ever wanted to be. I like to build them, maintain them, and run them. It gets in a man's blood. It's unreasonable. It's like falling in love with a beautiful lady when you're a young buck, and you can never get her out of your mind. Train men are train men for life. Now, as you know, I don't want to fight with farmers, ranchers, and especially grieving mothers. I've never had anything hit me like this. I think I'm goin' to retire, Miss Jolie."

She reached over and touched his hand. "Mr. Culburtt, you're so perfect for this job."

"Miss Jolie, I haven't slept in two nights. I just keep thinking about that boy. His eyes. His pleading eyes, and I couldn't do a thing for him. My word, Miss Jolie, I would have gladly traded places with the lad. My pain is so great, and I know I'll have to carry it the rest of my life. There have been moments in the past two days that I wished his mother had done a better job of shooting me."

"Mr. Culburtt, don't say that. We need you here. The railroad is so necessary for everyone in western Nebraska, and it can be so cold and impersonal. You make it real, human, reasonable. You *are* the railroad in our minds. We need you."

"Miss Jolie, those are kind words. I expected it from you. I don't think the Bowerses know how to be any other way. Steel rails run through my veins, but it's the Lord's tender mercy that seems to be in yours. Railroad men come and go. I can be replaced. It's you, your mama and your daddy, your family, that can never be replaced. I think it best that I retire. I've got some friends up in Deadwood. Maybe I'll move up to the Black Hills."

"But you're a railroad man, Mr. Culburtt. Accidents happen often. This isn't the first death you've been associated with, is it?"

"Heavens no, but this was not a railroad worker who understood that it's a hazardous job. Nor a passenger aware that there's potential danger in fast-moving trains. Just a lad hiking down the tracks. Oh, my, Miss Jolie. I can't get his image off my mind. It haunts me like an Edgar Allan Poe novel."

"Mr. Culburtt . . . you just can't blame yourself. You had the yard posted. You have a watchman. You did what you could."

"It wasn't enough," he coughed.

"Was it your idea to station the dogs?"

Culburtt opened his eyes but refused to look at hers. "No, the idea for yard dogs came from Monroe and the bunch at headquarters. They trained the dogs and shipped them out. They said it would end our problem."

Jolie held her hat in her lap and wiped dust off the nightstand with her fingertips. "What problem was that?"

"Ever since the unrest last month, we've been having cars randomly broken into at the yard."

"And items stolen?"

"Yes, but only good things. They seem to know which cars hold the most valuable merchandise."

Jolie picked up a glass from the nightstand. "Would you like a sip of water, Mr. Culburtt?"

"Yes, thank you."

She held the short glass as he sipped. "If they're selective in what they take, perhaps it's someone who works for the railroad and has access to the invoices."

"There's always that chance. But even when I deliberately mislabeled several cars to try to catch our own people, the thieves knew where the best goods were anyway. It's always a random night, a random time of the night, and never the same location in the yard. Even when I post a guard, he's in the wrong location."

"I hadn't heard of any of this happening."

"We were trying to keep it quiet," Culburtt explained. "With sentiment being what it is, we didn't want to give anyone else ideas. A boy's death and me getting shot is not exactly keeping things quiet."

"Neither of which is your fault, Mr. Culburtt," she said.

"I accept the responsibility for this district. That's my job. Anyway, headquarters sent the dogs, and we had them two weeks. Now this. I've penned up the dogs. I won't let this happen again. I try to do things right, Miss Jolie."

"I know, Mr. Culburtt."

"I can't believe she shot me."

"Mrs. Mitchell seems to be a very distraught woman. I believe she had some emotional struggles before all of this."

"Are you saying she's crazy?"

Jolie gave a deep sigh. "She's had a lot of tough things in her life — losing a husband, a couple of sons running off. She wasn't very balanced. That doesn't excuse her actions, but she didn't even know whom she shot. She was so mad that she lashed out. Mr. Culburtt, even a well-mannered dog will lash out and bite his master if he's hurt or scared enough."

"Yes, but we aren't dogs."

"That's very true. Very true. There's no excuse for it. But we need you here, Mr. Culburtt. Please reconsider."

The gray-haired man reached out his hand toward Jolie. She took it and held it with both of hers. He just shook his head. She watched the tears roll down his leathery cheeks. He tried to open his mouth to speak. No words came out.

"It's okay, Mr. Culburtt. You get your rest. I'll check back on you next time I'm in town." Jolie placed his hand back on the covers, patted his forehead, and turned to leave.

His voice was barely a whisper. "Thank you, Miss Jolie. . . . You'll never know how important your words are to me."

She descended the stairs of the hotel. *Lord, Mr. Culburtt is a good man. It's not easy representing an unpopular company, but he does it with compassion and fairness. This hardly seems like a just reward for his patience.*

Essie and DirtDoug waited for her on the sidewalk in front of the hotel.

"How was Mr. Culburtt?" Essie asked.

"Recovering but melancholy. He blames himself for Sudsy's death."

"I thought it was an accident."

"He thinks it could have been prevented."

"Celia DeLaney is looking for you," Essie informed her.

"Oh, yes. Where is she?"

The big, fat cat rubbed up against Jolie's black lace-up shoes.

Essie pointed toward Saddler's. "She was at the grocery store, but I think she went home after that."

"We'll take the wagon over to her house and give her a ride," Jolie said. "Mr. Dix wanted us to escort her to the jail so he could have his lunch."

The girls hiked across the street. Jolie rubbed the horses' ears and then climbed up on the wagon.

"Can DirtDoug come with us?" Essie asked.

Jolie looked down at the disinterested black-and-white cat. "Do you think he wants to?"

"Oh, yes," Essie squealed. "He said he likes the wind in his face."

Jolie laughed and reached out her arms. "Hand him up, and he can sit with us."

The huge cat perched on the wagon seat

between Jolie and Essie as the team bolted into the street and raced toward Third Street. He sat perfectly still and leaned to the right as they turned up the street.

Celia DeLaney stepped out on the porch. "Can we go see Honey now?" she called.

"Yes, do you need any help with things?"

"No. I'll get my basket, hat, and shawl."

Essie scooted over and put DirtDoug in her lap. "Honey? She calls Maxwell Dix Honey?"

Jolie studied the small poplar trees planted in the DeLaney yard. "She's crazy about him, Essie." *We need to plant trees next spring. I like a yard with trees. Of course, by next summer I'll be living in a one-room apartment behind a gun shop with nothing but . . . a new wardrobe closet.*

"You think Max likes her that much too?"

Jolie nodded. "Yes, I do."

Celia DeLaney's hat ribbon was the same color as her yellow hair. Her gingham dress was freshly starched and ironed.

"You look beautiful today, Celia," Jolie called out as the blonde climbed up in the wagon.

"Jolie, as long as I don't have to stand

103

next to you, I believe I do look quite handsome today."

Jolie glanced back down the street. "That's nonsense."

"No, but you're very kind. I see you have the monster kitty from the meat market."

"His name is DirtDoug. He likes fast wagon rides. I hope you do too," Essie announced. "Hold on to your hat."

The team sprinted up the street.

With one hand Celia DeLaney clutched the iron rail of the wagon seat. Her other hand kept her cotton skirt from billowing. DirtDoug leaned into the wind. Essie's long hair flagged out behind her.

Jolie Bowers let out a long, slow sigh. *Lord, the faster I drive, the more relaxed I am. It must be wonderful to drive a train and feel that rush of air in your face. Some days I just want to run these horses down the road and never stop. I wonder if You created wind because You like the feel of it on Your face.*

"My word, Jolie, you drive faster than anyone in Nebraska," Celia shouted.

"Mama drives faster," Essie hollered.

Men tumbled out of saloons and shops, and children gawked in awe as they thundered up to the sheriff's office. Celia looked at the men watching them. "It does have some benefits," she murmured.

Two men strolled toward them from the direction of Saddler's Grocery. "Miss Jolie," the taller one called out, "did you hear about that openin' for a stagecoach driver in Chadron?"

Jolie climbed down off the farm wagon. "No thanks, Raymond. I'm a school-teacher, and stage driving would be too boring."

The other man let fly with a wad of chewing tobacco that splattered the dust in the middle of the street. "It might be borin' to you, but it would be a spiritual experience for the passengers."

"How do you figure that, Luke?" she asked.

"They'd be praying for their lives the whole time. Some churches don't have that many faithful."

Jolie clapped her hands and grinned. "Oh, I like that. But if I weren't here to drive down the street, who would put the fear of God in you?"

"Don't you ever change, Miss Jolie," Raymond urged.

"Thank you, boys. That's very sweet of you to say."

"DirtDoug doesn't want to get down," Essie announced. "I think he likes ridin' with you, Jolie. Besides, he gets tired real easy."

"You stay there so he doesn't spook Stranger and Pilgrim," Jolie instructed.

Celia waited on the sidewalk with her basket. "Jolie, how did you talk all those ladies into going home? When I came by, I thought they were going to tear Honey apart limb from limb."

She led Celia to the sheriff's office. "I merely reasoned with them and gave them something else to do." Jolie paused by the door. "I wonder what happened to Minnie Clover and Mary Tarnes? They were going to represent the ladies in case the sheriff or judge returned."

"Perhaps they thought of something better to do."

"I hope so. Riotous behavior never produces righteousness." Jolie knocked on the door. "Max? It's Jolie and Miss Celia."

They waited a moment. Then Celia knocked. "Honey, it's me — Celia Lou."

"Celia Lou?"

"He calls me Celia Lou."

"Is that your middle name?" Jolie asked.

"No, but it's so cute the way he says it. I pretend it's my middle name."

Jolie opened the door a few inches. "Max? Celia is here with your lunch."

There was no response.

Jolie opened the door all the way and marched in. Celia DeLaney slipped in behind her. "Max? He's not here!" Celia's voice cracked.

"Perhaps he's with Mrs. Mitchell." Jolie rushed over to the door leading to the cells. It was unlocked. She swung it open. "Mrs. Mitchell?" Jolie turned back to the main office. "She's gone too."

"Where are they?"

"Maybe the judge did show up, and they are at the courthouse."

"But what about Honey's lunch?" Celia asked.

"You could leave it here or just wait for him."

"Could I wait here in the office?" Celia asked. "I mean, it's not illegal, is it?"

"Of course not."

Celia plopped down in the chair. "This is a fine shinley. I'm just trying to fix my Honey some lunch, and nothing seems to work out."

Jolie raised her chin and sniffed. "Celia, what's that smell?"

"It's sauerkraut and ham sandwiches."

"No . . . it's worse than that," Jolie insisted.

"Does it smell that bad? Sauerkraut

doesn't spoil, does it?"

"No, I smell something . . . It's way too familiar." Jolie hiked back to the cells.

"What is it, Jolie?" Celia called out.

Jolie stopped at the open cell door where Dusty Mitchell had been incarcerated. Her hand went over her mouth and nose. "Oh, no!"

"What is it?" Celia repeated from the doorway.

"Vomit."

"In the cell?"

"Mrs. Mitchell lost her stomach." Jolie turned and scurried back.

Celia fanned her face with her hand.

They were both startled when the front door banged open. Maxwell Dix strolled in with a wide grin. "Ain't this nice? The two purdiest gals in Nebraska are in my office. No offense, Miss Jolie, but I do have a fondness for the yella-haired one."

Celia hurried to his side. "I brought you lunch."

"Thank you, Celia Lou, darlin', but I have a mess to clean up first."

"I'll clean up the cell," Jolie offered. "Mrs. Mitchell ate something that didn't agree with her, I take it. Where is she?"

"Over in Gering at Dr. Fix's hospital."

"She was that sick?" Jolie asked.

"I think she stopped breathin' there for a moment. Scared me plum to death; so I raced her over there."

Jolie patted her fingertips together in front of her. "What was the problem?"

Max dug into Celia DeLaney's basket. "Doc says it's classic shellfish allergy."

"What?" Jolie probed.

He glanced up with half of a ham and sauerkraut sandwich in his hand. "She's allergic to shellfish."

"How can she be? She's from Louisiana. She would know if she's allergic to shellfish or not. That's what she ordered for lunch."

Max sniffed the sandwich and stuck it back into the basket. "She asked for the shellfish?"

"Yes."

He rubbed his blond mustache. "That doesn't make sense. Why would you purposely make yourself sick?"

Jolie stormed around the office. "She's at Dr. Fix's? Who's guarding her?"

"She's sick, Miss Jolie. She ain't goin' nowhere," Dix insisted.

"She's also a prisoner."

"Dr. Fix and her driver are there," Max explained. "They said it would be all right for me to come back here. The doc said she wouldn't feel like getting out of bed for a couple days."

"Something's not right," Jolie said. "What if she purposely made herself sick, and now she isn't being guarded?"

"You don't think . . ." Dix stammered.

"Yes." Jolie nodded. "I do."

Four

"Miss Jolie, that woman was deathly sick. She turned blue and stopped breathin'. It don't make sense for her to go to that extreme." Maxwell Dix held his hat down with his hand as they rounded the corner and hit the bridge to Gering. "No one would do that to herself on purpose."

"It doesn't have to make sense to us. It has to make sense to a desperate and confused, grieving woman," Jolie called back.

DirtDoug sat in Essie's lap and leaned into the breeze.

"Miss Jolie, you ought to slow it down a little on this bridge," Dix shouted.

"She did slow it down," Essie replied. "Where's your sense of risk and adventure?"

"I was hopin' to make it to the weddin'," Dix mumbled.

"Yours or Jolie's?" Essie pressed.

"Mine."

Jolie threw her entire weight straight back and jerked the lead lines. Stranger and Pilgrim settled down to a trot. Yet the wooden bridge creaked as if a convoy of

Prussian cannons were crossing. "You and Celia? Oh, that's wonderful. When is the date?"

"I didn't say anything," Dix mumbled.

"You said you were getting married," Jolie replied.

"You two must be listenin' to squeakin' axles. I promised Miss Celia not to say a word and let her announce it in her own way. Now don't you make my life miserable for me. It ain't for months yet."

"June 7?" Essie asked.

"I — I — how — how . . ." he stammered.

"Yes! I did it. I figured it out," Essie squealed. "Jolie and Tanner are getting married on the 14th. Celia is a traditional kind of bride. She wants a June wedding, but she doesn't want to be compared with Jolie Bowers; so she picked the Saturday before Jolie's wedding, but she doesn't want to announce it yet because she thinks Jolie will be angry, but Jolie won't be. She'll just clap her hands and say, 'Oh, yes!' "

"You are amazin', little sis." Dix grinned.

Essie flashed a wide grin. "Yes, and I'm quite fetching too!"

"And I am way too predictable. I don't even need to be here. She knows what I'm going to do and say ahead of time." Jolie hugged her sister. "You impressed all of us."

"Except for DirtDoug," Essie said. "Cats are not easily impressed."

"I've noticed that," Jolie remarked as they rolled up in front of Dr. Arbuckle Fix's office and hospital.

Max leaped off the wagon. "Wait here. I'll check to make sure the patient is secure."

"Perhaps I overreacted," Jolie admitted. "There's just something so strange about Mrs. Mitchell. I can't really explain it."

Essie stroked the fat cat's head. "There's something strange about DirtDoug. He smells like a meat market. I think he needs a bath."

"I hope you don't intend to be the one to give him one." Jolie stroked the cat's back. "My, he really does have a fine purr."

"He's very happy today. Did you see him smile?" Essie asked.

"No, I don't believe I did."

Essie held the long-haired cat's tail straight up. "Did you know that he's considering moving?"

"No, really?" Jolie asked.

"Yes. He said he has always wanted to live in the country."

Jolie studied the front door of the doctor's office. "Perhaps Strath and Landen Yarrow could take him in."

"No! That's not what I . . . what DirtDoug meant," Essie protested.

Jolie studied her sister's brown eyes. "You may not haul off Mr. Bengsten's cat."

"Just because he eats in the alley behind the meat market doesn't mean —"

Jolie glanced up to see Maxwell Dix sprint out of the doctor's office.

"She did it, Miss Jolie. You were right," Dix fumed. "Fine deputy I am. Can't even guard a woman prisoner."

Jolie's eyes searched the street. "How did it happen?"

"She wouldn't use the bedpan and insisted on goin' out to the privy. Dr. Fix had another patient; so her driver stepped out to the backyard with Mrs. Mitchell. She must have slipped out of the yard when he turned his head. They can't find her."

"How long has she been gone?" Jolie asked.

"They figure twenty minutes. They've been searching the entire neighborhood since."

Jolie shook her head back and forth. "That is one troubled woman. She just keeps making poor decisions."

"I better get back and warn Culburtt," Dix proposed. "Who knows what she'll try."

"Yes, and warn them at the train yard," Jolie added. "I don't think she's very choosey about which railroad man she shoots."

"I'll probably get fired over this. I told Miss Celia I couldn't do this kind of work. I've let her down," Dix lamented.

"Miss Celia thinks you can do almost anything short of walking on water," Jolie assured him. "She'll stick with you, Maxwell Dix, through anything."

He climbed back into the wagon. "I reckon you're right about that part. Can you help me look for Mrs. Mitchell?"

Jolie glanced at the watch that hung on a silver chain around her neck. "Yes, after I get Bill and Bob started digging a grave for Sudsy. I promised to meet them at 1:00."

The cemetery, like all of Scottsbluff, lay on flat, treeless ground. The oldest marker was barely more than a year earlier. At the center was a circular dirt turn-around, and Jolie parked her wagon alongside Bill and Bob's topless old surrey. In the center of the circle were six dead popular seedlings no more than two feet tall.

"Howdy, Miss Jolie," Bill called out as she strolled up to them. "Say, that ain't your mama waitin' in the wagon, is it?"

"Oh, course it ain't her mama," Bob scoffed. "It's her little sis."

"Her mama's little too, Bob."

"That's true but she's older."

"Her mama don't look too old. She wears her hair in a braid."

"That don't mean anything," Bob insisted.

"That's right," Bill pondered. "Aunt Beulah sometimes used to wear her gray hair in a braid."

"I told you that was an accident," Bob growled.

Jolie found an iron spike driven in the ground just north of the circle. "Boys, this is where the grave should be dug. Let me draw it out with the heel of my boot." Jolie hobbled around, scratching out a huge rectangle in the dry west Nebraska dirt. The ground was much softer than when she had etched out a hopscotch court for the children at school. Though she had not touched the dirt, she brushed her hands together before she spoke. "There. Now, listen to me. It should be as wide as that pick handle, as long as one step past the shovel length, and as deep as the shovel.

Do you understand?"

Bill tugged off his old felt slouch hat. "Yes, ma'am."

She pointed to the south side of the rectangle. "Could you please stack all the dirt over here on this side so that the casket can be lowered from the other side?"

"Whoa, did you hear that, Bob? It's goin' to be one of them fancy casket funerals. Don't reckon we ever been to a casket funeral. Except maybe Aunt Beulah's."

Bob Condor glared at his younger brother. "I done told you that were an accident."

Jolie broke into their mutual scowl. "Boys, did you hear what I said?"

"Yes, ma'am." Bill grinned. "You said you wanted it as wide as that pick handle, as long as one step past the shovel length, and as deep as the shovel."

"And she wanted all the dirt piled over here," Bob added.

"I was comin' to that part," Bill pouted.

"This dirt is soft, Miss Jolie. Do we get the whole cash dollar each even if the dirt is soft?" Bob asked.

"Yes, you do. And I'll need you to fill it in after the service is over."

"And leave the casket down there?" Bill questioned.

"That's right."

"I reckon that makes us legal grave-diggers now." Bill grinned.

"Professional," Bob boasted. "If we get paid cash dollars for it, we're professional gravediggers. Ain't that right, Miss Jolie?"

"I believe so." She turned back to the wagon, then paused. "I won't be back for a couple hours; so if you get done, just relax and enjoy the afternoon."

"Yes, ma'am." Bill nodded. He walked back to the wagon with her. "I see you're totin' that meat market cat."

"Essie is thinking about taking him home."

"Isn't that a fine shinley?" Bill exclaimed. "You do that, Bessie. I won't miss that cat one bit. It can put up a real tussle, especially when you're both eyin' the same piece of meat. You know what I mean?"

I have no idea in the world how to think like these two. "We haven't decided if he's going with us. That's up to Mr. Bengsten. I believe the cat belongs to him," Jolie explained.

Bill rubbed his clean-shaven chin. "Old man Bengsten told us he'd give us a pork chop each if we'd kill that cat."

"He did?" Essie hugged DirtDoug.

"But there's some things a man won't do." Bill nodded.

Jolie glanced at Bill's hollow brown eyes. *Somewhere in there is a spark of Your image, Lord.*

"Besides," Bill continued, "me and Bob is out of bullets, and that cat's too dadgum mean to wrestle with your hands."

Perhaps not. "I'll see you boys a little later."

Bob Condor strolled up. "Say, Miss Jolie, if that boy at the livery comes lookin' for his spade and pick, tell him we'll bring 'em back as soon as we're done."

"You stole them?" Essie gasped.

"No, ma'am. We just borrowed them without telling him. He was sleepin' on the hay, and we hated to wake a boy up from his nap."

"How considerate," Jolie said.

"Thank you. That's the way Mama raised us," Bill boasted.

Jolie climbed back into the wagon and drove toward town.

"Bill and Bob are surely strange, but I sorta like them," Essie admitted. "I wonder why that is?"

"Because Estelle Bowers has spent her life befriending strays."

"Do you like them?"

"Yes, I do," Jolie admitted. "Sometimes I have trouble remembering not to expect too much from them."

"I'm impressed. They must have had to save some money even to buy that old surrey. Those black horses of Mrs. Mitchell's might be the fastest sprinters in the county," Essie remarked.

"They got that rig from Mrs. Mitchell? Why did she give it to them? How do you know they're fast?"

"Sudsy used to brag about how his mama and him could go to Scottsbluff after dark and make it back home before midnight."

"He did? Why did they come all the way into Scottsbluff after dark?"

"His mama needed some medicine."

"What kind of medicine?"

"I don't know," Essie replied. "Maybe it was shellfish allergy medicine."

"I'm surprised there was a drugstore open after dark." The wagon rumbled up to the front of the Platte River Armory, and Jolie parked it halfway out in the street. She shoved the lead lines into Essie's hand. "Here, hold the boys while I run in to see Tanner for a minute."

"Did you need a smooch that bad?" When Essie took the lead lines, DirtDoug sat on the wagon seat beside her.

"No, of course not. I want to ask Tanner to help with Sudsy's funeral."

Essie stroked the black-and-white cat. "You mean, you aren't going to smooch him?"

Jolie paused on the sidewalk and tugged off her straw hat. "I didn't say that."

Even before the bell above the door quit ringing, there was a shout from the back of the room. "Hi, Jolie."

She glanced back to see her youngest brother sitting on a stool next to Tanner Wells. "Hi, Gibs. I see you made it to town after all."

"Yep. We got back about half an hour ago. I drove as slow as I could." He grinned. "I didn't see you around town but figured you'd come by and see your sweetie."

"Yes, and I should have known you would be here talking guns with Tanner."

"We weren't talking guns," Tanner declared.

"Oh?"

"We were talkin' about girls." Gibs blushed.

Jolie laughed and stepped over close enough to put her arm around her brother's shoulder. "Oh, you were? Just what were you discussing?"

"Jolie, did you ever notice how many fine-lookin' women live around Scottsbluff?" Gibs asked.

"Now that you mention it . . ." She winked. "I did notice it. I take it Mr. Gibson Hunter Bowers is a tad smitten with Miss Candace Clevenger."

Tanner wiped his hands on his shop apron. "Perhaps *tad* is not quite the right word."

"Did you know that Miss Candace plays the fiddle?" Gibs asked.

Jolie studied her youngest brother's sparkling eyes. "Oh my, I'm sure there are lots of things I have to learn about Miss Candace."

"Me, too. She's goin' to come visit me."

"She is?"

"She said next time Strath is home, she'd like to come visit me," Gibs declared.

Jolie glanced at Tanner, who just shook his head. "Little brother, that's very nice. Be sure and let me know so I can cook a fine dinner. Perhaps we should invite Strath and Landen to come over that night."

"Why?" Gibs asked.

"Perhaps you're right. Now I think Deputy Maxwell Dix could use some help from Junior Deputy Gibson Bowers. He's had a prisoner escape."

Gibson grabbed his Winchester .22. His eyes widened. "Did Mysterious Dave Mather escape?"

"No, I don't believe the sheriff has captured him yet. But Sudsy's mother escaped."

"Why was she in jail?" Gibs asked.

"Attempted murder."

Gibs scurried out the door while Jolie explained the situation to Tanner.

"So you're goin' ahead with a funeral even though Mrs. Mitchell's on the loose?" he asked.

"What choice do I have? For health reasons, he must be buried by sundown, and Mrs. Mitchell isn't here to give instructions. Could you come up to the cemetery with me and read over him? It will just be me, Essie, the Condor brothers, and maybe Gibs."

He hugged her shoulder. "I'll be there. You got yourself into quite a complication."

"Yes, I seem to be good at that."

"Do you reckon it'll be that way your whole life?"

"I imagine so. Do you want to change your mind, Mr. Wells?"

His strong arm grabbed her around the waist and lifted her off the ground, and his lips met hers. They were a little chapped. Warm. And very enthusiastic. He plopped her back down. "Do you think I've changed my mind?"

Jolie could feel her grin stretch her cheeks. "Perhaps we should elope."

"What did you say?" he laughed.

"Oh, nothing." She sighed. "You have very unreasonable kisses, Tanner Wells."

"Unreasonable?"

"Yes, you kiss me like that, and I lose all sense of reason."

"Maybe I should kiss you again."

"Kiss me like that again, and I could lose more than reason." Jolie paused and put her hand over her mouth. "I can't believe I said that."

"Neither can I. Go on, Jolie Bowers. I'll see you at the cemetery. What time should I be there?"

She put on her hat and tied the ribbon under her chin. "At 3:00 p.m." She glanced at the door to the backroom. "Is it oak, maple, or walnut?"

"What're you talkin' about?" Tanner scowled.

"My new wardrobe. Is it oak, maple, or walnut?"

"Jolie Bowers, you promised you wouldn't peek!"

"Mr. Wells, if you think you can surprise me with something merely by hiding it in the backroom, you sorely underestimated my ingenuity."

"Obviously."

"And?"

"It's oak."

She threw her arms around his neck and slammed her lips into his.

When she exited the shop, Essie and DirtDoug were waiting for her in the wagon.

"That's the most ridiculous thing I've ever heard in my life," Essie grumbled.

"What?" Jolie climbed back into the wagon.

"Gibs told me that Miss Clevenger just might be the most beautiful woman God ever created, and he reckoned he would just up and marry her someday. It's pitiable. She's way too mature, eh, old for him."

"He's a boy just starting to feel like a man, and she's a pretty lady. Let him enjoy his crush. You enjoy Leppy."

"I wish you would stop comparing us. There's nothing the same. Where are we going?" Essie asked.

"To park this team at the livery. We need to help the deputies search for Mrs. Mitchell. I think we should go door to door."

"We need to eat lunch. All I've had is some butterscotch."

While Max and Gibs scouted the south side of the river, Jolie and Essie searched the streets and alleys of Scottsbluff. Nadella Ripon organized a ladies' brigade to hunt for Mrs. Mitchell. An hour of searching uncovered no clues.

"Maybe she stole a horse and just rode off," Essie murmured as they headed toward the Full Moon Café.

"That would be the smart thing to do if a person was wanting to get away." Jolie paused and waited as a milk wagon rattled along. "But she hasn't made a lot of smart decisions."

Essie skipped across the street ahead of her. "Mr. Bengsten made a smart decision. DirtDoug is quite excited about moving to our place."

"I hope he gets along with Francis, Little Max, and MudBall."

"He really likes Stranger and Pilgrim," Essie noted.

Jolie held the café door open for her sister. "And I can't believe that Stranger allows a thirty-pound cat to sleep on his back."

Essie plowed into the crowded café. "DirtDoug is warm and snuggly."

Jolie led her to a table near the rear window. "We'll just have some soup. We still have a lot to do in town."

Essie plopped down in the oak chair. "I have to go to Rawlins. Really, Jolie, if I don't go, I'll regret it the rest of my life. That's not just a little girl talking."

Jolie reached her hand across the table and took her sister's. "I know, Essie. I promise we'll go and see Leppy at the first possible moment. I just need to take care of one crisis at a time."

They were just finishing bowls of bean soup when a short, balding man at a neighboring table slammed his newspaper down on the table. With his back toward them, he waved his finger at the gray-haired man who sat across from him. "They're squatters — that's what they are. The deputy had no right to say what he did. He's supposed to come with me and toss them out on their ears."

"What're you going to do?" the gray-haired man asked.

"I'll wait for Riley to come back. The sheriff knows me."

"Yes, but what about them? They put a lot of work into the place."

"They can move on down the road — that's what. It's not a homestead. I own it outright."

"I still say you better take it slow and get the feel of things. A lot has changed around here. You did abandon the place."

"I most certainly did not. I was just gone longer than I expected. Maybe I'll just go out and take care of it myself. You're beginning to sound like that gun-slinging deputy. I will not be intimidated by the likes of him."

"Just make sure you don't call him out," the other man muttered.

Essie leaned toward Jolie and whispered, "Sounds like another crisis."

"Yes, and he can have it. My basket is quite full already. Let's go by Rev. Leyland's house one more time. Perhaps he's home by now. I would so like for him to do the graveside service."

At 2:30 p.m. Tanner Wells and a clerk at the furniture store loaded the pine casket into the back of Jolie's wagon. Jolie leaned back on the lead lines so that the team moved slowly across town. Tears streamed down her cheeks. Essie sat between Tanner and Jolie. Both of them too wiped tears from their eyes.

DirtDoug sat in Essie's lap. He was unmoved.

At the cemetery, Bob and Bill Condor were stretched out asleep in the shade under the surrey. They crawled out as Jolie brought the wagon to a stop.

"Howdy, Miss Jolie." Bill grinned. "Howdy to Miss Jolie's fella."

Tanner nodded at Bill and Bob. "Looks like you boys got it dug."

"Yes, sir." Bob nodded. "And if I do say so, it's a mighty fine hole. We did a little extra."

Jolie tied off the lines and let Tanner lift her to the ground. "What do you mean, a little extra?"

"The diggin' was so easy," Bob began.

"And you said we should just relax and enjoy ourselves," Bill continued.

Jolie looked down into the hole. Her hand flew to her mouth. "Oh, my! How deep did you dig it?"

Tanner studied the gravesite. "I'd say it's about ten feet deep."

"Wow!" Essie peeked over the edge. "You could bury a whole family in there."

"Ain't it a beauty? And it don't cost you one penny more," Bob announced.

"But — how — how . . ." Jolie stammered.

Bob squatted by the edge of the deep grave. "Diggin' was easy, Miss Jolie. It was getting out that was difficult."

"He stood on my shoulders and got out. Then he tossed me a rope and hitched it to the surrey," Bill explained. "Shoot, he pulled me straight out, just like he was skinnin' a buffalo."

"Sorry about them popular trees, but they was dead anyway," Bob apologized.

"How're we going to let the casket down so far?" Essie asked.

"I reckon we can tie it off to the wagon and let it down with the ropes," Tanner replied. "You want me to go ahead?"

Jolie glanced around at the vacant cemetery. "Yes, I think we should go ahead."

"Here come Gibs and Maxwell Dix," Essie called out.

By the time the casket was sunk deep in Nebraska soil, Ophelia Sitmore and Pearl Anderson had joined the other seven.

"I'm sure Nadella will be here," Mrs. Sitmore announced.

"Perhaps we should wait a moment more," Jolie suggested.

Gibs scooted over by Jolie. "Max got

word that the sheriff had Mysterious Dave Mather cornered up on the Niobrara River. He said to release Mrs. Mitchell on bail and come up and help him."

"Oh, that's nice." Jolie glanced around at the barren cemetery. "Too bad she's not here to be released."

"Can I go up with Max and help the sheriff?" Gibs asked.

"I don't think so. You're a little young still."

"I ain't afraid, Jolie," Gibs pleaded. "And I can shoot straight."

She put her arm around her brother's shoulders. They were about the same height. "I know, Gibs. You're without doubt the bravest fourteen-year-old in the West."

Gibs scratched his head. "I can't wait until I'm as old as you."

"Yes, this whole family seems to want to grow up quick. I suppose I'm the same way."

"I think there're some more ladies walking up here!" Essie exclaimed.

"Jolie, I got an itch in my hair," Gibs said. "Can you see if I have a tick?"

Lord, he's not too grown. He still needs big sis to look for ticks. Jolie dug through his scruffy, thick dark brown hair. "Oh, my,

131

there is a bite of some kind, but I don't see a tick."

"Lice?"

"No lice," she noted. "Just a rather large bite. Perhaps a spider out of the hay or something."

Maxwell Dix sidled up to Jolie. "Did Deputy Bowers tell you about lettin' her out on bail?"

"Yes, he did."

"I don't know how to do that when she isn't around. Am I suppose to go help the sheriff and tell him I let the prisoner escape?"

"You didn't let her escape. You treated her with compassion and sincere concern. Maxwell, you need never apologize for that."

Max jabbed his hands in his vest pockets. "Listen, I don't know exactly how to bring up this subject, Miss Jolie, but an ol' boy stopped by the office and claimed that —"

Minnie Clover and Mary Tarnes hiked up to join the other ladies.

"Miss Jolie," Minnie called out, "I need to talk to you in private. This is an emergency."

"Max, tell me about your visitor in just a minute." Jolie left him and Gibs and scooted over to where the four women huddled.

"Miss Jolie," Minnie whispered, "Nadella is waiting down the street with Mrs. Mitchell."

"You found her?"

"She found Nadella."

"Is she still sick?" Jolie asked.

Mary Barnes looked puzzled. "Sick?"

"A violent reaction to shellfish, remember?"

"Oh, she seems as well as can be expected," Minnie replied. "We helped her find something black to wear and were coming to the funeral, but we spotted the deputy. What're we going to do?"

Jolie studied the women's anxious faces. "Do you have twenty-five cash dollars among you right now?"

Mrs. Sitmore clutched her bosom. "Of course I do."

"Would you be willing to use it to pay Mrs. Mitchell's bail? Deputy Dix received word that he can let her out on bail. If you pay him right now, I believe Mrs. Mitchell is legally out on bail, and she can come to the funeral."

Mrs. Sitmore turned away from the others and dug in her bodice. When she spun back around, she had twenty-five dollars in her hand. She shoved it at Jolie. "Here!"

"You realize that if Mrs. Mitchell doesn't show up in court, you'll forfeit the bail?"

"A mama should be able to come to her boy's funeral," Mrs. Sitmore murmured. "Besides, I'll make sure she's there."

Jolie gave Max the bail money.

He cleared his throat. "I reckon that solves my dilemma, but as I was sayin', this man stopped by the office and —"

"Max, if you don't leave right now," Jolie insisted, "Mrs. Mitchell won't come to her son's funeral."

"But this old boy said that —"

"Really, Max, you can tell me tomorrow at church," Jolie said. "The sheriff needs you, and we need you gone."

He shook his head and jammed his hat back on. "You're the hardest-workin' woman I ever met, Jolie Bowers."

"Posh, that's not true. You've met my mother."

"The two of you are tied then. She runs the farm, and you run the rest of the world."

"That's not true," Jolie protested. "Now go on and let a grieving mama get to the graveside of her baby boy."

"I reckon nothin' serious can happen

until the sheriff gets back," he murmured.

"Wish I was goin' with you, Max," Gibs blurted out.

"Little Deputy, so do I. Mysterious Dave got his name for mysteriously escaping ever' time he seems to be pinned down."

"Look for him where he shouldn't be," Gibs advised. "I read in the *Gazette* that most of the time criminals are where you think they ain't."

As soon as the deputy was out of sight, Minnie Clover retrieved Nadella Ripon and Dusty Mitchell.

Bob and Bill Condor squatted on top of the mound of dirt.

Tanner thumbed through the small Bible.

Essie and Gibs stood to one side.

DirtDoug lounged on Stranger's back.

The women gathered around a black-veiled Mrs. Mitchell.

Jolie stood a step behind Tanner Wells.

He cleared his throat. "Let me begin by sayin' that it seems to me there are at least three things we can agree on at a moment like this. First, Devon Sudsy Mitchell's death is a great and grievous tragedy. We stand with Mrs. Mitchell, and our hearts hurt too. Second, we can agree that God is among us. He has promised to comfort those who mourn. And He said, 'Lo, I am with you always, even to the end of the age.' Third, God's ways are sometimes mysterious."

"Yes," Essie called out. "Here comes Rev. Leyland!"

They waited for the clergyman and his wife to arrive. Then with obvious relief, Tanner surrendered the service. He and Jolie stood alongside Essie and Gibs. After the final words were said, Mrs. Leyland invited the women to her house. A sobbing Mrs. Mitchell rode off with the Leylands.

"I thought you did good," Essie declared.

Tanner hugged Essie's shoulder. "Thank you, little sis, but I was so nervous I was afraid my knees would give out, and I'd tumble into that grave."

Gibs stared down into the black hole. "We're all afraid of tumbling down there. I surely wish I had gone with Max. Sometimes it don't seem fair that it takes so long to grow up." He scratched his head.

"Miss Jolie, is it time to pull out the ropes and toss in the dirt?" Bob Condor asked.

"Yes, and I appreciate the fine job you did. I know you'll do just as good a job filling it in." She reached into her purse and pulled out four coins. "Here you go, boys." She handed two coins to each man. "One dollar each, as agreed on. And a bonus of twenty-five cents apiece because you did such an outstanding job."

"Did you see that, Bob? We got a bonus," Bill boasted.

"Miss Jolie always does us good, Bill."

"Except for that time she knocked us cold with that fryin' pan," Bill noted.

"I reckon we deserved that," Bob mumbled.

Bill stared at the coins in his hand. "I don't reckon I've had this much money in my hand since . . . well, since that day at Aunt Beulah's house."

"I told you I was sorry for that. How come you keep bringin' that up?"

Bill turned to Jolie. "Don't mind Bob. He's sort of touchy about some subjects."

Essie and DirtDoug sat between Tanner and Jolie in the big wagon. Gibs stood behind the seat, his hat flopped on his back, held to his neck by a horsehair stampede string.

Jolie circled the horses, and Bob Condor trotted after the wagon. "Miss Jolie! Miss Jolie!"

She pulled on the lines and stopped the

wagon. "What is it, Bob?"

"You did want us to leave the body down in the hole, didn't you?"

"Of course," Jolie replied.

"And the casket too?" Bill added.

"Yes. Cover them up."

The farm team lurched forward.

"Are you three headed home now?" Tanner asked.

"We need to stop at the meat market and grocery," Jolie said. "I didn't know we were spending the entire day in town."

"It's been a rather full day," Essie declared.

"Say," Gibs said with a grin as he scratched his head, "while you two are shoppin', maybe I ought to go by and see Mrs. Fleister."

"Mrs. Fleister, and not her niece?" Jolie challenged.

"I told Mrs. Fleister that I'd give her a report on the situation with Sudsy's mama. They had heard that she was in jail."

"Yes, and I, for one, am worried about Mrs. Mitchell being out on bail. I believe she's on the edge of doing irrational acts at all times," Jolie said.

"Are you saying she's crazy?" Gibs asked.

"I'm saying she's capable of doing crazy,

even violent things at any given moment," Jolie explained. "It's very bizarre behavior."

"Yeah," Gibs mumbled, "that's what I meant."

"It won't take us more than an hour to shop, and then we need to hurry home. So don't dally."

"When are we goin' to bust Leppy out of that Wyoming jail?" Essie whined.

"We'll discuss it with Mama and Daddy. Maybe Daddy can go with you. Or even Strath Yarrow to provide legal help. I just don't know how to get out of teaching school. It would take most of two days to get to Wyoming. One to Kimball by stage, and a second to Rawlins by train. Besides, what can a schoolteacher do?"

"Yes, but what good is an attorney after he's been convicted by a stacked jury?" Essie complained. "I need Galen Faxon and that bunch of Texas gunmen."

"I believe they went to Helena," Jolie said. "Besides, you need to take one thing at a time. Today you need to haul DirtDoug home and introduce him to Francis, Max, and MudBall."

"That's true." Essie let out a long sigh. "Since they are now four, I wonder if they'll want to play whist without me?"

Tanner slipped his arm around Essie's shoulders. "You taught them how to play whist?"

"I tried. But MudBall never pays attention."

"The big cat looks more like a poker player to me," Tanner observed. "He never shows any emotion."

"I believe you're right," Essie agreed.

"I'll swing by Mrs. Fleister's house on our way back to the grocery. Where do you want to meet us?" Jolie asked her brother.

Gibs licked his fingers, mashed down his cowlick, and then pulled on his hat. "Let's meet at the sheriff's office. I promised Maxwell I'd make sure it's cleaned up and locked before we go home."

"You have a key to the sheriff's office?" Tanner asked.

"Sure. I'm a junior deputy," he boasted.

"And part-time janitor," Essie giggled.

Jolie yanked back on the lead lines and stopped the wagon in front of the Fleisters' two-story wood-frame house. "Be nice, don't be a pest, and try not to scratch in public."

Gibs leapt off the wagon, his Winchester pump .22 still in his hand. "Yes, Mama!"

"Mama would say the same things if she were here."

"Yes, she would." Gibs grinned. He looked up at the gunsmith. "Tanner, you're gettin' one fine woman for a wife. I reckon you know that, don't you?"

Tanner laughed. "I do know that, little brother, and I appreciate your reminding me."

Jolie snapped the lines, and the horses bolted back out into the middle of the street. "Did my little brother just call me 'one fine woman'?"

Tanner shoved his hat back. "I believe he did, Jolie Bowers."

"He's only fourteen," Essie pointed out. "How would he know a fine woman?"

"He knows, little sis. Believe me, he knows," Tanner laughed.

With groceries and meat carefully boxed in the back of the big farm wagon, Jolie parked the team in front of the sheriff's office. Essie sat beside her. DirtDoug slept in her lap.

"Hold the lead lines, little sis. I'll go get Gibs. No reason to wake the cat."

"Did you notice what a good sleeper he is? Sleep is very important for the health and stability of a cat."

Jolie grinned as she climbed down. "Yes, I believe you're right about that."

There was no one in the office when she pushed inside the front door. "Gibs?" Dust still fogged the air from a fresh sweeping. There was a hint of acrid sulfur match smoke lingering in the air. "Gibs?" she called out again.

"Is that you, Jolie?" a voice filtered from the backroom.

She stepped toward the door that led to the three empty jail cells. "Yes. Are you about ready to go?"

"Almost," he called back.

When she opened the door, she spotted her brother in the rear cell. "Are you cleaning up after Mrs. Mitchell?"

"Sort of," he mumbled.

"Do you need any help?" she asked.

"Sort of."

"What can I do for you?"

"Could you get the cell keys out of the top left-hand drawer in the office and sort of come unlock this cell?"

Her hand went to her mouth. "You're locked in?"

"Sort of."

"How did that happen?"

"I don't want to talk about it," Gibs mumbled.

"No, I don't suppose you do."

Within a minute she had him liberated,

and they glanced around at the office. "Are we ready now?" she asked.

"Jolie, you don't have to tell anyone about this, do you?"

She hugged her brother's shoulders. "Gibson Hunter Bowers, any brother who calls me 'one fine woman' can be assured that I will never tell a soul."

He hugged her back. "Jolie, you're a great sister. I'm just glad it was you and not Essie who found me."

"Now little sis is great too," Jolie insisted.

"Yeah, but she ain't 'one fine woman' . . . yet."

Jolie laughed and took her brother's hand. "No, but she certainly will be soon."

They were hand in hand when the door was flung open. An older bald man holding a bandanna to his face pushed his way inside.

"Where's the sheriff?" he demanded.

Jolie rushed to his side. "Oh, my, are you hurt? Do you need to go to the doctor?"

"Not until I get that man arrested. Where's the sheriff?" the wounded man blustered.

"He's up north chasing down Mysterious Dave Mather," Gibs reported.

"Where's that yellow-haired deputy I talked to earlier?"

Jolie led the man over to a side chair. "Deputy Dix went to assist the sheriff."

"Who in blazes is in charge?" the man fumed.

"I reckon I am," Gibs offered. "What can I do for you?"

From behind a bloody bandanna, the man studied Gibs. "Is this a joke?"

Jolie stared at what she could see of the man's face. *The voice belongs to the man from the café. . . . But I've seen this man someplace before.* "Gibs is a deputy. He can take your report and make sure the sheriff gets an account."

"I need a real deputy."

"Gibs can handle most any situation."

"Are you his wife," the man needled, "or his mama?"

"Thank you for both compliments," Jolie said. "I'm his sister. Now what happened? Did you get robbed?"

"Not if I can help it. The man busted my nose. I want him arrested and thrown out of my place."

"Do you have an establishment in town?" Jolie probed.

The man adjusted his bloody bandanna. "Out of town a ways," he mumbled.

Gibs sat down at the sheriff's desk and pulled out a piece of paper. "Who is the man who busted your nose?"

"He's a squatter who tried to take over my place and wouldn't leave when I demanded them to go."

Jolie continued to study the man's eyes. *I know I've seen him before. But not here. Maybe in Montana. I wish he'd pull down that bandanna.* "Do you know his name? Which is your place?"

"The neighbors said his name is Matthew Bowers, and my name is Joseph Avery."

"What?" Gibs shouted and jumped up.

"I rode out to tell them to vacate my farm because the deputy refused to do it, and one thing led to another. The dynamite went off, the woman got hurt, and the man busted my nose, and a kid pointed a shotgun at me and said he'd kill me if I ever came back. That whole family's crazy."

Five

With one fluid motion, Gibson Bowers slammed his Model 1890 rifle into the midsection of Mr. Joseph Avery. "Should I shoot him, Jolie?"

Avery dropped the bandanna, and blood dripped on the wooden floor. His now grotesque nose was mashed to the right. "My word, what are you doing? This whole town is bizarre," he gasped. "I should have stayed in Greensboro."

He scooped up the bloody rag as Jolie marched straight at him, arms folded across her chest. "What did you do to our mother?"

"Mother? Your mother?" He stared at Gibs, then at Jolie, then back at Gibs. "What are you saying?"

"I'm Jolie Bowers, and this is my brother Gibson. You said that our mother is hurt. What did you do to her?"

Avery backed toward the door. "Does that woman have children scattered all over Nebraska?"

Jolie felt every muscle in her neck and shoulders tighten. "Shoot him, Gibs. No one can insult Mama like that."

"No! Wait!" Avery screamed and held up his hands. "I apologize. I don't even know your mother."

Gibs left the rifle poked into the man's ribs. "What did you do to her?"

"I didn't do anything," Avery mumbled, still holding the bandanna to his nose. "I merely yelled at her to quit cowering behind the wall and leave the premises. She stood up to say something, and the dynamite went off. How was I to know she had a dynamite charge set to go off?"

Jolie felt her heart race, her voice tighten. Her head seemed to be spinning. "Dynamite?" she gasped.

"Mama was blown up with dynamite?" Gibs now had Avery pinned to the door.

"Wait! She was alive . . . I think. . . . I didn't see any blood. Until your father went wild and broke my nose."

"Daddy doesn't fight," Jolie declared.

"I assure you, I didn't do this to myself."

"Let me shoot him, Jolie," Gibs pleaded.

Jolie clasped her hands together so tightly her fingers turned white. "We have to go take care of Mama. We don't have time for this."

"But what about Avery?" Gibs pressed. "You want me to coldcock him?"

"What kind of children are in this town?" Avery moaned.

"Loyal ones, Mr. Avery." Jolie glanced around the office. "Lock him in the jail cell."

With bandanna still at his nose, Avery threw his shoulders back. "You can't do that. That's my property out there. You can't steal my land."

"Mr. Avery, I was in Helena with my mother and my father when you laid the deed to that place on Judge Winthrop's bench and had him and the clerk witness the sale."

"I've never been to Helena in my life," he declared.

"You're a liar!" Gibs shouted. "I was there too."

"That's impossible! It must have been someone else."

"You have a very distinct face, Mr. Avery. It was you."

"It's goin' to be even more distinct," Gibs threatened. "I can give you a distinct gut if you want one."

"Put him in the cell," Jolie ordered. "We have to leave."

"I won't be intimidated by a whiskerless youth," Avery barked.

Jolie fought to keep from screaming.

"Gut-shoot him, Gibs."

Gibs's finger tightened on the trigger.

Sweat dripped off Avery's forehead and mingled with the blood on his face. "No! I'll go. I'll go. But you don't have any charge against me."

"Trespassing and reckless endangerment to start with," Gibs announced. "Until I think of other ones."

Avery staggered toward the cell door. "But that's my place."

"You signed the papers over in Helena. You have no ownership there, no matter how many times you try to sell it."

"What're you talking about? The papers are in the Platte River Bank in Gering."

"You should get twenty years in jail for fraud, Mr. Avery. You're an evil man," Jolie said. "Lock him up, Gibs, and hurry."

"I'll need to write a note for the sheriff or Max."

"Just hurry," Jolie shouted.

She ran out the door, her boot heels signaling anger and anxiety. "Mama's been hurt," she shouted at Essie.

Gibs soon followed her out and leapt into the wagon. "Here comes Lawson!"

The smaller wagon rattled down the street toward them. "Mama's hurt!" he hollered.

"We know. We just talked to Joseph Avery," Jolie reported.

Lawson stared up and down the street. "Did you shoot him?"

"I would have, but Jolie had me throw him in jail," Gibs said.

"How bad is Mama?" Jolie asked.

"I don't know." Lawson shook his head and wiped tears from his eyes. "Daddy was cryin' when he carried her to the house."

"Daddy doesn't cry," Essie protested.

"Except when it comes to Mama," Jolie put in. "What did he want you to do?"

"He just said go get Jolie and Dr. Fix."

Jolie glanced over at her youngest brother. "Gibs, go with Lawson and get the doc. She has a fast rig. Essie and I will get straight home to help Daddy."

Stranger and Pilgrim sensed the urgency and responded to a slap of the lines as if a grizzly bear were clawing at their hooves. Jolie and Essie were both thrown straight back, and they struggled to sit upright.

DirtDoug leaned into the wind.

"Jolie, Mama's got to be all right," Essie cried.

Jolie kept her eyes focused on the dirt street as they bounced along. "Mama's tough. She can survive."

150

"She ain't tougher than dynamite," Essie sobbed.

The tears blew off Jolie's cheeks as they thundered out of town. "The Lord will take care of her."

"Jolie, I'm scared."

"I'm scared too, baby sis."

For the next two miles neither spoke. The road dipped and swerved.

Hooves thundered.

Dust swirled.

Wheel hubs squeaked.

Wagon boards rattled and snapped.

And Jolie's head thumped like a military drum on the parade grounds.

DirtDoug slept in Essie's lap.

"Jolie," Essie sobbed, "if Mama goes to heaven, will you take care of me?"

The tears poured down Jolie's face until she couldn't see the road. She tried to wipe her eyes on her sleeve.

"Please, Jolie. Daddy would be too crushed to take care of me," Essie pleaded.

"You know I'd take care of you until the day I die. Mama will be okay, little sis. Some griefs are just too much to bear. The Lord will spare us," Jolie insisted.

"Then why are you cryin' like me?" Essie wailed.

Jolie put her arm out, and Essie scooted

151

over and laid her head in Jolie's lap. Jolie stroked her sister's hair as the team strained to race faster.

Lord, when I was young, the thought of losing Mama or Daddy never entered my mind. I knew I would grow up. I knew that someday I would marry. Since I was eight years old, I've been wanting my own house. Since I was nine, I've been cooking and taking care of my family. But I never could imagine life without Mama or Daddy.

When we went back to Aunt Charlotte's funeral, I finally accepted the fact that someday . . . someday in the far-distant future Mama and Daddy would finish their earthly chores and go to heaven to be with You. It crushed me to think about it, but I reckoned I would be able to bear it because I would be more mature and trusting. Lord . . . I'm not there yet. I'm just like Essie. I'm a little girl who is scared. Oh, I'll take care of Essie, Lord, but who'll take care of me? Mama has been my very best friend in the world ever. I'm just not mature enough, strong enough, coura-geous enough to lose my mother and my best friend all at the same time.

Maybe later, Lord . . . perhaps when I am . . . fifty and have grandchildren, and

. . . Lord, Jesus, I am not nearly as strong and independent as everyone thinks. I just have a wonderful family that makes me look good.

"Can't you make them go faster, Jolie? Make them go faster," Essie sobbed.

"Essie, Mama wouldn't want us to run them to death."

"I'm not having a good day," Essie said. "DirtDoug is having a good day, but I'm not. Did you ever notice how bad things come in bunches. It's as if the Lord is busy someplace else and leaves the backdoor open by mistake."

"That's a good analogy, Estelle Cinnia . . . but it doesn't hold. The Lord doesn't make mistakes."

"I know. I know that's true, Jolie. But sometimes . . . just sometimes it feels in my heart like He made a mistake."

"I know," Jolie admitted.

When they reached the second crossing, Essie waved toward the east. "There's Chester! He's in the middle of the road."

"What's he doing?" Jolie shouted.

Essie tried to stand, but the jolting wagon made her lose her balance and plop back down. "He just laid down in the road. I guess he's trying to stop us."

"We can't stop," Jolie called out. "We have to go home."

Essie cupped her hands around her mouth. "Get out of the way, Chester!"

The noise of the wagon and pounding hooves drowned out her holler. DirtDoug opened one eye, then closed it.

Essie tugged on Jolie's arm. "What will we do?"

"We'll circle around him," Jolie said. "The shoulder of the road is flat."

"He'll probably jump out of the way at the last minute," Essie said. "He always does that with the trains."

"He does?" Jolie gasped. "Which way will he jump? Perhaps toward his house. There's safety in the yard, I suppose."

"I say he'll jump across the road to the other side," Essie shouted. "If we don't stop, Chester will be mad. When he's mad, he likes to throw things. There are no rocks in his yard to throw at us."

Jolie loosened the lead lines. "You may be right."

"So which side will you drive on?" Essie asked.

"Straight!"

Lord, I don't understand Bullet Wells. It's amazing that he has lived this long. I pray he'll live even longer.

Jolie stood up in the thundering wagon and yelled, "Bullet! Get out of the road!"

Stranger and Pilgrim galloped faster. Essie held her hat down with one hand and clutched the iron railing with the other.

DirtDoug opened both eyes.

And Chester "Bullet" Wells dove for the sagebrush across the road from his sod house.

Jolie plopped down. Essie shoved DirtDoug to the floorboard and leaned behind her sister.

"I was right, Jolie. Chester grabbed some rocks!"

"At least he moved," Jolie replied. "That was an answer to prayer. I'm glad he's a lousy shot with the rocks."

Essie sat back down beside her. "He's sort of a good shot."

Jolie glanced at her sister. A narrow ribbon of bright red blood trickled down her left cheek.

"Did you get hit with a rock?" Jolie gasped.

Essie bit her lip, fought back the tears, and nodded her head.

With the lead lines still in hand, Jolie leaned over and kissed Essie's bloody cheek. "Did you stop that rock for me?"

Essie nodded. "I knew he would throw it

at you. I didn't want you to get hurt."

Jolie sat up straighter and could feel tears puddling at the corners of her eyes. She reached over and rubbed her sister's back. "Estelle Cinnia, if Mama goes to heaven, will you always take care of me?"

Essie patted Jolie's knee. "Jolie Lorita, I'll take care of you until the day I die. You know that. Mama will be okay, big sis. Some griefs are just too much to bear. The Lord will spare us."

Jolie let the tears flow and nodded her head. "We need each other, little sis. I reckon we always will, won't we?"

"Yes. Life is too hard to go through sisterless. Do you know what I mean?"

Jolie looked at her sister and grinned.

"What are you smiling at?" Essie asked.

"You know, Leppy Verdue might just be too young for you. Sometimes you are much, much older than twelve."

"I know." Essie sighed. She picked up the hem of her long yellow cotton dress, wiped the blood off her cheek, blew her nose on the dress, and then brushed it back down.

Jolie shook her head and stared at the road ahead. *Lord, I love my sister so much. She's delightfully herself, some- where between eight and twenty-eight.*

Stranger and Pilgrim were lathered when they slowed to turn south at Strath Yarrow's house. Landen and a young girl ran out in the yard and waved.

Essie waved back as they picked up speed on the narrow road to the river. "Who's that girl with Landen?" she called out.

"That's Stacy Edgemont."

"Where's her mama?"

"Inside with Strath, I presume."

Essie put her hand over her mouth. "Do you think they're doing something naughty?"

Jolie felt her grin widen. "Landen and Stacy?"

"No, Strath and Mrs. Edgemont."

"Estelle, Strath is a widower, and Larryn is a widow. I don't think they're doin' anything except getting to know each other. It's none of our business."

"Do you and Tanner ever do anything naughty?" Essie probed.

Jolie gasped. "You're not supposed to ask me that!"

"Oh." Essie's eyes widened. "That's all the answer I need."

Jolie held her head high. "We do not do anything naughty."

Essie stroked the sleeping cat. "Then

why don't you let me sit out on the bench and watch?"

"Because a man and a woman who are going to get married need some time to be alone — that's why."

"You mean, to sit around and think about doing something naughty?"

"Estelle Cinnia!"

The yard was empty as they raced past the concrete and river rock footings for the new house. Jolie rolled the wagon right over to the three-sided barn.

"I'll take care of the horses," Essie offered. "You go check on Mama."

"Really?"

"I'm too scared to go see Mama. You go on. Then come tell me. Really, I can do the horses. Besides, I need to introduce DirtDoug to everyone."

Jolie handed Essie the lead lines and climbed down off the wagon. "Stand on the nail keg and wipe them down real good. I'll be back as soon as I have a report. I need to unload the groceries."

Jolie sprinted to the two-room sod house. She shoved the door so hard it banged against the wall and bounced back at her.

"Daddy, how's Mama?"

Matthew Bowers sat beside the front

158

room bed, holding the limp hand of a small woman with a long auburn braid who lay on her back on the bed. There was a blank stare in his brown eyes.

She hurried to his side. "Daddy, it's me — Jolie. I'm home now. How's Mama?"

"She still has a pulse," he mumbled, then held out his arms.

Jolie hugged his shoulders and cradled his head against her stomach. Matthew Bowers clutched his daughter and sobbed.

She held him tight. "It's okay, Daddy. Mama will be okay. Lawson is bringing Dr. Fix. She'll know what to do."

"I've been praying and praying," he sighed.

"The Lord will hear us, Daddy." She continued to hug him. "Let me loosen her collar and wipe her brow. Did you try the smelling salts?"

"I — I — I didn't know what to do," he mumbled. "You've always been here, Jolie, to take care of doctoring us. I just sent Lawson to town to find you."

"I'm here, Daddy. You keep praying. Let me take care of Mama."

He kept clutching her.

"Daddy, let me tell you a story. Last month when you were in Lincoln and got arrested, Mama got a cryptic telegram about violence, and it sounded like maybe you had been hurt or even killed. Mama almost died that day, Daddy. That woman can't survive sixty seconds without your love. But with your love she thinks she could live forever. So you sit right here and hold her hand and pray and tell her you love her. She'll come around. Her desire to be with you is much greater than the power of death. Whisper in her ear, Daddy."

Jolie brought some lukewarm water in a porcelain basin to the other side of the bed. She unfastened the three pearl collar buttons on Mrs. Bowers's dark green dress. Then with a slightly damp tea towel, Jolie wiped her forehead, cheeks, and neck.

Mr. Bowers kissed his wife's ear and whispered something. Then he sat up. "I don't understand, Jolie. Joseph Avery showed up yelling and screaming about this place being his. Mama forgot she had set the charge and stood to tell him to get back . . . and the dynamite went off. I was at the edge of the cornfield. She wouldn't wait for me to finish with the corn. She wanted to blast that granite boulder. You know Mama; I couldn't talk her out of it. I heard the rider and scurried toward the house. Lawson saw it all." Matthew

160

Bowers shook his head. "I was so mad at him. I can't believe anyone would be such a fool. I reckon I busted his nose."

"Yes, you broke it all right."

"You saw Avery in town?" Mr. Bowers asked.

"At the sheriff's office," she informed him.

Mr. Bowers stroked his wife's arm. "What did Sheriff Riley say?"

Jolie cupped her hand on her mother's cheek. "He wasn't there. He's up north chasing Mysterious Dave Mather."

"Has he got a deputy yet?"

"Max is his deputy, but he's up with the sheriff."

"Then who's running the office?"

"Deputy Gibson Hunter Bowers and I were there."

"What happened?" Mr. Bowers asked.

"Gibs arrested Avery and tossed him in jail."

"For fraud?"

"And reckless endangerment. Daddy, how can Mr. Avery show up and claim this place belongs to him? He's sold it a dozen times over."

Mr. Bowers stood and stretched his arms. "Darlin', this homestead is the least of our worries right now." He stared down at the woman on top of the faded quilt-top comforter. "What am I going to do, Jolie Lorita?"

"I'll take care of Mama for a minute. You go talk to Essie. She needs her daddy's hug. Lawson will have the doctor here soon. Get some fresh air, Daddy. You know I'll take care of her." She stepped to her father's side and handed him the wet rag. "You've got dried tears all the way to that handsome mustache, Mr. Bowers."

He wiped his face and hugged her shoulders. "I sat there for hours tellin' her it will be okay, that Jolie will be home soon. I feel so helpless, Jolie. I'm supposed to be taking care of her, and I failed again."

"Go on, Daddy. Go talk to Essie. You can't protect Mama, me, or anyone from the fools of the world like Avery."

Matthew Bowers trudged out into the Nebraska sunset.

Jolie unfastened the long sleeves on her dress and began to roll them up. She soaked the rag in the basin and wrung it out. "Now, Mama . . ." Jolie wiped the neck of the unconscious woman on the bed. "Your man is dying inside. You are his whole life. All he's ever wanted is to impress Melissa Pritchett and prove that he is worthy of the one he considers to be the finest woman God ever created." Jolie wiped her mother's forehead with the damp rag and brushed scattered auburn bangs back. "You really need to come around. He's quite pathetic without you. In fact, you two are the most pathetic couple over sixteen on the face of the earth. And I love it, Mama. Lawson, Gibs, Essie, and I might be the luckiest children ever. We get to see every day what real love is supposed to look like. Speaking of which, you should see your youngest son sigh over Mrs. Fleister's niece. He makes Essie look like an amateur."

Jolie was examining her mother's arms and legs for any signs of wounds or bleeding when she heard a carriage roll into the yard. "That's the doctor. You'll be all right, Mama. She'll take care of you."

Mr. Bowers ushered Dr. Fix to the steps. "Jolie, check on Gibs. He's tending the doctor's horses. I think he's getting sick. I'll stay with the doctor."

Essie ran over to her, the black-and-white cat draped around her shoulders. "Gibs drove the doctor's rig. He said she likes to go as fast as you and Mama."

"I take it DirtDoug doesn't like walking."

"MudBall was being very rude."

"How about Max and Francis?"

"Francis is jealous, and Max is a little intimidated."

Jolie hiked toward the doctor's carriage. "Where's Lawson?"

"Gibs said he and April are on their way."

"April is with him? How convenient."

"The Vockneys were in town looking for the doctor. April came out with Lawson," Essie explained.

A wagon rumbled into the yard, and the girls waited for it to roll to a stop with Mr. Wells and Bullet on board. "We saw the doctor follow you back. Delila insisted I come see if you're all right. I hope I don't seem presumptuous."

"Thank you, Mr. Wells, for your concern. Mama got hurt in a dynamite blast. The doctor is with her now."

Mr. Wells climbed down off the wagon. "Is that how Essie's cheek got cut? A rock blast?"

Essie stared at Bullet Wells, who frantically shook his head. "Yeah," she murmured, "it was a rock blast."

"What can I do to help?" Mr. Wells asked.

"Just pray, Mr. Wells. I think we're all right now that Dr. Fix has arrived," Jolie informed him.

"Jolie, could you ask the doctor to stop by our house on her way back? Theo can't decide if he has the chills or a fever. I want her to look at him. I think he's getting a rash."

"I'll tell her," Jolie assured him.

"Can I stay and play with Estelle?" Bullet asked.

Essie scooped up a jagged piece of granite rock. "Sure, Chester and me can play catch." She cocked her arm back, and he dove into the back of the wagon.

"On second thought, I need to go home," Bullet mumbled.

"Thanks for checking on us, Mr. Wells."

"I hope it wasn't too nosy. You seem like our daughter-in-law already. Delila and I were worried."

"Not at all. And I certainly think of you as relatives too."

The Wells wagon rolled north at twilight.

"I'm not related to Chester," Essie sighed. "Even after you and Tanner get married, I'm not related to Chester."

Gibs hiked toward them from the barn. Each step dragged in the dry Nebraska dirt. "Jolie, I don't feel good. I almost vomited driving out here. I'm goin' to get a drink. My head hurts."

"It looks like you're sweating."

"But I'm cold."

"Perhaps you need to lie down. Why don't you slip past everyone in the living room and go lie down on your bed. It looks like you have a spider bite on your forehead."

"After that he must have crawled all the way down into my trousers. I've got a bite on my, eh . . . you know . . ." He blushed.

"Your hip?" she offered.

"Yeah. Ain't that a fine shinley? Ever'thin' happens at once." He pulled off his coat. "It surely is hot tonight."

"I thought you were cold," Essie declared.

"I don't know what I am. Tired, mainly. You don't reckon I'm allergic to Miss Clevenger, do you?"

"Talk about a fine shinley." Jolie smiled. "There must have been some mild poison in that spider bite. I'll have Dr. Fix peek in on you when she gets a chance."

Gibs had disappeared into the house when a square-shouldered man on a black horse galloped into the yard. He wore a suit and vest, but no tie or hat.

"Strath Yarrow, what brings you here?" Jolie asked.

"I hate to be nosy, but first you and then

the doctor rattled down here faster than a train going downhill."

"I always drive fast."

"But you had a doctor following you."

"It seems to have stirred up the whole neighborhood," she said.

"I just talked to Mr. Wells. He told me what happened. Is there anything I can do for your mother?"

"Thank you, Strath. I like having neighbors who care. But we don't even know what the situation is. You'd better get back to your company."

Strath Yarrow dismounted. "Larryn is cooking supper for Landen and me. Then we're taking the ladies back to town."

"You don't need to explain to me." Jolie smiled.

"Yes, I do, Jolie Bowers. You're not only the queen of western Nebraska, but you're the moral and spiritual conscience as well."

"That's absurd," Jolie protested.

"Estelle, was I right?" Strath asked.

"I didn't know it was limited to western Nebraska," Essie responded.

"Really, you two exaggerate so."

"Say!" Strath turned to the younger Bowers girl. "Is that a new fur wrap, or do I see the butcher shop cat?"

Essie's eyes sparkled. "This is DirtDoug, and he decided to move out with us."

"Landen will be delighted," Strath said. "He's been eyeing that cat for a month."

"The cat likes everyone here except MudBall."

"Your hog?"

"Yes, and I need to go talk to them about it." Essie spun around and marched back to the barn.

"Jolie," Strath said, "did you know how unique each member of your family is?"

"Little sis is the hidden jewel. She's a bulldog like Mama and yet has such a tender heart."

"Jolie, I'd like to stay to get the doctor's report," Strath added. "Your mother and father have become like family to Landen and me. But I suppose I need to get back to my company. I know there's not much a lawyer can do at a time like this. Still —"

"Strath!" Jolie called out. "There is something you can do."

For the next several minutes they sat on the front step as she filled him in on Avery's return and his claim to the place.

"Strath, the judge in Helena, his clerk, and our whole family are witnesses that Mr. Avery sold us this place. I just can't understand how a man can lie like that."

Strath ran his fingers through his short, thick hair. "I'll do some preliminary investigation tonight."

"Oh, I don't want you to have to start tonight. Monday would be —"

"I'm going to town tonight, remember?" Strath winked. "I have to make sure a certain widow lady and her daughter get home at a proper hour. So I'll ask around."

"Am I really that domineering?" Jolie quizzed.

"Yes. Most folks say that God and Jolie Bowers have everything under control. But everyone, including Landen and myself, like it that way."

Jolie shook her head. "The sad part is, I don't know if I can be different. I can't remember when I was any other way."

"Jolie, you make everyone want to be on your side. No one wants to oppose Jolie Bowers. I haven't heard anyone complain."

Jolie tried to listen to the voices inside the house, but she could only hear a murmur. She stared across the yard to the hog pen where Essie was giving a lecture. "Strath, I don't know Larryn Edgemont well, but she seems like such a sweet lady. She has the most relaxed, pleasant smile."

"She's a treasure, Jolie. She makes me

feel at ease. I don't have to watch my every word and action."

Jolie raised her eyebrows. "Like you do around me?"

He grinned and revealed his straight, white teeth. "I didn't say that. But I'm just not sure it's fair to her. Mamas or wives who die young are always wonderful, never age, and have no faults. That's hard for a new wife to compete with."

"So are husbands who die young," Jolie reminded him.

Strath took her hand and nodded. "Maybe that's my biggest fear, Jolie. I can never live up to his perfection. Peter Edgemont seems to have been a saint of a man."

"I'll be praying for you," Jolie offered.

He released her hand. "And I'll be praying for your mother."

Essie strolled back to them.

"Where's your cat?" Strath asked her.

"He's taking a nap on Stranger's back."

"He sleeps on a horse?"

"Horses are quite comfy."

Strath turned back to Jolie. "I reckon I should go back. You know Landen and I have two extra bedrooms. If for any reason your family ever needs to use them, let me know."

"I can't imagine why we would. Our sod house is quite sufficient," Jolie bristled.

"I'm just trying to find some way to offer help."

"Thank you very much, but we have plenty of room."

He shook his head. "Jolie Bowers . . . never mind."

"Go on, Mr. Yarrow, say it. The Lord's timing is always perfect."

He grinned and mounted the black gelding. "Essie, has your sister ever made a mistake?"

"No, but I'm only twelve." Essie grinned. "Daddy said she was quite bossy when she was two."

He tipped his hat. "Somehow I think I knew that. Please let me know how your mother is. I'll report back if I learn anything in town."

"Strath, I really appreciate your offer. I'm sorry I was curt with you. I guess I'm worried about Mama."

"Jolie, you need not apologize for being human. It catches us by surprise, that's true. But it's a pleasant surprise."

Lawson and April Vockney rolled into the yard as Strath turned to ride north.

"How's Mama?" Lawson called out.

"Dr. Fix and Daddy are with her. We're

just waiting to find out," Jolie replied.

Lawson glanced around the bare dirt yard. "Where's Gibs?"

"He's kind of sick. He went to his room. He got bit several times by a spider. I think it made him weak," Jolie explained.

"Mary is sick too. That's why we went to town," April told them.

Jolie strolled to the side of the wagon. "What was her problem?"

Sixteen-year-old April Vockney waited for Lawson Bowers to lift her off the wagon. "We didn't get her checked out. The doctor was coming out here; so I came with Lawson and will ride with the doctor over to our house when she's through here. It sort of looks like —"

Mr. Bowers stepped to the doorway and called out, "Jolie, come here!"

"Is Mama okay, Daddy?" Essie hollered.

"Dr. Fix is still examining her, but she came to."

"Can I come see her?" Essie asked.

"I need Jolie's help for a minute. Then you may," Mr. Bowers stated.

When Jolie entered the front room, Dr. Fix had a sheet pulled up to Lissa Bowers's chin.

"Jolie," Dr. Fix said, "come around and hold your mother's hand. I need to look for any rock fragment damage."

Lissa Bowers's eyes followed her daughter.

"Mama, it's so nice to see your eyes open. My, you had us worried, but we were trusting the —"

"Jolie," Dr. Fix interrupted, "did your father tell you?"

Jolie, still holding her mother's hand, turned back to stare at her father, who stood near the door.

"Mama can't hear, Jolie."

Jolie felt her throat tighten. "She's temporarily deaf?"

"It may be permanent," Dr. Fix told her. "The dynamite was too shallow or too big a charge. The concussion of the air blast did considerable damage to her eardrums. I can examine the middle ear, but not the inner ear."

"She can't hear anything?" Jolie asked.

"Probably just some ringing in her ears," the doctor explained.

"But in time she'll regain it, won't she?"

Dr. Fix rubbed the back of her neck. "Perhaps. Just perhaps." She rolled Lissa Bowers over on her side, facing Jolie.

Jolie bent over, with her face right in front of her mother's. She mouthed the words. "Mama,-it's-okay.-I'll-take-care-of-you."

Lissa Bowers reached up and laid her callused hand on Jolie's smooth face. Her voice was a coarse whisper. "I know, darlin'. . . . I know you will."

"You-can-talk-fine."

"Yes, and I don't have to hear myself. That part is nice. All I hear is a million crickets in my head."

"The-doctor-said-your-hearing-might-return-in-time."

"I hope so," Lissa murmured. "I couldn't bear never again hearing my Matthew sing or my Jolie lecture a crowd of ruffians."

"Mama,-you'll-hear-again. I-just-know-you-will."

"What about Avery? What was he shouting at me about?"

"Avery-is-just-up-to-his-old-tricks. He-claims-the-place-is-still-his.-Strath-came-over,-and-I-have-him-looking-into-it."

"He's a good man."

"Did-you-know —"

"Yes. . . . I like Larryn," Lissa Bowers said.

"She-seems-very-sweet-and-sincere."

"Does he"

"Yes,-and-Landen-gets"

"That's what I"

"I-think-they"

"So do I. Are you"

"Of-course,-Mama.-I-couldn't-be"

"I know, darlin'. You have your Tanner."

"He's-a-rock,-Mama."

Lissa reached out and hugged her daughter. "I already miss your sweet voice."

When Dr. Fix finished the examination, Jolie helped her gather her things.

"Could you step in the backroom and take a look at Gibs? He has some strange bites, and it's not like him to go to bed before supper," Jolie requested.

After a moment in the backroom, Dr. Fix stood at the doorway between the two rooms. "Matthew, I need you two to exit this room and gather everyone out at your barn."

"Wh-what?" he stammered.

"You too, Jolie," the doctor insisted.

"But . . . I need to stay with Mama."

"She's asleep right now. Please go out there immediately. I'll explain in a moment," the doctor ordered.

Jolie, her father, Essie, Lawson, and April all hiked out to the barn.

"What's going on? Why can't I go see Mama?" Essie squealed.

"Here she comes," April called out from the open side of the barn.

Dr. Fix's dark hair was tucked up under her straw hat as she pulled on her long black coat. The high lace collar on her white blouse made her neck look stiff.

"What is this all about?" Mr. Bowers asked.

The doctor folded her arms across her chest and paced back and forth. "Let's start with Melissa. She does not seem to have any other damage except her ears. With granite chips flying as they did, it's a miracle she did not get hit. It was to her great advantage to be so tiny. Let me give you the best case first and then move to the more serious. It could be a temporary hearing loss. In which case in a few weeks or months . . . or up to a year, her complete hearing will be restored. Now more serious — it could very well be . . . that the damage is irreparable, and she will remain deaf forever."

"Not forever," Essie piped up. "She won't be deaf in heaven."

Dr. Fix nodded. "Yes, that's quite true, Estelle. And that promise makes doctoring worthwhile. But there's more."

"What else?" Jolie asked.

"Sometimes . . . there is eye damage from an explosion like this."

"But Mama can see fine," Jolie pointed out.

"Now she can. The eyes work the opposite of the ears. They see fine at first, but may have been so weakened . . . that vision becomes more dim day by day . . . until . . . well, until she becomes blind."

"No!" Essie cried. "No, not our mama!"

Jolie fought back her tears and clutched her father's arm. "How will we know about her eyes?"

"It could take weeks for them to stabilize," the doctor replied. "Normally, by then she will have the vision that will be permanent."

"Does she need to rest her eyes now?" Matthew asked.

"No. And she doesn't need to be told this. Let her tell you how her vision is. She'll know."

"Isn't there anything that can be done?" Matthew Bowers asked.

"Medical science offers no help."

"We can pray," Jolie murmured.

"Yes, you can. And you might want to pray for Gibson too," the doctor added.

"What's the matter with Gibs? What bit him?" Lawson asked.

"Nothing bit him," Dr. Fix answered. "Your brother has varicella, better known as chicken pox."

"Chicken pox?" Jolie gasped.

"He'll have chills." Dr. Fix set her medical bag on the nail keg and opened it. "He'll have flashes of heat, pains in the head, thirst, and restlessness, and sores all over his body. After four or five days they should dry up, form scabs, and fall off."

"I've had chicken pox," April chimed in. "I think that's what Mary has too. She's the only one in our family who hasn't had it."

"And maybe Theo Wells," Jolie added. "Mr. Wells said he has the chills."

"It's highly contagious. That's why I sent you out here." The doctor sorted through glass vials. "I need to quarantine the house."

"What? But my wife is in there," Matthew Bowers protested.

The doctor set two small glass jars on the wooden keg. "Have you had chicken pox?"

Matthew Bowers rubbed his square jaw. "When I was about five, and we moved to the house in Michigan."

"How about Melissa?"

"She had it a few months before Jolie was born. We were scared to death of losing the baby."

"Okay, that means that Melissa, Matthew, and April can be in the house. I'm afraid the others are quarantined. Do you have someplace else to stay?"

"This is our home!" Jolie pleaded.

"It will only be for a few days, perhaps a week."

"Can we stay in the barn, Dr. Fix?" Lawson asked.

"Yes, as long as you don't go in the house."

"But — but — but I have to cook . . . and take care of Mama. I promised to take care of Mama!" Jolie wailed.

The doctor closed up her bag. "Absolutely not."

Jolie paced back and forth. The barn seemed to be swirling around her head. "But who will cook? Who will take care of Mama?"

"I will," April volunteered.

"But you're not her daughter," Essie blurted out.

"She's goin' to be Mama's daughter-in-law," Lawson mumbled.

April Vockney grabbed Jolie's arm. "Please, Jolie. Let me prove to your mama and to myself that I can take care of a home. I know I can't replace you, but let me do it for a week."

"But . . . I can't . . ." She turned to her father. "Daddy?"

He hugged her. "Darlin', we have to go along with the doc on this one. Lawson and I will need to harvest corn all week."

"We can stay in the barn. We've done that before," Lawson offered.

"I heard Strath Yarrow say he had a couple extra rooms in his ready-wall house," Essie called out.

"I can't abandon my family," Jolie sobbed. "I have to take care of them."

"Perhaps you could stay at the school for a week," Mr. Bowers suggested.

"She could stay there." Dr. Fix nodded. "But of course there can be no school."

Jolie hugged herself. "What?"

"The only way to stop a pox outbreak is to isolate and quarantine. You'll need to cancel school for a week if indeed several of your students are infected."

"I can't take care of Gibs and Mama. I can't teach school. What am I supposed to do?" Jolie wailed.

"This is an answer to my prayers," Essie shouted.

"What prayer?" Lawson challenged.

"To go to Rawlins, Wyoming."

"If you show no sign of pox in the next twenty-four hours, a trip would be fine. Do you have family in Rawlins?" Dr. Fix asked.

"No," Essie declared. "Leppy Verdue is my sweetie, and I need to go bust him out of jail 'cause they're goin' to hang him for murder."

Dr. Fix stared at the youngest of the Bowers clan. "My, she does have an active imagination."

Matthew Bowers put his arm around his youngest daughter's shoulders. "No, that pretty well sums it up."

Dr. Fix shook her head. "I do think they're right."

"Who?" Jolie asked.

"Those who say there has never been another family like the Bowerses in the entire history of Nebraska." Dr. Arbuckle Fix smiled.

Matthew Bowers sighed deeply and with straight face mumbled, "Nebraska is still new."

"Daddy, I can't go running off," Jolie protested.

Dr. Fix took April aside. "See to it that Mrs. Bowers's forehead keeps cool. Feed her liquids until she's no longer dizzy when she walks."

Jolie inched closer to them.

Mr. Bowers pulled her back.

"And as for young Gibson," the doctor continued, "make sure he has a spare diet, cool drinks, and a mild aperient."

"A mild what?" April asked.

"I'll give you this sulfate of magnesia and acetate of ammonia. Boil water and let it cool. Then mix an ounce of sulfate and three ounces of ammonia in half a glass of the boiled and cooled water. Maybe every three or four hours."

Jolie cleared her throat. "I didn't hear all of that, Dr. Fix."

"Jolie, dear, I wasn't speaking to you. I'm afraid April is the nurse this time."

Jolie's neck stiffened.

Matthew Bowers took her arm and led her straight out into the Nebraska twilight.

Six

Essie ducked behind the stall as she pulled on her yellow dress. Her full bottom lip curled between a pout and a pucker. "It seems strange that only you, me, and Lawson are going to church."

Jolie stared in the mirror propped on the anvil and combed her wavy auburn hair. "What's totally foreign is that someone else is taking care of Mama and cooking and tending my house. Essie, I just don't think I can camp out here in the barn for a week. I don't have it in me. I'll go mad. I'm supposed to be inside."

Essie licked the palm of her hand and smashed down her errant bangs. "We need to go to Rawlins."

The barn air tasted musty, and Jolie fanned her face with her hand as if that would improve things. "I've been thinking about it. But I don't know how I can leave Mother."

"She has Daddy and April." Essie scampered over and jammed her head between Jolie and the mirror. "I reckon that's as cute as I'm goin' to get."

Jolie rubbed her sister's shoulder. "You look darling."

"Yes, but I never know what that means. You said a red ribbon tied around a pig's tail looked darling too."

"Estelle, you're a very cute girl."

Essie's grin widened. "There's no one I would rather hear say that."

"Not even Mr. Leppy Verdue?"

"Maybe him. Are we going to Rawlins?"

"I just can't leave my household. I'm supposed to be here."

"And I'm supposed to be in Rawlins. Leppy sent me a letter because he knows I'll help. I have to go, Jolie, even if I run away on my own. I just have to go."

Jolie hugged her sister's narrow shoulders. "There will be no running away, Essie. We'll get this figured out."

"When?"

Jolie propped her foot on the rail of the stall and laced up her high-top black shoes. "As soon as I figure out my role around here. I'm supposed to take care of my family."

Essie handed Jolie a yellow ribbon, then turned around and waited. "Until you get married. Then you'll have another family to take care of."

Jolie tied the ribbon in her sister's brown

hair. "I'm not married yet."

"Why don't you and Tanner get married today?" Essie spun around. "Then you'll have him to look after, and you won't have to worry about us."

"That's nonsense. Of course I'll worry about you always." Jolie fastened the top button on Essie's yellow dress. "And I'm not getting married today."

"Neither am I." Essie strolled along the stall and petted DirtDoug, who perched on the top rail. "Jolie, you have to teach me how to cook everything before you get married. I already know how to cook eggs and toast."

Jolie tied her other shoe and brushed down the green cotton dress with her hands. "I believe Mama is planning on doing the cooking after I'm married."

"Why is that?" Essie paused and chewed on her lower lip. When she spoke again, her voice was soft. "You were doing all the cooking when you were nine, but I'm not able to do it when I'm twelve. Why do you suppose that is?"

"That's a very good question, Estelle Cinnia. I'll have to give it some thought."

"Thank you, Jolie Lorita. Perhaps there's hope for me yet." Essie meandered to the open side of the barn. "Here comes Daddy!"

Jolie tucked her hair back in combs and took one last glance in the mirror.

"May I come into the girls' room?" Matthew Bowers called out.

Essie ran up to him. "It's just a barn, Daddy."

Mr. Bowers wore his suit, but no coat. His tie was loose, and the top button on his white shirt was unfastened. "Yes, and I'm sorry to inconvenience you like this."

Jolie scooted up to his other side. "How's Mama?" She felt his strong arm surround her.

"She's feeling better. She's sitting up on the side of the bed now."

"How about her eyesight?" Jolie asked.

Matthew Bowers rubbed his thick brown mustache and glanced back at the sod house. "All of us are a little blurry-eyed when we first wake up."

Jolie fought back the tears. "Daddy, this is driving me insane. I couldn't sleep at all last night. I don't think I can do this staying out in the barn."

Mr. Bowers lifted her chin. "April is doing a fine job."

"Did she sleep on a pallet on the floor?" Essie asked.

"No, I had her sleep in your bed."

Essie raised her light brown eyebrows.

"In our bed? I feel like the three bears when they found that someone was sleeping in their bed."

Mr. Bowers glanced around the barn. "Where's Lawson?"

Jolie stepped out into the dirt yard. "He went to hitch up the team."

"Stranger and Pilgrim?" Mr. Bowers asked.

"Of course," Jolie replied.

"I think you should take the other horses." He turned to his youngest daughter. "Estelle, go tell Lawson to hitch up Leppy and Pullman instead."

Essie started toward the corrals, then turned back. "Why?"

"Mama and I were talking this morning, and we think you two ought to go to Rawlins."

Essie's brown eyes widened. "By ourselves?"

"You could take the stage down to Kimball and catch the Union Pacific. Lawson can drive the team home. I don't think he could handle Stranger and Pilgrim without you two along."

Essie skipped off toward the rock corral.

Jolie clutched her father's arm. "I can't leave Mama, Daddy. Don't ask me to do that, please."

"Darlin', listen to me. School is closed for a week. You and little sis need to stay away from the house. Lawson and I will work from daylight until dark harvesting the corn. April will be here with Mama. If there's an emergency, she can come get me. That means you sit in the barn and pet the cat for days."

"What about Mr. Avery?"

"Between the sheriff and Strath Yarrow, we'll get that figured out too. I don't know what his game is, but this is our place, and I won't give it up."

"And poor Mrs. Mitchell — what's to be done about her?"

"That's for the sheriff and the judge to decide."

"But . . . Gibs needs me."

"Gibs is better this morning. He's ready to eat, but he can't leave the house for a while. And you can't do one thing for him. He can spell off April watching Mama."

"It's . . . like my family doesn't need me anymore," Jolie mourned.

Mr. Bowers nodded toward the corral. "Little sis needs you, Jolie."

"But that's not the same."

"Jolie Lorita, think about what you're saying. You and Essie just might have an opportunity to save Leppy's life. I don't believe he's guilty of murder. If you stay home, you won't be able to take care of anyone, and you certainly won't save anyone's life. Mama will need you next week . . . and the week after and next month. It's only for a few days. We were just thanking the Lord that if such a thing as this had to happen, it's better now than after you get married."

"Daddy, I would come home and —"

"Jolie, a woman only has one home. Tanner will need you. Don't you dare shortchange him."

She slipped her hands around his waist. "Daddy, I can't go off now. I just can't."

"What're you going to say to Essie if something happens to Leppy while you're sitting out here in the barn doing nothing? There are times, Jolie Lorita, when we have to release our responsibilities to the Lord's care. It will all be waiting for you when you come back. Trust me, you have lots of time to take care of Mama."

"Daddy, are you kicking me out?" she sniffed.

"Only for a few days, Jolie. I'm asking you to take care of little sis and her Leppy. Your family needs you to do that."

"But what will Mama say if I leave?"

"It was her idea. Go ask her," he suggested.

Jolie stared over at the uncovered porch of the sod house. "You mean, go into the house?"

"No. You stay in the yard. I'll walk her to the door."

Jolie released her father. "Can she walk okay?"

"She seems to like clutching onto my arm a lot," he said.

"Daddy," Jolie smiled, "Mama likes clutching onto your arm even when she isn't injured."

"You noticed that? Let me go bring her to the door." He started across the yard, then paused. "Jolie, April is a wonderful girl. Mama and I are learning to love her dearly. But she isn't our Jolie Lorita. No one will ever replace you. The Lord created only one like you, and it's our privilege to have you in the family."

Jolie let out such a deep sigh that she felt her dress tighten a little at the waist. "Thanks, Daddy. I think I needed to hear that."

Jolie pulled a burgundy knit shawl around her shoulders as she walked to the northeast corner of the rock and cement foundation for the new house. She stared at the doorway of the two-room sod house. Walking slowly, clutching her man's arm, Lissa Bowers appeared at the door. She wore a long flannel gown. Her waist-length, wavy auburn hair was combed out and draped down her shoulders and back.

Jolie spoke slowly, her voice loud, deliberate. "Hi,-Mama.-You-look-very-nice."

Lissa Bowers laid her head on her tall husband's arm. "Good morning, darlin'. Thank you. And you look beautiful, of course."

"How-do-you-feel,-Mama?"

"Feel? I'm dizzy, and my head hurts. But it's better than last night."

"I-don't-want-to-go-off-and-leave-you,-Mama."

"We need you to take Estelle to see her Leppy. When you're in Cheyenne, would you look for some material for my mother-of-the-bride dress?"

"Really?-You-want-me-to-look?"

"I want you to pick it out for me."

"On-my-own?"

"Darlin', you know how to buy for me better than I do."

"Are-you-sure,-Mama,-that-you-want-me-to-go?"

"It'll make me rest easy, knowing you're

191

checking on Leppy. Will you do it for me, please?"

"I'll-do-it-for-you,-Mama.-But-I'll-miss-you."

"I need practice, darlin'."

"Practice?"

Lissa Bowers nodded her head slowly. "Practice getting along without my Jolie."

"I'll-only-be-gone-a-few-days,-Mama."

"That's all my heart can stand right now. Be careful. Let the Lord lead you. I need to lie down now."

"You'll-be-in-my-prayers,-Mama."

"I'm counting on that. And you have been in mine since many days before your birth."

"You-read-lips-good,-Mama."

A wide smile broke across Lissa Bowers's pained face. "Darlin', I'd know what you were saying even if I was blind."

Jolie's hand went over her mouth, and she glanced at her father's anxious eyes as he ushered his wife back inside.

Lawson crawled up into the smaller wagon. "Are you really goin' to let me drive?"

Jolie handed him the lead lines and then straightened his tie. "Yes, I am. This is a new day for me, Lawson Pritchett Bowers.

192

I'm letting others do things for me."

He slapped the lead lines on Pullman's rump and tipped his hat at the blonde girl in the doorway.

"I'm goin' to miss her," he mumbled as they rolled north along the rutted drive that led to the railroad tracks.

"April?" Essie asked. "You'll see her again in a few hours."

"I know," he said. "But when I'm with her, my heart sings, and my spirit runs across a field of spring wildflowers. Do you know what I mean, Jolie?"

She gripped her brother's arm. "Yes, I do, Lawson, and I'm happy for you."

"I think DirtDoug's heart is singing," Essie announced as she stroked the cat in her lap.

"He's certainly purring." Jolie retied her hat ribbon under her chin and fought the urge to tell Lawson to drive faster. "I can't believe DirtDoug wants to go to Wyoming."

Essie lifted the cat's limp paw and waved it at Jolie. "He didn't think it was a good idea to be left with MudBall."

Jolie grabbed the paw as if shaking hands. "I'm sorry they don't get along."

"He's such a gentleman," Essie declared.

"DirtDoug or MudBall?" Jolie laughed.

Essie raised her nose as if insulted.

"DirtDoug. I think he would straighten MudBall out if he whacked him on the nose. But DirtDoug prefers diplomacy to violent aggression."

"Oh, my!" Jolie clapped her hands. "I hadn't realized that cats were so thoughtful."

Essie rolled the big cat on his back and clapped his front paws together. "You don't think they just sit around and stare at the wall all day, do you? No, they're pondering the whole time. They probably think too much," Essie maintained.

"What a wonderful title for a story," Jolie said. " 'The Cat Who Thought Too Much.' "

"I'll have to write it sometime," Essie said.

"Maybe you and DirtDoug could co-author it," Lawson laughed.

"I was thinking the same thing," Essie murmured.

As they approached the new two-story house at the corner, Lawson nodded at the corrals. "Strath's rig and horses are gone. I reckon he went to church already. I sure do like him, Jolie."

"Yes, he's a very good friend."

"He's the smartest man I ever met, next

to Daddy, of course. But he don't know a buffalo chip about farming. I showed him how to rig up the plow. He has a lot to learn."

Jolie studied the two-story house that had been assembled in a little over two weeks. *Lord, I wonder if I'll ever have my own balcony? I'm not coveting Strath's house.*

Perhaps, just a little.

"I'm surprised he would give up being a lawyer. He seems like such a perfect attorney."

"He hasn't given it up. He still does legal things for us and for the school and for the farmer's association."

"I heard Mrs. Fleister wants to hire him," Essie stated.

"I'm sure she does," Jolie murmured. "With all that work, I'm not sure he'll have time to do much farming."

"Do you know what he told me?" Lawson blurted out.

Jolie rocked back and forth with the rhythm of the rig. "What?"

"Now you can't tell Mama and Daddy this," Lawson demanded.

Essie's brown eyes widened. "What did he tell you?"

Lawson slowed at the corner, then

turned west. "He watched me plow and said he ought to just hire me to do his farmin', and he'd concentrate on legal matters."

"He did?" Jolie exclaimed.

"He said I could work for salary or shares. I could save up for my own place if I worked shares."

"But Mama and Daddy need you," Essie pointed out.

"I know it. I was dreamin' about the future. When I'm with Miss April, it seems I'm always ponderin' the future. I told him I need to help Mama and Daddy get our place established. That's why I don't want you to tell them about this. I would never leave them if they needed me." He slapped the lead lines, and the team raced along the dusty road.

"The day will come soon enough, Lawson, when they don't need you," Jolie warned. She felt a tear slip down the side of her cheek.

Strath Yarrow nodded to Jolie and Tanner as they exited the church. Mrs. Fleister clutched his arm.

"Let's go rescue Strath," Jolie whispered.

"He does look desperate." Tanner smiled.

They scooted through the crowd. "Mrs. Fleister, you look so nice this morning," Jolie remarked.

"Oh, Jolie dear, that's so kind of you to say. I was just telling Mr. Yarrow —"

Jolie winked at Strath. "Mother always said that purple was a slimming color."

"Yes, well . . ." Mrs. Fleister stammered. "I'm so sorry to hear about your dear mother. Is she taking callers?"

"Not until the chicken pox quarantine is lifted. Now, if you don't mind, I have some serious legal matters to discuss with Mr. Yarrow."

"Oh, dear." Mrs. Fleister released his arm. "I had hoped he'd come over for dinner."

"I'm sorry," Strath apologized. "This matter is pressing."

With a flip of her hand, she brushed a piece of lint from the sleeve of her purple dress. "Yes, I do hope to see you later in the week. Candace will only be here a short while longer, you know."

"I promise to stop by at the first opportunity," Strath said. Then he strolled down the boardwalk. He whispered, "Thanks for liberating me. It makes a man want to avoid church."

"Do you have any news for me?" Jolie asked.

He glanced back over his shoulder at the crowd in front of the church door.

"Where's Larryn?" Jolie asked.

Strath Yarrow's blue eyes widened. "She stayed home. Stacy was feeling poorly, and Larryn wanted to make sure it wasn't the chicken pox."

"What did you find out about Joseph Avery?" Tanner asked.

"The sheriff released him on bail and took him to the doctor. I learned that he is indeed the Mr. Avery who proved up that homestead."

"Of course he is," Jolie acknowledged. "We met him in Helena, Montana."

Strath loosened his tie. "He says he has witnesses in Missouri that will prove he was in Springfield on the date your papers say he sold you the place."

"He's lying," Jolie snapped. "He was in Montana."

"How could he have been in both places?" Tanner quizzed.

"I'm not sure. When the bank opens tomorrow in Gering, he says he'll get the papers that prove he hasn't sold the place."

"That's nonsense. We have the original deed, and it's been properly filed."

"Is it possible they could lose the place?" Tanner asked.

Yarrow paused at the end of the wooden sidewalk and waited for two buggies to pass. "No," he declared.

Jolie put her hand on his arm. "How can you be sure?"

"Because I'm a very good lawyer." Strath grinned.

"I pray that you're right, Strath. Mama and Daddy can't withstand too much more," Jolie murmured as she released his arm.

"Trust me, Miss Jolie. You let me worry about this. That's what attorneys are for," Strath urged.

"It's a shame you're retiring," Tanner commented. "We could surely use a good lawyer to settle things out here. It seems to me, the frontier was first settled by Winchesters and Colts, but now it's time for laws and lawyers."

"You might be right, Mr. Wells, but I can't abandon Landen again. We only have each other."

Jolie arched her eyebrows. "And if that condition changed? What if Landen had a mama to look after him?"

"I have given that some thought. But I'm never going back to the city. Landen loves it out here." He glanced around. "Which reminds me, where did he go?"

"I believe he and Essie went to visit with DirtDoug, her new cat," Jolie offered.

Strath shook his head. "You know, we've always lived in the city, and the only people we could count on to look in on us were my relatives. I've been in Scottsbluff a month, and it seems like all of western Nebraska has adopted us. You don't know how much I appreciate that."

"We're hoping you stay a long time, Strath."

"Me too, Miss Jolie."

Jolie nodded at Mr. and Mrs. Maynarde as they drove by. Then she turned back to Yarrow. "I need to go to Rawlins for a couple days, Strath. Is there any way you can keep Mr. Avery off our homestead until I return?"

"I believe the combination of reckless endangerment charges, a broken nose, and the chicken pox quarantine will hold him back for a while," Strath said. "And if that doesn't work, Sam Colt and I will keep him out on Telegraph Road."

"Do you have any suggestions for us in dealing with Leppy Verdue?" she asked.

Strath rubbed his clean-shaven, square chin. "He's been convicted and sentenced?"

"Yes, and the judge will not recognize an appeal."

"He can't do that," Strath declared.

"He's doing it."

"You can hire a lawyer in Cheyenne and try to file an appeal there," Strath suggested.

"The longer it drags out, the more likely there'll be a lynching," Tanner warned. "I heard they want to show the coal mine owners and the railroad they mean business. Leppy seems to be the test case of who has the power."

Strath tugged at his black tie. "Then the best thing that could probably happen is for Leppy's pals to yank him out of there. He could surrender to the U.S. Marshal in Denver."

"From the sound of things, that's what they want," Tanner said. "They'd like nothing better than for another armed group to ride in and give them an excuse to shoot Leppy and a few others in the guise of self-defense."

"If we get Leppy out, could you negotiate with the U.S. Marshal's office so that he won't have to face that mob in Rawlins?" Jolie pressed.

"You're giving Strath lots of work, darlin'," Tanner observed.

"You get him out, and I'll see that he doesn't go back to Rawlins until it's cleared up."

"You're that confident of yourself?" she pressed.

"Yes, ma'am. I don't know a teacup full of farming, but I do know law." He glanced back at the crowd in front of the church. "And I know that I need to find Landen and head home, or I'll be stuck at Mrs. Fleister's all afternoon with another niece."

"Candace is a very pretty, charming lady," Jolie remarked.

"I hear she has another suitor." Strath grinned.

"Really?" Jolie pressed.

"Essie said that Gibs was setting his eyes on her."

Jolie's smile stretched her cheeks. "Yes, he's like a pup discovering a butcher shop"

"I'm not the sort of guy to cut in on a pal like Gibs," Strath said.

"Chicken pox might just have cut his romance short," Jolie responded.

A gray-haired man on horseback rode toward them.

"Miss Jolie." The man tipped his broad-brimmed hat. "Tanner . . . Strath."

"Sheriff, I missed you at church." Jolie fanned her face with her straw hat.

He shook his head. "Boys, I do believe the good Lord sent Jolie Bowers to western Nebraska to scorn us all back to the faith."

"Does it work?" Jolie asked.

"Yes, ma'am. But things are crazy today. I had too much sheriffin' to do to take a break. Miss Jolie, I need to talk to Mrs. Mitchell. Nadella claims she doesn't know where the woman is."

"But Dusty was to stay with Mrs. Sitmore."

Sheriff Riley leaned back in the saddle. "They said she took off in the middle of the night."

"Oh, dear." Jolie glanced up and down the street. "That is one troubled woman."

The sheriff stood in the stirrups. "Now I have to comb town for her again. This time she stays in jail, no matter how many ladies camp out at my front door."

"Essie and I need to catch the stage down to Kimball, or I would help you look for her," Jolie explained. "I'll ask around before we leave."

The sheriff plopped back down. "You goin' after Verdue?"

"Essie and I are goin' to visit him. The whole situation seems strange."

"If he were my kin, I'd bust him out. The sheriff and judge are crooks down there. If that sheriff ever crosses into Nebraska, I'll arrest him for bribery. We had Mysterious Dave Mather trapped up near Ft. Mitchell last spring. He slipped right through that sheriff's side of the loop during broad daylight. Three days later the sheriff buys himself a house on the hill in Rawlins. Now you tell me . . ."

"You think he was bribed?" Strath asked.

"He's bragged about it. Meanwhile, I've got to find a crazy woman, not to mention keepin' an eye out for Mather himself."

"What happened up on the Niobrara?" Tanner asked.

"I kept him pinned down on the riverbank until Maxwell Dix rode up. We swung out and closed in on him. And he wasn't there! He just disappeared."

"Did he swim down the creek?" Tanner asked.

"Swim? It's not six inches deep. But we did find some mud on the rocks below there. If that was him, then he's headed southeast."

"Toward the bridge on the North Platte?" Jolie queried.

The sheriff scratched his one-day-old gray beard. "Maybe. Maxwell Dix rode out that way to let folks know to keep an eye out."

"If he comes across the plains and drops down, do you think he'll be headed by my folks' place . . . and the Bowerses'?" Tanner asked.

"If he took a straight line, he'd cross the Vockney farm. But if he took a straight line, he'd be crazy. That's where we're looking for him. That is, if I can locate the Mitchell woman. There are days, Miss Jolie, when I just feel like tossin' in my chips and ridin' west."

"But you can't do that, Sheriff, because we need you," she insisted.

He pulled off his hat and wiped his forehead on his dark blue shirtsleeve. "Yes, ma'am, I reckon you're right. But that don't mean I'm not tempted."

The sheriff rode east as Lawson, Essie, Landen, and DirtDoug drove up in the wagon.

"Are we goin' to eat in town, Jolie?" Lawson asked.

She glanced at those in the wagon. "I was planning on it."

"Do you think it would be all right for me to head on home. You don't need any help catchin' the stage, do you?" Lawson asked.

Jolie studied her brother's face. "You're in a hurry to get back?"

"April was cooking him some sweet potato cakes," Essie reported. "He's afraid they'll all be gone."

He's crazy about her, Lord. April Vockney, you're one lucky girl. "Yes, that does make one in a hurry."

"Can you give me a lift?" Tanner asked Lawson.

Jolie spun around. "You aren't having dinner with us?"

"I think I should go check on Theo and warn my folks about Mather being on the loose out there," Tanner reported.

"Mysterious Dave Mather is out east of town?" Lawson asked. "Gibs will want to sneak out and hunt for him."

"Tanner, how can you go home? Your house is quarantined just like ours," Jolie protested.

"I had the pox when I was eight." Tanner swung up into the wagon as Landen climbed down.

Essie said something to Tanner, then handed DirtDoug down to Jolie. She jumped off the wagon and retrieved the carpet bag satchel from the back.

Landen tugged on his father's suit coat. "I'm hungry, Strath."

"You two are welcome to join Essie and me at the hotel," Jolie offered.

"Eh, well," Strath said, "we have a commitment."

"At Mrs. Fleister's?" Essie asked.

"Of course not." Jolie grinned. "You're going to Mrs. Edgemont's, aren't you?"

"Yes, we are," Strath said.

"But she cooked for you last night," Essie noted. "Is her cooking that good?"

"Estelle!" Jolie cautioned.

"What did I do now? I don't even know when I say the wrong thing."

"What your sister is saying is that I would be going to Larryn's house even if she were a lousy cook."

"Is she?" Essie asked.

"No."

"Can she cook as good as Jolie?"

"No," Strath said. "But who can?"

"That's true." Essie shrugged. "Jolie's going to teach me how to cook good."

"You'll have to come over and cook for me and Landen sometime."

"Me?" Essie gasped.

"You'll need to practice those lessons, won't you?" Strath suggested.

"Yeah, but I was goin' to practice on Gibs and Lawson," Essie mumbled, "not real people."

"If you change your mind, we'd be happy to have you." Strath Yarrow tipped his hat. "Now, ladies, if you'll excuse us. We'll visit the Widow Edgemont and her charming daughter."

With their satchel beside the table and DirtDoug asleep on the floor, Jolie and Essie ate dinner at the window table of the Imperial Hotel restaurant.

"What time does the stage to Kimball leave?" Essie asked as she tried to stab green peas with her fork.

Jolie finished chewing a bite of garlic-buttered whitefish. "Three o'clock every day," she announced.

Essie glanced down at the sprawled cat. "Do you think DirtDoug likes peas?"

"I think you should eat everything on your plate, young lady."

"Who made up that rule anyway? I mean, if the buttermilk is rotten, we don't have to drink it. So why do I have to eat something that tastes rotten?"

"Essie, eat your dinner. We might not have anything else to eat today. The train leaves Kimball right after we get there. We'll be in Rawlins by daylight."

"Do we get dessert today?"

"No. We should ask around for Mrs. Mitchell. Perhaps we have time to look in a couple places." Jolie stared at a layer of scalloped potatoes. *They're undercooked and unsalted. How such a person can claim to be a chef is a mystery.*

Essie piled her spoon high with peas and shoved the whole bite into her mouth. "Aimmghe dummmm."

"Yes, I can see you're done. It might be best if you chewed them before you swallowed them."

They left the hotel with Jolie toting the satchel and her handbag. Essie carried DirtDoug like a baby that needed to be burped.

"Are you going to carry him everywhere?" Jolie asked.

Essie held the cat like a limp rag and stared at his sleepy eyes. "He doesn't like to get his paws dirty."

"But he's a cat. He's supposed to walk on his paws," Jolie insisted.

"He likes it when I carry him."

"Yes, I imagine he does."

Essie spied a man walking toward them. "Hey, here comes Trip Cleveland. Hi, Trip."

"Hi, little darlin'," the tall man called out. "Did you buy a fur coat?"

"This is my cat DirtDoug."

"A cat, eh? Is he lame?"

"No. He likes to be carried."

"How is my hero?" he asked her.

"I'm goin' to Rawlins to bust my Leppy out of jail."

He pulled off his dirty brown hat and stared at Essie. "I reckon you are."

"You believe me? No one ever believes me."

"Essie, you saved my life after that wreck at Bobcat Gulch. I'd believe most anything you said." He stepped between the sisters. "Miss Jolie, could you come over to see Mr. Culburtt before you leave town?"

She surveyed Cleveland's narrow eyes. "We're in a slight hurry."

He leaned down to Jolie's ear. "Mr. Culburtt has something to tell you about that Mitchell woman."

"Does he know where she is?" Jolie asked.

"No, but he's got some news that he wants to tell you."

Jolie marched toward the Nebraska Hotel alongside the long strides of Trip Cleveland.

Essie dropped back. "DirtDoug doesn't like me to hurry."

"You can wait in the lobby," Jolie called out.

"We'll wait out in front. Did you know that some hotels don't cater to felines?"

Cleveland shook his head. "Little sis is really something."

"She's unique, isn't she?" Jolie replied.

"Shoot, Miss Jolie, there ain't another family like yours anywhere in the West."

"I'll take that as a compliment."

"It was surely meant that way. Most ever'one deems it a privilege to be counted as a friend of the Bowerses."

"That's a very nice thing to say, Trip. You're a kind man."

"No, Mr. Culburtt is kind. I'm just learnin' to be."

Trip Cleveland stayed at the bottom of the stairs as Jolie hiked up to Mr. Culburtt's room. Cutter Davenport greeted her at the door, his hand on the grip of his Colt revolver. "I hear Mrs. Mitchell is on the prowl again."

"I afraid so, Mr. Davenport. Please be careful."

"Don't worry. I'll guard Culburtt. That's my job."

"Yes, and I meant for you to be careful yourself."

"Thanks, Miss Jolie. I think he wants to talk to you alone."

Edward Culburtt was propped up on several pillows as she entered the room. He was clean-shaven, and his hair was neatly combed. He motioned to the chair beside the bed.

"You look good today, Mr. Culburtt."

"Thank you, Miss Jolie. Every day I'm alive, I get stronger. That's a good sign."

She sat down in the chair and tugged off her hat. "Did you want to talk to me about Mrs. Mitchell?"

"Yes, I had some rather disturbing news."

"I know she's out wandering around again," Jolie stated. "The sheriff is looking for her."

"No, that's not what I wanted to talk about."

"Oh?" The room had an aroma somewhere between menthol and ammonia. Jolie pulled out her handkerchief and patted her cheeks.

"As soon as I heard she was out and stalking, I sent a couple of the boys to her place to wait and see if she showed up there. I thought they might bring her back to the sheriff."

"Did she go home?" Jolie asked.

Culburtt pulled the white sheet up to his neck. "No. But while they were peeking in the windows to make sure she wasn't there, they discovered some interesting things at her house."

"What?"

"A crate of Swiss clocks, for instance," Culburtt announced.

"Swiss clocks?"

"Is it cold in here?" he asked.

Jolie stood and tucked the quilts around Culburtt. "Now what about the clocks?"

"Thank you, Miss Jolie." He turned his head toward the window. "The clocks were ordered by Mr. Ephraim Mendez at the Colorado Furniture Emporium and stolen from our train two weeks ago."

"She has stolen merchandise?"

"Quite a number of things. All from our trains."

"I don't understand." Jolie sat back down. "Do you think she's the one robbing your trains?"

"One thing I know for sure — someone in that house got ahold of our merchandise."

Jolie leaned closer and could smell tonic water on Mr. Culburtt's face. "But . . . it was just her and Sudsy who lived there."

"How did she make a living? Did she have a job in town?"

"I don't think so," Jolie replied.

"I know this sounds strange," Culburtt continued, "but was the lad very athletic?"

"He was quite strong and agile for a boy," Jolie admitted. "What does that have to do with anything?"

"That's what I've been lying here

thinking about. I believe an athletic boy could climb to the top of a train car, pop open the small hatch, and lower himself to the top of the goods. He could then signal someone if it was something worth stealing. Another person could drive up alongside the rail car, bust open the lock, and load the goods. With a fast rig, they could be down the road before anyone spotted the robbery, especially in the dark."

Jolie sat back and let her hands drop to her lap. "Are you accusing Mrs. Mitchell and Sudsy of train robbery?"

"I believe I am."

"What did the sheriff say?"

"I haven't told him yet."

"Why?" she asked.

The railroad man leaned toward her. "I wanted to talk to you first."

"Me?"

"Miss Jolie, we can recover much of the goods. That boy can never be recovered. I don't care if she's in jail or not. She's paid dearly for her sins. The Lord can settle the rest. I just want her to leave the state. I was hoping you could talk to her."

"What should I tell her?"

"Tell her that she'll be prosecuted for burglary and attempted murder if she stays, that now would be a good time for a trip on out west . . . or east. . . . I just don't want her around here."

"Mr. Culburtt, did you have a crate of Winchester 1873 saddle-ring carbines in the 352,000 serial number range stolen from the train?"

"My word, where did you find them?"

"Mrs. Mitchell sold them to Tanner. He contacted the factory to see whom they really belonged to."

"I didn't think she'd be so brazen as to sell them in town. That's an easy way to be caught," Culburtt said.

"I'm not sure she thinks rationally." Jolie reached over and held the older man's rough, callused, cold hand. "Do you think the dogs were chasing Sudsy because he was looting a train car?"

He squeezed her fingers. "I think it's very possible."

"Oh, my, no wonder she's acting so strange. She would be feeling horrible guilt if she knew her illegal actions got her son killed."

Culburtt's voice lowered to a whisper. "She might even have seen him die."

"Oh, no!" Jolie gasped.

"If my idea is right, she waited on the far side of the tracks for him to signal. Then she rolled up, and he jumped down to load the goods they wanted. But this time when he got down, the dogs chased him. She would have witnessed it all."

"That would be impossible to live with," Jolie offered.

"It would surely drive a person mad."

Jolie released his fingers and patted his hand. "She's lashing out at you because she can't accept the truth."

"I know it's just a theory." Culburtt shrugged. "But she does need to explain her receiving and selling stolen railroad goods. If it's true, how does a woman get to such a place as that? I would have hired her as a crew cook if she'd asked for a job."

"I suppose at some point she convinced herself it was the best option she had."

"And people hate the railroads," he mumbled.

"The Mussel Slough Tragedy out in California didn't exactly garner people's support for the railroads. I wouldn't say hate, but many mistrust any company that is big, powerful, and autocratic."

"I'm not saying we don't deserve that reputation," Culburtt murmured. "I know that many think that stealing from the railroad isn't stealing. But the truth is, any theft chips away at a person's moral integrity. I don't think they realize what they're doing to themselves. I do think I'm goin' to retire."

"Mr. Culburtt, you do what you have to do, but I wish you'd stay. I think the next ten years will be crucial in the development of western Nebraska. We'll need men like Daddy . . . and men like you."

Culburtt used the sheet to wipe his eyes. "Miss Jolie, you are something. You make an injured, tired, old railroad man feel important still. I thank you for that."

"Then you'll reconsider retirement?"

"I'll think about it. If I stay, and I say 'if,' can I count on your support?"

"Mr. Culburtt, I should be offended that you have to ask that. Of course you have my support."

"One problem at a time. First, I'll need to deal with the Mitchell woman. If she stays in town, I'll have to get her back in jail. Davenport and I both need some solid sleep without worrying that a crazy woman will march in here, gun blazing."

"I'll relay your message as soon as I see her," Jolie promised.

Essie and DirtDoug sat on the bench in front of the hotel when Jolie exited.

"Bill and Bob stopped by. They wanted

217

to know if you had any more bodies to bury," Essie reported.

"I trust I'll never have to go through that again."

"Mama and Daddy will die sometime," Essie murmured. "Do you ever think about that, Jolie?"

"No. Because I think they're goin' to live until they're ninety."

"Jolie, is Mama goin' to be blind?" Essie asked.

"No, she won't. I just can't handle that."

"She talks a little loud now, doesn't she?"

"Yes. We'll have to help her find the right volume level."

"Have you ever heard DirtDoug yell?" Essie quizzed.

"No, I don't believe I have. Does he yell often?"

"Only at MudBall." Essie shrugged.

They had only gone a block toward the stage station when a commotion in the alley caused Jolie and Essie to stop and stare.

"Is that Mr. Mendez?" Essie asked.

"It looks like he's bleeding!" Jolie exclaimed. She set the satchel down. "Wait here and let me check it out."

She jogged down the narrow pathway

between the furniture store and the hat shop. Ephraim Mendez appeared with his suit coat wrapped around a bloody arm.

"Mr. Mendez," Jolie called out as she approached, "what has happened to you?"

"That woman is crazy," he shouted.

"What woman?" Jolie looked up and down the alley.

"The one who came into my store and started slashing my furniture with a hunting knife, screaming that I shouldn't be open on Sundays," he said.

"Where is she?" Jolie pressed.

"She's behind those two barrels. I tried to stop her. I have a gun, Miss Jolie, but I couldn't pull the trigger. I can't shoot a woman. I don't know if I could shoot a man. At least, I locked her out of the store."

"Go find the sheriff," Jolie instructed. "And get the doctor to look at your wound."

Mendez stepped toward the side alley. "What will you do?"

"I'll think of something." *Lord, this is way beyond me now. It's almost demonic. Help me, Jesus.*

Mendez scurried toward the street.

She stepped closer to the barrels. "Mrs. Mitchell, come out now. It's Jolie Bowers.

219

Mr. Mendez is gone; so you can come out. You don't have to hide. Are you hungry? I'll get you a meal and a warm place to stay."

"You come any closer, and I'll kill her," a deep, menacing voice threatened.

Jolie scouted up and down the alley but could see no one. "You'll kill whom?"

"The Mitchell woman," the voice growled.

The hair on the back of Jolie's neck tingled; her shoulders stiffened; her tongue stuck to the roof of her mouth. She swallowed hard, then choked out, "Stand up and show yourself."

Dusty Mitchell in tattered brown dress stood up, holding a huge hunting knife to her own throat.

Seven

Jolie tried to back away but couldn't move. *I don't want to be here, Lord.*

"I meant it. I'll slit her throat!" the deep voice threatened.

Jolie opened her mouth but couldn't speak.

Get me out of here, Lord. Now!

"Leave us alone!" the raspy voice shouted.

Jolie felt perspiration slide down her cheeks and drip off her chin. *I don't know what to do. I don't know what to do!*

"Maybe I'll kill you too," the woman hissed.

Jolie could feel goose bumps on her arms. She couldn't keep from shivering.

I want my daddy. I want my daddy here right now.

"I'll slice up that pretty face of yours," the voice growled. Mrs. Mitchell took a step forward, the knife, streaked with Mendez's blood, held to her own throat.

Jolie couldn't quit staring at the wild woman's dark, terrified eyes.

She's scared to death, Lord, and she

can't stop this from happening. No one can stop it. Oh, Lord Jesus . . . oh, Lord.

"Jolie, what's all the yelling? Why does she have that knife? What's wrong with her? Did she cut herself?"

Jolie spun around to see Essie standing in the walkway between the buildings.

"I'll kill her first!" Mrs. Mitchell ranted. She lunged toward Essie.

Essie screamed and jumped back.

"No," Jolie screamed at the top of her voice. "In Jesus' name, stop!"

The woman turned toward Jolie. "What did you say?"

Jolie's voice was barely a whisper now. "In Jesus' name throw down that knife."

The woman turned back toward a frozen Estelle Bowers. "You must be joking."

Jolie scurried between the woman and Essie. *No one threatens my little sis.* Jolie ground her clenched teeth. "Drop it now!" she barked.

As if suspended in time, Mrs. Dusty Mitchell stood perfectly still. Color fled from her face. Her eyes brightened and then slipped to a blank stare. The knife slid from her hand. She collapsed, unconscious, in the dirt.

Essie ran to Jolie and clung to her. "Jolie, what was that?" she sobbed. "I was scared,

Jolie. I was really scared."

Jolie stared down at the woman. "I know, baby sis. I know. I've never been so scared in my life."

"What was that?"

"I don't want to know." Jolie hugged her sister and shook her head. "I really don't want to know."

She heard footsteps behind her and turned to see Sheriff Riley run up, gun in hand. "Did you kill her?" he shouted.

Jolie knelt in the dirt beside the unconscious woman. She cradled the woman's head and brushed thick, uncombed bangs back out of her eyes.

"No, Sheriff, I didn't kill her. She needs help. She needs the state asylum, poor dear. She just can't live with it. I think she caused poor Sudsy's death, and she can't live with it."

Sheriff Riley knelt beside her. "Do I need to get Dr. Arbuckle Fix?"

"No, you need to get her in a locked cell and make sure she can't hurt herself. I'm certain she'll try to take her life."

"She went crazy?" he asked.

"There are other enemies besides insanity," Jolie murmured, then softly laid the woman's head down. "She needs Rev. Leyland more than she needs a doctor. I believe she's chased by demons within and without."

The sheriff enlisted the help of two by-standers to tote Mrs. Mitchell to the jail. Jolie hiked back to the boardwalk where DirtDoug slept on top of the carpetbag.

Essie clutched her sister's arm. "Jolie, I was really, really scared. I thought she was going to stab me for sure. I kept wanting to scream, 'Jolie, help me,' but my mouth didn't work." She lowered her voice. "I wet my underwear. I thought I was going to die."

Jolie hugged her. "That's okay. You can change at the hotel."

"Then all of sudden there you were, protecting me, just like a guardian angel."

"We have to look out for each other," Jolie assured her. "You know that."

Essie started to cry.

"It's okay, baby." Jolie hugged her sister tightly. "It's okay. She can't hurt you now."

"That's not why I'm crying. I'm crying because I'm horrible, and I hate myself."

"What do you mean?"

Essie stared down at the boardwalk. "When I thought she was going to stab me, you jumped over in front of me, and I thought to myself, *Good. She'll stab Jolie instead of me.* Oh, Jolie, I'm so ashamed of myself. I'm horrible. You are so noble, and I'm so horrible. I was so scared. I've never seen anything like that before."

"That's okay, Essie. Really. All of us have a natural urge to save our own lives."

"But you didn't give in to it. You jumped over to save me."

"I was pushed."

Essie looked around. "What do you mean?"

"I was so terrified I couldn't move. It was as if the Lord swatted me on the backside, and I jumped forward. It was involuntary heroism. I didn't know what to do."

"Really?"

"Yes, I believe the Lord can do a better job at looking after us than we can. Don't you agree?"

"You mean, I should be thanking Him instead of you?"

"Yes."

Essie wiped her eyes on her dress sleeve. "Thank you, Jesus. And thanks, Jolie. You're the best sister in the world."

DirtDoug sat on the bench in front of the Imperial Hotel. Next to him Jolie Bowers leaned back against the unpainted wood siding.

Lord, give Mrs. Mitchell some peace. I

don't know what went on back there, but she was battling You . . . not me. I hope I never have to face that ugliness and hatred again. I felt so totally helpless. I don't like feeling helpless. I like being in control of everything. I know . . . I know . . . and in control of everyone. I think it's time I changed.

She stared down at her hands.

I'm still shaking. Maybe I'll never know why I've wanted to grow up so fast. I go from crisis to crisis. My only joy is taking care of my family, and now that's removed.

That's not true, Lord. I delight in my class. I love being a teacher.

And.

Jolie felt her cheeks stretch as a wide smile broke across her face.

I love being on Tanner's arm. Oh, my. I bet I'm blushing. How I love being with him, Lord. Maybe Essie's right. Maybe we should get married before next summer. Hmmm. That's the most peaceful thought I've had in days.

An old surrey pulled by two long-legged black horses rattled up in front of her. Bill Condor tipped his hat. "Howdy, Miss Jolie. You and that butcher shop cat takin' a siesta?"

"Hi, boys. I'm waiting for Essie. You two look very nice."

Bob sat up and tugged at the tight collar of his new white shirt. "Yes, ma'am, we got ourselves a shave, haircut, and bath."

"They even had hot water, Miss Jolie," Bill added. "Shoot, I haven't bathed in hot water in five years."

Jolie stood and strolled to the edge of the sidewalk. "You two look so handsome all cleaned up. You know, you really should do that more often."

"That's what I said, didn't I, Bob?" Bill grinned. "If a man could afford it, he ought to do this once ever' few months."

Bob Condor picked at his teeth with his fingernail. "We had enough money left to buy ourselves a roast beef dinner."

"With forks and spoons and ever'thin'!" Bill grinned. "It surely was fine, Miss Jolie."

"You did all of that with the money I paid you?"

"No, ma'am. We got ourselves another grave-diggin' job this mornin'," Bob announced.

"On a Sunday?"

"You see," Bill gloated, "I told you this was Sunday."

Bob tugged off his hat. "We hated to

turn down two more cash dollars."

"Especially when the diggin' is easy. We dug a grave right next to that one for the boy," Bill explained.

"Who hired you?" Jolie asked.

"The boy's mama," Bill announced. "She let us have this here rig and team, but we ain't supposed to tell anyone where we got it."

"You just told her," Bob grumbled.

"Telling Miss Jolie is like tellin' somethin' to your mama," Bill declared. "That don't count as tellin'."

"Who was she planning on burying?" Jolie asked.

Bill glanced over at Bob. "I don't reckon she told us that, did she, Bob?"

"No, ma'am. It didn't seem right to ask such a personal question."

Jolie held her forehead with the palm of her hand. *She was trying to get killed, wasn't she, Lord? Even shooting Mr. Culburtt. She marched in there, hoping someone would shoot her. Poor lady. Some things must be just too horrible to bear.*

"Are you feeling peaked, Miss Jolie?" Bill asked.

"It's just been a long day already, and now we have a long stage ride."

Essie strolled out wearing a fresh brown dress and carrying the carpetbag.

"Hi, little sister!" Bill called out.

"Hello, William . . . Robert . . . How are you?"

"Did you hear that, Bob? She called me William."

"And me Robert."

"Ain't no one called us that since Aunt Beulah —"

"And I told you, that was an accident!" Bob fumed.

Essie plucked up the cat. "DirtDoug is very excited about riding on a stagecoach."

"Are you two goin' to stay in the hotel and catch the mornin' stage?" Bob asked.

Jolie glanced at the small watch hanging from the silver chain around her neck. "No, we're going to catch the afternoon stage."

"The one to Kimball?" Bill pressed.

"Yes."

Bill glanced at his brother. "Shoot, Miss Jolie, it left nearly an hour ago."

Jolie folded her arms across her chest. "No, the southbound stage leaves at 3:00 p.m."

"I'll be! They changed the stage time, Bob."

"We need to hurry." Jolie grabbed the

satchel. "We've only got a few minutes."

"I seen it leave with my own eyes," Bob mumbled. "The stage pulled out at 2:00 p.m."

"If Miss Jolie said it leaves at 3:00, then it leaves at 3:00," Bill declared.

"It left an hour ago," Bob insisted.

"Maybe her watch stopped. I had a watch like that once. It always read ten minutes till ten no matter what time of the day it was," Bill reported.

"Did we miss the stage?" Essie asked.

Jolie grabbed her hand and trudged east. "Of course not. I've been watching the time."

"Did you notice anything heavy about that satchel?" Essie asked.

"No. Should I?"

"No." Essie shrugged. "I was just wondering. Can I sit by the window in the stage?"

"It probably won't be crowded."

"I haven't been on a stagecoach since we moved down from Montana."

"I've taken the Kimball stage a couple of times." Jolie glanced down at her watch.

"I don't see anyone waiting for the stage," Essie called out as they turned the corner.

"You see, I told you it wouldn't be

crowded. We shall both have a window seat."

Essie glanced up and down the street. "I don't even see a stagecoach."

"It must be running late. I suppose we didn't need to hurry after all." Jolie glanced up at the green sign on the outside wall of the stage office. "You see, it says right there: 'Departures south, 7 a.m. and 3 p.m. daily.' I knew I was right."

"There's a little asteroid by the time," Essie pointed out.

"You mean an asterisk?" Jolie questioned. "I wonder why."

"Look!" Essie scooted the bench away from the sign. "The asteroid is down there. 'Except Sundays.' Those aren't the Sunday hours."

"Of course they are," Jolie insisted.

Essie stroked the head of the fat cat. "Then where is the stage, the ticket man, and more passengers?"

"I'm sure . . . What do you mean, except Sundays?"

Essie's nose was pressed against the window of the stage office. "I think it says 2:00 p.m. on Sundays."

"That's nonsense. I know when the stage leaves."

"So do we sit here until morning?"

Jolie looked at her watch, then held it to her ear. "I can't imagine why there aren't —"

"Did you miss the stage?"

Jolie spun around to spot a bearded man in a wool suit and bowler and a thin man in canvas coveralls. "Luke. Raymond. Is the stage late today?"

"It left at 2:00, like always," Luke reported.

"The stage doesn't leave until 3:00," Jolie contradicted.

"Except Sundays, Miss Jolie," Raymond reported. "Just one southbound on Sundays. It leaves at 2:00 p.m."

"It most certainly does not," she huffed.

Luke pulled off his hat and scratched his dark brown-and-gray hair. "She don't exactly like bein' wrong, does she, little sis?"

"Jolie's never wrong," Essie commented. She and DirtDoug plopped down on the bench. "Even when she's wrong, she's never wrong."

"Are you hinting that we missed the southbound stage?" Jolie fumed.

"No hint," Raymond drawled. "You missed it, Miss Jolie."

"Well . . . well . . . I really can't accept that!" Jolie huffed.

Luke shrugged. "Miss Essie, if you need

anything, we're headed over to see the McMasters sisters."

"They invited us for cake." Raymond grinned.

Luke tipped his hat, and the two men shuffled down the sidewalk.

"I think we missed the stagecoach," Essie mumbled.

"That just can't be!" Jolie declared.

"I was talkin' to DirtDoug. He thinks we missed the stage too."

Sheriff Riley rode up on his buckskin horse.

Jolie pulled off her straw hat and fanned herself. "How's Mrs. Mitchell?"

"She came to, but she won't talk," the sheriff reported.

"Are you leaving her unattended?"

"Mrs. Leyland organized some of the church ladies to sit vigil outside her cell. I've got her shackled so she can't hurt herself. I'll put her on the train to Lincoln tomorrow. The judge over there will have to commit her. In the meantime, I have to get out and help Maxwell Dix. Mysterious Dave Mather is out there somewhere. I can't thank you enough for helping me find her. Strange how she passed out like that." He glanced up and down the street. "Sorry about you missin' the stage."

"Miss it?"

"I thought you were goin' down to catch the Union Pacific at Kimball. That stage leaves at 2:00 on Sundays."

Jolie plopped down on the bench beside her sister. "Yes, well . . . it seems that I miscalculated," Jolie mumbled.

"What're you goin' to do now?" the sheriff asked.

"She doesn't know," Essie replied. "Jolie has never miscalculated before. Isn't this a fine shinley?"

Jolie sat straight up. "We'll just rent a rig and drive down."

Sheriff Riley pulled his watch out of his vest pocket. "You might want to hurry. It'll take a rig as fast as those two big horses of your mama's to get down there in time for the train. Good luck to you." He tipped his hat to them and rode east.

"What're we going to do, Jolie?"

Jolie Bowers stood up and grabbed the satchel. "We're going to make the train. I simply will not allow anything else to go wrong in this day."

They hadn't taken three steps when the Condor brothers rattled up.

"Did you miss your ride, Miss Jolie?" Bill called out.

Jolie glanced at Essie.

She nodded her head.

"No, we didn't, boys." Jolie shoved the satchel into the back of the tattered surrey. "Now you two scoot into the back. I'm going to drive."

"Where are we goin'?" Bob asked as he handed her the lead lines.

"To Kimball, boys."

Essie slid into the front seat next to Jolie. DirtDoug sat on her lap.

"We're not going to miss that train. I'll see to that," Jolie declared.

"What did she say?" Bill called out from the backseat.

"She said to hold on to your hat!" Essie called out just as the team broke for the middle of the street.

DirtDoug sat in the satchel with only his head peering out. Essie perched on the leather seat by the window. Jolie reclined on the seat by the aisle.

"Do you think they'll recover?" Essie asked.

"They're very strong. I told the livery man to liniment their legs every couple of hours and feed them some whole oats," Jolie replied.

Essie put her nose against the glass window. "I meant Bill and Bob."

Jolie grinned. "I believe they'll recover too, but I doubt if they ever let me drive again."

"I thought we were goin' to hit that antelope at the pass in Wildcat Hills."

"No one ever hits an antelope."

"No one ever drives that fast but you and Mama. . . . Do you think Mama will still like to drive fast?"

"Of course she will."

"Bill almost fell out when you swerved around that freight wagon. Bob had to grab his leg and pull him back."

The train lurched forward. Essie watched the twilight landscape roll by. "We barely made it."

"We had several minutes to spare," Jolie boasted.

"My rear is sore from bouncing in that surrey."

"My shoulders hurt," Jolie admitted.

Essie rubbed her sister's shoulders. "That was the second most fun, scariest ride of my life. Mama chasin' down the train was the first."

Jolie leaned forward with her arms on the seat in front of her. "I'm hoping we can sleep on this train."

"DirtDoug is asleep already. He didn't get much sleep last night. MudBall kept him awake."

Jolie closed her eyes and sighed as Essie continued to rub. "Was the pig talking too loudly?"

Essie stopped rubbing for a moment. "MudBall snores."

"I didn't know that."

"Cats have very sensitive ears." Essie began to rub again.

"I believe I've heard that."

"What are our plans, Jolie?"

Jolie sat up. "Let's sleep."

"No, I mean when we get to Rawlins. What do we do then?"

Jolie brushed her auburn bangs out of her eyes. "We'll go visit Leppy and survey our options."

"How long will that take?"

"Not long. We'll talk to the judge. The sheriff. Someone. There must be something that can be done."

"Sheriff Riley said the judge and sheriff are crooks," Essie reminded her.

"Perhaps he was mistaken. Maybe Leppy's already out."

Essie's bottom lip curled, and she closed her eyes. "Maybe he's already lynched."

"Estelle! Don't work yourself into a dither."

"I should have listened to Stuart Brannon," Essie mumbled.

"Have you been reading Gibs's dime novels?"

"In *Bad Water Below the Border*, Brannon told that Mexican senorita that a proper lady should never fall for a gunman. It would only cause her heartbreak."

"I see. And you just threw caution to the wind?"

"What's a girl to do when a guy has a dimpled smile?"

"True." Jolie grinned. "It does seem a tad unfair for the Lord to give gunmen such irresistible smiles."

"I was thinking the same thing. I think Leppy will settle down after we get married," Essie declared.

"I trust that won't be for a few years."

"Daddy said I have to be eighteen."

"That's over five years away."

"Yes, but it's better than last year."

"What did he say then?" Jolie asked.

"He said I have to be thirty before I get married. I think he was teasing."

Jolie leaned back in the seat and closed her eyes. "It'll be difficult for them to let you go, Essie. You're the baby. You'll be the last one at home."

"I think I'll get married before Gibs."

"Did you see the look on his face when he spied Candace Clevenger?"

"Maybe you're right. Maybe I will be last to get married. Leppy will wait. He told me the good ones are worth waiting for."

"I think we both need to get some rest, or we won't be able to help anyone," Jolie added.

"I don't know if I will be able to sleep. The train is noisy," Essie complained.

"It doesn't seem to affect DirtDoug. Perhaps if we set him on the floor, you could lay your head in my lap."

"Do you mind?" Essie asked.

"Of course not."

The only light was the lantern in the conductor's quarters. Jolie stroked Essie's long hair. The train car rocked back and forth as it rolled out of Nebraska into eastern Wyoming. Jolie could smell leather, sweat, onions, and rosewater perfume from the other passengers. She rested her chin on her chest, her wool shawl pulled around her shoulders.

Lord, please take care of Mama. She's the family treasure. Everyone thinks it's me, but You and I know better. It's Mama who keeps us all going. She is such a rock. She thinks her children are the most talented and gifted in the world. We've spent our whole lives trying to live up to

Mama's expectations.

And Daddy — no woman ever loved her man more than Mama loves Daddy. Sometimes it's embarrassing, but it's wonderful. I have no doubt all four of us will have wonderful marriages, and, if so, it's all Mama's doing. He is the center of her every dream. Even after almost twenty years. Don't let her lose her sight, Lord. Don't let her ever lose sight of Daddy. Please.

I need some sleep.

I need to sleep for a week and wake up with everything solved.

Jolie opened her eyes when they pulled into Cheyenne. At Laramie City, she didn't bother looking. When they stopped at Medicine Bow, she closed Essie's mouth and pulled her shawl back up to her shoulders. Daylight broke before they rattled into Ft. Steele, and she was combing her wavy auburn hair when they slowed before entering Rawlins.

The conductor appeared at the front of the car, a double-barreled shotgun in hand. "Folks, we have trouble here. If we didn't need to take on water and let two passengers off, we wouldn't stop. I want you to keep the windows up and move toward the center aisle."

"My word," a woman in front of Jolie called out, "what's going on?"

"The coal miners north of here are being stirred up by union agitators. They consider the railroad an enemy. They may try to attack the train."

Jolie woke up Essie.

"Don't stop!" another pleaded.

"We've got passengers for Rawlins. The railroad keeps its schedule."

"At the cost of lives?" someone shouted.

"We haven't lost anyone yet," he shot back.

Essie petted DirtDoug and jammed him back into the satchel. Then she turned so Jolie could comb her long hair.

"When are things going to settle down?" someone asked.

The train now was creeping up to the station.

"I hear there's a lynch party in town. They've been drinking for two days. They'll probably lynch the poor bloke after dark tonight. Then they'll all sober up, and perhaps we can get them to listen to reason," the conductor said.

A man with a clerical collar asked, "Why doesn't the governor call in the troops?"

The conductor strolled down the aisle.

"Because this is now the great state of Wy-oming, and he won't admit he can't handle local problems with local forces."

He paused next to Jolie and Essie. "Needless to say, ladies, I want you by the door for an immediate exit."

Jolie stood on the step right behind the conductor. She held her handbag. Her hat was pulled down in front and tied under her chin. Essie had tied her hat ribbon around her face in such a way that the hat looked more like a mask. She pushed DirtDoug's head down into the satchel and fastened it over him.

"There are some things a cat shouldn't have to see," she murmured.

"Get those passengers off. We're not takin' on water until we get to Fillmore," someone shouted from the platform.

The station was crowded with shouting, milling men. The conductor, shotgun in hand, shoved his way out, pulled Jolie and Essie to the platform, and then leaped back into the car. The train never came to a halt. Many in the crowd followed the movement of the train, throwing rocks at the windows. There were two gun blasts.

Jolie ran with Essie toward the depot.

"Who's shooting, Jolie?"

"I can't tell. It's crazy."

"It reminds me of Mrs. Mitchell," Essie murmured. "Only it's a whole mob of them."

"Are you scared?" Jolie asked.

"No, are you?"

"No. I wonder why that is?"

Essie opened the satchel, peeked in at the black-and-white cat, then fastened it. "I think I had all the afraid scared out of me in Scottsbluff."

"I know what you mean."

"How will we find Leppy?" Essie probed.

"That shouldn't be a problem. There'll be a big crowd of drunk men around the jail."

The sidewalk was empty, and the front of the hardware store was boarded up. A man with a shotgun stood near the door.

"If you gals need to shop, the store is open. Just tryin' to keep that crowd from bustin' us up and stealing everything, like they did at Umlodt's Grocery."

"No, we don't need to shop. Why doesn't the sheriff do something?"

"The sheriff is leadin' that bunch. Maybe it'll settle down after Verdue gets hung. I just wish they'd get it over with." He glanced down at the carpetbag. "Did you two come to town looking for your husbands? They're probably in that riot down at the jailhouse."

"Thank you." Jolie nodded, and they scurried on.

"He thought I'm old enough to be married," Essie giggled.

"You're almost as tall as I am."

"Yeah, but the rest of me isn't like you," Essie mumbled.

They turned the corner. "Oh, my!" Jolie exclaimed.

Several dozen men lounged on the steps in front of the jail. More were on wagons. Some had guns drawn; many had amber bottles in hand. Staying across the street from the crowd, Jolie and Essie inched closer until they paused at a clothing store. Jolie strained to listen to the crowd.

"Why do we have to wait until dark?" one of the men grumbled.

"The sheriff wants the cover of night."

"We could hang the sheriff too."

"He's the one who pays us. Besides, where else do we get free liquor?"

"Yeah . . . and I hear that ain't all that's goin' to be free!" someone chortled.

A man in a black frockcoat and top hat strolled up to the crowd, and they moved back to let him get to the front door and step inside.

"Who was that?" Essie asked.

"That's ol' man Phillips," a deep voice boomed behind them.

Jolie spun around and was shocked to see a woman who was almost wide enough to fill up the doorway.

"He's the undertaker. Probably wants to get a coffin built. Did you notice how men never look an undertaker in the eye? Guess they figure their time is coming," the woman reported. She glanced down at the satchel. "Don't tell me you came here on purpose."

"Yes," Jolie said.

"If you need to get away from that drunken crowd, you come in here," the woman offered.

"Thank you," Jolie said. "Essie, you stay here. I'll go see how difficult it is to visit with Leppy."

"Are you relatives of Verdue?" the woman asked.

"Yes, I'm his sweetie," Essie reported.

The woman stared at Essie from head to foot. "That's okay with me. He got a bum deal, but we can't stand up against that crowd."

"I understand." Jolie nodded.

The woman tugged on her tight white lace collar. "They'll loot my store and burn it to the ground if I protest what they're doing. None of them are locals."

"Essie, you wait here. I'll go over." She handed her sister her handbag.

"I'll go with you," Essie insisted.

Jolie put her hand on her sister's shoulder. "No, let me test the water first. If they allow me to go in, I'll signal for you to join me."

"You're crazy to go over there," the big woman huffed.

"Crazy, but not dumb," Jolie murmured.

The sun had risen above the Medicine Bow Mountains. Yet it still cast long shadows as she ambled across the dirt street.

Lord, I have no idea why this does not frighten me as much as facing Mrs. Mitchell. These are all paid, drunken gunmen. It's a sad life if that's as high as they have climbed. But they will not stop Jolie Bowers!

A short man with a half-empty bottle stopped her as she approached the group. "Where do you think you're goin'?"

"I need to talk to the sheriff. This is his office, isn't it?"

"Not for you, it ain't," another growled. "We're takin' care of business here. You walk on the other side of the street."

"I most certainly will not. Move aside."

He turned and shouted to the others, "She wants to talk to the sheriff."

"Maybe she's one of the Laramie City girls he's invited to the lynching," a man in a wagon called out.

A big, bearded man with no front teeth waded through the crowd toward her. "You see, I told you it would be worth waitin' around fer!"

Slowly they gave way, and she crowded between them. Most were sweaty, dirty, and reeking of whiskey. When Jolie reached the door, they huddled behind her so close she could feel them brush against her dress. She knocked on the door.

A short man in a dark brown suit and tie, with gray hair that hung to his collar, opened the door about two inches. "What do you want?"

Jolie cleared her throat and spoke as if quieting a classroom of unruly children. "I want to speak to the sheriff."

"I said, what do you want?"

"I told you, I want to speak to the sheriff."

"I am the sheriff. What do you want?"

"May I come in and talk to you?"

"No." He slammed the door.

She knocked again.

"You need help, lady? We'd like to get in there too." A big man slammed the butt plate of his Winchester carbine against the door. "Open up, Sheriff. Let's hang the son of —"

The door opened. "I told you we'd wait . . ." The man with the gray hair spied Jolie. "Are you still here?"

"I demand to see my brother."

"Who in blazes is your brother?"

Lord, You said we should treat all believers as brothers and sisters. "Leppy Verdue." *I'm not sure Leppy fits, but I'm willing to give him the benefit of the doubt.*

The crowd hushed. The big man mumbled, "Are you his sister?"

"Most men, no matter how despicable, have mothers and sisters," she replied. "Surely I don't pose any danger."

"He didn't tell me he had a sister," the sheriff maintained.

"I'm sure there are many things he didn't tell you. He was trying to protect us. I must talk with him. I demand you open up."

"Nobody makes demands of me, lady."

The sheriff slammed the door.

He can't do that! No one slams the door on Jolie Lorita Bowers. She nodded for the big man to bang on the door. He seemed happy to oblige. There was no response.

"I reckon he don't want to talk to you."

Jolie folded her arms across her chest. "I traveled a long way to see him."

"You can take your brother home to Mama after tonight," someone called out.

"I'm not leaving until you open this door," Jolie shouted.

A skinny, sour-smelling man staggered up to her. "You can wait with me, honey."

Lord, this is not the way I planned it.

"Please move aside. The baby can't breathe," a young woman's voice called out.

Jolie spun around to see Essie carrying something wrapped in a blanket on her shoulder. She wore Jolie's dark blue dress and had a fat stomach. A very, very fat stomach.

"I'm getting faint," Essie called out. "I think I'm goin' to vomit."

The men scooted back. She waddled up to Jolie.

"Jolie, have they let you see my husband yet?"

"Your . . ." Jolie hugged her sister. "Do you know what you're doing?" she whispered.

"I hope so," Essie said.

Jolie knocked on the door again.

"Sheriff, Verdue's wife and baby are here," the big man shouted.

The door swung open a few inches. "What is this — a family reunion?"

Estelle Lorita Bowers took a deep breath. "I want to see my husband."

The sheriff studied Essie. "Is this a joke?"

Tears flowed down Essie's cheeks. "Even a condemned man should get to kiss his loving wife and darling infant good-bye," she sobbed.

"Let her in, Sheriff," the big man demanded. "She's right. Ever' man should say good-bye to his wife and baby." The crowd pressed forward.

The door swung open, and Essie and Jolie were pulled inside. The door slammed behind them.

"You ladies are crazy."

"But we aren't dumb," Essie responded.

"Are you really his wife?" a tall deputy asked. He stood next to the undertaker.

"Ask him. Tell Leppy his sweetie is here to see him."

"What's your name?" the sheriff asked.

"Estelle Cinnia . . . but my Leppy calls me Essie."

The sheriff stepped back toward the cells and shouted, "Verdue, your sweetie is here.

What's her name?"

"Estelle Cinnia, but I call her Essie!" Leppy hollered back.

The sheriff shrugged. "Junior, you go back and keep an eye on them." Then he turned to the undertaker. "Can we have him buried before daylight?"

The deputy led them back down the dark, narrow hallway in the windowless building. In a white long-sleeved shirt and black vest, an unshaven Leppy Verdue leaned against the bars of the far cell.

"Essie, darlin', I knew you'd come."

"I had to see my husband."

"You told them we're married?" Verdue mumbled. "I didn't want to, eh, jeopardize your safety."

"We ain't goin' to hurt a woman with a baby in her arms and another on the way," the deputy declared.

"Another?" Leppy gasped.

"I wanted to surprise you," Essie announced.

"I'm surprised."

"Aren't you goin' to say hello to your sister?" Jolie pressed.

Leppy stared for a moment, then nodded. "Oh . . . yeah, howdy, sis. Eh, how's Mama takin' this?"

"She prays for you every day."

Leppy glanced up at the deputy. "I got a prayin' mama."

"You got about two minutes to talk. That's all," the deputy informed him.

"Could you open the cell so he can hold little Dougie?" Essie nodded toward the blanket-covered baby.

The deputy reached for his vest pocket, then backed away.

"No, ma'am, I'm not openin' the cell."

Essie stepped up to the bars. "Look, Daddy. Look at your darlin' baby."

Leppy reached through the bars.

"Keep your hands back, Verdue," the deputy growled.

Jolie leaned up against the deputy's arm. "Surely you'd let him touch his baby one last time."

"Okay." He shrugged.

Leppy reached over to the blanket and patted the baby. "And he looks just like me. Give us your opinion, deputy. Does he look more like me or like my Essie darlin'?" Verdue asked.

The deputy stepped closer to Essie and pulled back the blanket. "That's a dadgum cat!"

The barrel of the revolver crashed into the deputy's head, and he slumped to the floor.

Jolie covered her mouth with her hand. "Where did you get the gun?" she whispered.

"From my darlin' Essie," Leppy announced.

Essie faked a smile. "I borrowed it from Strath."

"Without telling me?" Jolie choked.

"You would have made me give it back."

"Unlock the cell door," Leppy requested.

"There are fifty armed men out there," Jolie cautioned as she turned the key in the lock.

"If we each shoot ten . . ." he suggested.

"That leaves twenty."

"What's your plan, Essie?" Jolie asked.

"I don't know." She shrugged. "I didn't think they'd believe I'm Leppy's wife."

"I think all that stuffing helped."

"It took a lot of stuffing to fill out your dress," Essie admitted. "What do you think we should do now, Jolie?"

"Leppy, you drag the deputy back into the cell. You stay in there with the door unlocked. Eh . . . give me the baby . . . little Dougie."

DirtDoug flopped across Jolie's shoulder. Essie covered him up with the blanket. "He's a very good baby."

"I'm glad he didn't meow at the wrong time." Jolie motioned to the floor. "Lie down there like you've fainted."

Verdue dragged the deputy inside the cell. "Is this going to work?"

"Today they seem to believe everything," Jolie murmured. "Give me the deputy's gun. It's my turn to coldcock someone."

"Have you ever done it before?" Leppy asked.

"No."

"She coldcocked the Condor brothers with a fryin' pan," Essie said.

"This is a little different," Verdue instructed. "Don't get softhearted. It will only be effective if you think about drivin' a sixteen-penny nail with one blow. Hit him like you're drivin' big nails."

Essie sprawled on the floor. "Should I have my mouth open or shut?"

"Open," Jolie replied. "Now lie still."

Carrying DirtDoug, Jolie walked slowly down to the sheriff's office. When she peeked in, the sheriff and the undertaker were counting gold coins.

"Excuse me, Sheriff, do you have any smelling salts?" she asked.

He looked startled. "What now?"

Jolie strolled into the middle of the room. "Mrs. Verdue fainted, and the deputy can't get her to come to."

"Okay . . . that's it," the sheriff groused. "Time's up. You two are leaving. I don't have smelling salts."

The undertaker reached in his vest pocket and pulled out a small milky blue vial. "I'm always prepared." He handed it to the sheriff.

"I don't care if she's passed out or not. You're leaving right now."

The sheriff marched down the hall and squatted next to Essie. "This is starting to . . ." Then he stared around. "Where's Junior?"

Like driving big nails. Jolie brought the barrel of the revolver down across the back of the sheriff's head. He slumped on top of Essie. Leppy dragged him into the cell.

Essie jumped up. "He was heavy."

"Now the undertaker," Jolie whispered.

Essie pulled the sheriff's gun from his holster. "It's my turn." She grabbed the gun by the barrel and practiced tapping it in the air. "Like driving big nails." She hurried down the hallway and climbed up on a bench next to the office door.

Jolie stepped back into the sheriff's office.

"Excuse me, sir."

The undertaker glanced up from the

255

stack of gold coins. "How's the little lady?"

"Better, thank you. Mr. and Mrs. Verdue have some questions about the burial. They want to pay you extra for something special," Jolie explained.

The undertaker pulled off his top hat and strolled ahead of her to the back hallway. "I always respect the wishes of the family," he assured her.

He had just stepped into the hall when the grip end of the Colt slammed into his head. The man didn't drop. He turned toward Essie, who stood on the bench.

"I did it wrong!" she gasped.

"Wait," Leppy called as he swung the cell door open.

The undertaker raised a finger at Essie . . . then slumped to the floor.

"Okay, that makes three of them. What about the other fifty?" Leppy asked.

"We'll walk right through them," Jolie announced.

"We will?" Leppy replied.

With all three men unconscious in the back locked cell, Jolie, Essie, and Leppy huddled by the sheriff's desk.

"I look silly in this," he complained.

Jolie stared at the long black coat and silk top hat. "You look fine. No one looks at the undertaker. It's as if it's bad luck."

"It can't work," he mumbled.

"None of this can work, but it has. Essie, you keep them focused on you by crying."

Essie's brown eyes grew wide. "But what if I can't cry?"

"What if you had just been cast to play Juliet in the school play?"

"That doesn't make me cry."

"And Bullet Wells is going to be Romeo, and you have to kiss him."

"Aggghhhh!" Essie sobbed. She clutched DirtDoug to her shoulder.

Jolie pulled open the front door and pushed her way into the crowd.

"My baby, my sweet baby will be father-less," Essie sobbed. "Oh, what am I to do? What am I to do?"

Leppy walked by her side, holding her arm. "Now, Mrs. Verdue, let me assure you, your husband will have the finest marble headstone and . . ."

Jolie slammed the door behind her and hustled to Essie's other side. "Hurry," she whispered.

They had almost made it through the crowd when DirtDoug meowed.

The men grew silent.

"What was that?" someone mumbled.

Jolie grabbed her handkerchief from the

sleeve of her dress and blew her nose.

Loudly.

Then they slipped into the alley.

Leppy glanced over his shoulder. "Where now?"

"Back of the bakery," Essie instructed. "I do have a plan from here."

The big woman from the clothing store held the lead lines of a two-horse buggy. "I didn't think you'd make it," she greeted them. "Here, go straight east toward Ft. Steele."

Within minutes, they were racing along the dirt road with Jolie driving the team. Jolie and Essie sat in the front. DirtDoug leaned into the wind, sitting on Essie's lap. Leppy Verdue sat on the duffle bag behind them. He clutched the railing. "I knew that my Essie darlin' would come for me. I just knew it."

"We barely got there in time," Jolie mused.

Leppy tossed the top hat on the floorboard. "You got there at the perfect time. Any earlier and they would have been too sober to believe all of that."

"I still can't believe they fell for it." Jolie shook her head. "Estelle Cinnia, you amazed me. You were very convincing."

Essie petted the cat. "And I thought

DirtDoug did quite well for his first acting experience."

"Yes, he did." Leppy grinned.

Essie held the cat up in front of her and studied his face. "I think you're right. He does look like you."

Eight

Leppy leaned back on the leather seat and pulled his new hat down across his eyes. "I can't believe you had a train waiting for us at Ft. Steele."

Jolie sat across from Leppy and Essie. She glanced out the window and stared at the barren Wyoming countryside. "I told you to give the Lord credit for a stalled eastbound. We were so unsure of ourselves in Rawlins. I had no idea there was an eastbound at this time of the day. There was no plan as to how to leave town."

Essie held on to Leppy's arm. "If she had thought about it, she could have gotten the train to wait. Everyone obeys Jolie, except maybe Chester Wells."

Through the dust and grime of a dirty face, two dimples framed Leppy's grin. "You two will be happy to know that I do give the Lord a lot of credit for that escape. He's the only one who could pull it off without any gunfire. But He surely cuts it fine, don't He? They were goin' to hang me tonight."

"Why tonight?" Jolie asked.

"They heard that a U.S. Marshal and the Wyomin' Attorney General were on their way. They wanted the spontaneous lynchin' to be over before anyone took a closer look," he reported.

"I wanted to come on Saturday, but Jolie said we had time to wait," Essie offered.

Jolie looked over at Essie and Leppy. "I mistakenly believed you had until December 20."

He patted Essie's knee. "Saturday might have been too soon. It was early Sunday mornin' when me and the Lord settled up." His voice softened. The dimples faded. "Now that I'm out of there, I'm glad I had that time to ponder things."

Jolie watched out the window as a dozen pronghorn antelope on a bluff stared back at the train. Her hands were folded in her lap. "What made you send Essie a letter in the first place? Did you really think she could break you out?"

He hugged Essie's shoulders. "Jolie, I really thought I was a dead man. They hated the men the mine owners hired. They wanted to prove they had power. They needed to convict and hang someone. It didn't matter if I was guilty or not, and the mine owners deserted me there. There was no reason to write to a lawyer. They would never have mailed it anyway. And it's for sure I couldn't write to Chug or any of the boys. An armed band of men would have meant lots more would die. They had just chased one posse out of town."

"You thought a letter to your sweetie would be delivered?" Essie giggled.

"I was hopin'." When Leppy pulled off his hat, his dark, unwashed hair curled out. "I figured if the letter got to the Bowerses' house, they would help me if there was any way possible. And if they couldn't come help, they would pray for me. I guess at the time it was my only hope. And my Essie darlin' didn't let me down."

Jolie winked at her sister. "She's a bulldog for you, Leppy Verdue."

He wiped the corners of his eyes. "Kind of a dusty old train, ain't it? . . . I've never known a family like yours. Jolie, I do know that I don't deserve the devotion Essie gives me."

"The Lord spoils us, Leppy," Jolie commented.

"Him and me made a deal on Sunday morning."

"If He let you get out of jail, you would go off to India and be a missionary?" Jolie grinned.

"Wouldn't that be a fine shinley? No,

I'm afraid there are a million Sunday school kids who would do a far better job at that than me. I told Him that I'd make a confession of faith, start learnin' how to live right, and try to find employment that doesn't depend upon my gun."

"That sounds serious," Jolie observed.

Leppy leaned back against the leather seat. "Facin' that lynch mob was not a time to be trivial with God. So Sunday mornin' me and Him struck a deal."

"What time Sunday morning?" Essie asked.

"What time? I reckon it was around 7:00 a.m. They were supposed to bring me some breakfast at 7:00," Leppy said. "Why do you ask?"

Jolie raised her eyebrows. "At 7:00 a.m. Daddy came out to the barn and told Essie and me that he thought we should come see you."

"Jolie didn't want to come."

"Oh?" he said.

"Mama got hurt, and I thought I should stay home and help her. Daddy insisted that we come, and he was right."

"But it was Jolie who confiscated Bill and Bob's rig and raced it all the way to Kimball so we wouldn't miss the train."

"I'm a grateful man. The Lord surely

kept His end of the deal."

Essie patted his knee. "Go ahead then, sweetie."

"Go ahead with what?"

"Make your confession of faith," Essie pressed.

"Right here?" he gulped.

Essie glanced behind them at an elderly Mexican man and woman who held a sack of onions in their laps. "Why not right here?"

Sweat beaded on Leppy's forehead. "Don't I need to say it to a preacher or something?"

Jolie reached over and stroked DirtDoug's head as the cat slept on top of the satchel. "No, Essie's right. You can do it right now."

"Out loud?" he gasped.

"Yes, of course."

Leppy Verdue sat up and glanced around at the other passengers. "I don't want to offend anyone."

Essie spun around toward the Mexican couple. "My sweetie wants to confess Jesus Christ as Lord and Savior out loud. Is that all right with you?"

The startled gray-haired man looked at his wife. She nodded.

"Es bueno," he mumbled.

"No, his name is Leppy," Essie declared. Then she turned back. "They said it's okay with them . . . or something like that."

Verdue took a deep breath and squinted his eyes shut. "Eh, God . . . this isn't easy for me. . . . I ain't much . . . but, well, You did a good job of gettin' me out of jail, and I'd like You to keep on takin' care of me . . . so I'm trustin' Jesus with my life ever' day. Amen." He swallowed hard and stared over at Jolie. "Did I do it right?"

"Did you mean it in your heart?" she challenged.

"I reckon I did."

"Then I reckon you did it right."

The Mexican woman tapped him on the shoulder. When Leppy turned around, she grinned and handed him a big yellow onion.

Jolie, Essie, and DirtDoug finished supper at the Kimball Hotel and then waited at the stagecoach office as the sun sank into Wyoming.

"I wish we had waited to see him off in Cheyenne," Essie said.

"We needed to buy some material for Mama's mother-of-the-bride dress," Jolie explained.

"I don't know why he had to go to

Denver," Essie mumbled.

"He needed some advice. Leppy has some friends there."

"He has some friends near Scottsbluff too," Essie pouted.

"Now, little sis, you have to let Leppy follow the Lord's leading."

"What if the Lord was telling him to come be with me?"

"Then he'll come be with you. The Lord doesn't need you to guide Leppy. God can do that easily enough."

They stood as the stagecoach pulled up in front of them.

"You know, Jolie . . . for a few minutes at the jail I actually forgot I'm only twelve."

Jolie hugged her sister. "Estelle Cinnia, you were marvelous. I can't believe you came up with that plan and pulled it off."

"I think it helped that they were mostly drunk."

"For a few minutes back in Rawlins," Jolie added, "I felt like the younger sister."

Essie's brown eyes widened. "Really?"

"Yes, and that has never happened in my entire life. You acted exactly like Mama."

"I did? I must be growing up." She plucked up the satchel with the cat's head protruding from it. "Come on, little Dougie. Mama is goin' to take you home."

Two men in suits and ties waited for Essie and Jolie to climb into the stage. The girls sat facing the front of the rig; the men sat across from them. One man was large, and his tight tie seemed to turn his face red. The other wore his vest unbuttoned.

"Evenin', ladies," the thinner man greeted them. "Looks like we'll be sharing the stage for a while. I'm K. M. Walther, on my way up to Rapid City, then Lead. Thought I'd stop by to see an old friend near Gering."

"Mr. Walther, I'm Jolie Bowers, and this is my sister Estelle."

"You can call me Essie."

In the twilight he motioned at the satchel. "I see you have a fine cat."

"Yes," Essie said. "This is DirtDoug."

The stagecoach bolted forward with a lunge at the driver's whoop. "Are you girls going on a trip or going home?"

"Going home," Jolie replied. "We have a homestead east of Scottsbluff."

"Jolie is a schoolteacher," Essie announced.

"That's fine, ma'am. I reckon in the twilight you look a tad young for a teacher," he said.

"That's quite all right. I am one of the youngest teachers in western Nebraska."

"But she's engaged," Essie reported.

"Yes, well, congratulations to all." Walther turned to the other man. "And you, sir? Are you headed to Gering? Rapid City?"

The rotund, white-haired man tipped his crisp hat. "Oh, excuse me. My mind was elsewhere. I just came from Deadwood. Miller is my name. Hawthorne Miller."

"Wow," Essie grinned, "does anyone ever confuse you with the Hawthorne Miller who writes dime novels?"

The man struggled to unfasten the top button on his white shirt. "I am that Hawthorne Miller!"

"You are?" Essie's chin dropped. "Then you write all those Stuart Brannon books."

He cleared his throat as if to address a throng of adoring fans. "Actually I write many other books as well as those."

Essie leaned over with her elbows on her knees. "My brother has nearly all of the Stuart Brannon books."

Miller held his round hat in his hand. "I trust that they have been a source of good moral lessons for him."

"He loves them," Jolie put in. "Though he does chuckle at your confusion over guns."

"Confusion?" Miller sat straight up. "All

of my books are arduously researched."

"Next time you probably should not have a Winchester 1876 in 45/70 caliber," Jolie said. "It was the Winchester 1886 that comes in that caliber. The '76 came in 45/75 and a few other calibers, but not 45/70."

"Schoolteachers are experts on munitions?" Miller huffed.

"Her fiancé is a gunsmith," Essie announced.

"Hmm . . . I do believe that."

"She's right, Miller," Walther confirmed. "I was in the army in the '70s, and no Winchester shot the government 45/70 cartridge. I suppose that's why we all carried the Springfield trapdoor single shots."

"Hmmm . . . I'll make a note of that."

Jolie rocked back and forth with the rhythm of the stage. "Mr. Miller, why are you going back north if you just came down from there?"

"I did some interviews with old Brazos Fortune up in Deadwood concerning a novel. I had just returned to Cheyenne when I heard the news of that big jailbreak in Rawlins."

"What jailbreak?" Jolie asked.

Miller pulled out a folded envelope, struck a sulfur match, and held the envelope close enough to read.

"From what I heard in the train depot . . . a killer by the name of Leonard Ventura was awaiting hanging when his gang swooped into town and helped him escape."

"His gang?" Essie asked.

"Yes, they are called . . ." He lit another match. ". . . the Medicine Bow Renegades."

"They are?" Essie said.

"How many in the gang?" Jolie asked.

"Now that's what makes it interesting," Miller said. "I understand the sheriff over there had at least six deputies guarding the prisoner and a dozen local upstanding citizens patrolling the street. But this gang of two dozen men and two dance hall girls came swooping —"

"Dance hall girls?" Essie grinned.

"A rougher lot there has never been. May you two ladies never have to view this degraded type of womanhood," Miller puffed.

"Yes, go on. What happened?" Walther asked.

"According to my sources, while this Ventura was in jail, his gang filtered into town one by one until they took all of Rawlins captive."

"The whole town?" Jolie gasped.

"Apparently. Then while the dance hall girls diverted the deputies' attention —"

"How did they do that?" Essie asked.

Miller leaned forward and lowered his voice. "Young lady, there are some things your delicate ears should never have to hear."

"I appreciate your discretion for my sister's sake, Mr. Miller," Jolie said.

"Certainly. I will try to edit the account, keeping in mind my listeners."

"So thoughtful of you." Jolie nodded.

"Thank you. Anyway, the six deputies and sheriff were shot, and Ventura rode away."

"Shot?" Walther replied. "Someone was shot?"

"Actually the telegram said the sheriff and all his men, plus a local businessman were incapacitated," Miller reported.

Essie reached over in the dark and poked her sister. "Their heads were chopped off?" she gasped, suppressing a giggle.

"No, not decapitated but incapacitated — taken out of the fight. I believe we can assume that means they were shot."

"Oh, my, what a violent and vicious gang." Jolie bit her lip to keep a straight face.

"Yes, it's horrible," Miller mumbled. "And some say the West has been tamed."

In the dark Jolie slipped her fingers into Essie's moist, warm hand. "Of course, that does make an interesting story for you."

"Quite so. I'm just a chronicler. I see myself as one recording history for a future generation," Miller puffed.

"With some fiction, of course?" Jolie challenged.

"Oh, here and there a word or two needs to be added to keep the story flowing, but being brutally honest, I merely call it a fiction book so no one will take offense."

"How noble of you," Jolie commended.

"I assure you, miss, I am no ordinary novelist."

Jolie leaned her head back and closed her eyes. "Yes, I can tell that."

In the darkness of the rattling stage, Jolie heard the other man shift his position. He cleared his throat and spoke. "Miller, what happened after the daring, despicable raid on Rawlins?"

"Hmmm, my word, that's not a bad title — *The Daring, Despicable Raid on Rawlins* . . . by Hawthorne H. Miller."

"What a wonderful mind you have, Mr. Miller," Jolie gushed. "I too am curious. What happened after the raid?"

"The sheriff reported that Ventura led his gang back up into the Medicine Bow Mountains. Naturally, the lawman is leading a big posse after them."

"I'm glad to hear the sheriff recovered from his gunshot wound enough to give chase," Jolie said.

"Quite so. Wyoming lawmen are a tough breed. Not like that California bunch," he blustered.

Jolie found herself shaking her head. *Lord, it's hard to imagine anyone more pompous than Hawthorne Miller.* "I didn't know that."

"It's true. You can trust my word," Miller boasted.

"I'm sure we can," Jolie said. "But why are you here? Why didn't you head up into the Medicine Bows to get an interview or something?"

"Writer's instinct. You either have it, or you don't," Miller declared.

"And you have it?"

"A double dose, I'm afraid. I checked with the agent in Cheyenne, and he said that a couple of dance hall girl types were on the eastbound out of Cheyenne."

"Are they going to Gering?" Essie asked.

"He said he overheard them mention the Wildcat Hills. I did some checking around and found a man who said two women who fit that description live in a cabin in Carter Canyon in the Wildcat Hills."

Jolie clutched her shawl to keep it from slipping off her shoulders. "And you're going to Carter Canyon for an interview?"

"Precisely. Perhaps I'll get to meet this Ventura fellow as well."

"Oh . . . he'll be there too?" Jolie asked.

"They said the blonde is his . . . eh, how shall I say this? His paramour."

"What does that mean, Jolie?" Essie probed.

"His sweetie," Jolie said.

"That almost sounds romantic," Essie replied. "Are your books romantic?"

"Hmmmpht. Of course there are elements of romance in every good story. Always quite tasteful, you may be sure."

"Yes, of course," Jolie echoed.

Three miles south of town, DirtDoug fell asleep. By the time they rattled their way to the first stage station, Essie was sleeping on Jolie's shoulder, and Mr. Hawthorne Miller's snore sounded like something between an oboe and a flute.

At Harrisburg Mr. Miller exited the stage and retreated to the only boarding-house in town. Jolie strolled around in the lantern light of the station as the horses were being changed. Mr. Walther strolled with her.

"Last time I was here, this town was called Randall," he said.

"I heard it was Centropolis for a while," she added.

"Sounds like something a schoolteacher would call it."

Jolie laughed.

"Oh, yes, sorry, Miss Bowers. You are a schoolteacher. No disrespect intended."

"That's quite all right, Mr. Walther. Schoolteachers do gain a certain reputation."

"As do writers. Miller has quite a high opinion of himself, doesn't he?" Walther ventured.

"I think that's probably necessary for a writer. You have to think you can do it."

"I suppose self-confidence is good in any field. I imagine you believe you have something to teach your students."

"Yes, you're right. I enjoy it, and I do believe I can help the children." She brushed her auburn hair back over her ear and pulled her shawl up closer to her neck. "How about you, Mr. Walther? Are you confident in your work, whatever it may be?"

"I'm an engraver by trade."

"You engrave plates, trophies, guns?"

"Oh, no. I used to make engraving plates for the Treasury Department. Stamps, seals, and the like."

"Oh, my . . . that does take some artistic talent. You said you used to do that?"

"Yes, now I'm in the authentication business. I'm a professional authenticator," he announced.

Jolie could smell fried ham, but all the lights in the buildings were turned off, and the street was dark. "What does such a person do?"

"For the past year I've been in Santa Fe, New Mexico, and Mexico City examining some of the Spanish land grants to see which ones are genuine."

"Those are still in question?"

"Oh, my, yes."

"But the Mexican War was forty-five years ago," Jolie declared.

"Our courts move slowly."

"Did you work on the Peralta claim?" Jolie asked. "I read about it."

"Yes, they sent me to Spain on that one."

"So are you finished in New Mexico?"

"For a while. The Homestake Mine in Lead had some shares show up that seemed to be a forgery. They hired me to go look at them."

Jolie felt the dry dirt compress beneath the heel of her lace-up shoes. "It sounds like a very interesting business."

"Thank you. Most think it sounds quite boring. But it's like a game. I do enjoy it."

Jolie paused near the raised wooden sidewalk. "Mr. Walther, could you look at a handwritten document and tell if it's the original or just a copy?"

"Usually I can spot the original. The first time through, a person is thinking of what to say next, and the writing shows halting, starting, pausing. The ink is often heavier in more places as a person starts and stops. There are several other things to look for."

She stepped up on the wooden sidewalk and found herself just as tall as Walther. "I have a document that I need authenticated. It's a deed to our homestead. What would it cost for me to hire you to look at it?"

"I hope I don't sound like Hawthorne Miller, but I am quite good at it. Usually I'm paid two dollars an hour."

"An hour?" she gasped.

"Sorry, Miss Bowers. That's my standard rate. However, if you just have a simple deed, I would authenticate it for two dollars total, no matter how long it took."

She stepped off the sidewalk and meandered toward the stagecoach. "I just might take you up on that."

"Do you have a document that has been challenged?"

"Not yet. But I expect it will be."

Walther held the door open, and Jolie climbed back inside. Essie was stretched across the seat.

"Do you mind if I sit over here with you?" she asked.

"Not at all. I trust I don't snore like Mr. Miller."

"My brother snores; so I suppose I'm used to it," Jolie said.

The night was still, the sky moonless, the air cool as they rattled north.

"Mr. Walther, will you be in Gering for a few days?" Jolie finally asked.

"It depends upon whether my old neighbor is still here. He travels a bit. I haven't seen him in several years. Last time I came through, he was in St. Louis or somewhere. We were neighbors as children back in Ohio."

"What is his name?"

"Joseph Avery."

"Oh, no!" Jolie gasped.

"Good heavens, did something happen to him?"

"Eh, no," Jolie replied.

"You seemed startled."

"To be frank, Mr. Walther, the document I want you to look at is from Mr. Avery."

"You bought his homestead?" Walther asked.

"Yes, we did. He was in Helena trying to sell it."

"Helena? That rascal. He told me he'd never been farther west than Nebraska. What seems to be the trouble?"

"He's a crook!" Essie called out in the dark.

"Estelle!" Jolie scolded.

Essie sat up. "Well, he is. He sold the place ten times."

"Essie's right, Mr. Walther."

"Which Avery are you talking about?" Walther pressed.

"Which one, what?" Jolie asked.

"Which one of the twins?"

"Twins?"

"Joseph Avery has an identical twin brother, Jacob, you know."

The stage hit a boulder at the top of Wildcat Gap, and for four hours Jolie tried to sleep as the driver, guard, and Mr. Walther struggled to repair the right rear wheel. At daybreak they inched their way down the grade, and after several more stops, rolled into Gering at 8:30 a.m.

Essie stood wrapped in a green wool shawl, the cat hugged to her shoulder. "Are we going to walk over to Scottsbluff?" Essie asked. "DirtDoug is very hungry."

"I imagine he is. But it feels good to stretch my legs." Jolie dropped the satchel and stretched her arms. Pale gray clouds swirled high in the west Nebraska sky. "I don't think I want to ride on a stage again for a long time."

Essie lifted her nose. "Do you smell something funny?"

"Only you and me. We need to clean up."

"Can I have the bath water before you this time?" Essie requested.

"I do believe it's your turn to bathe first. Hot water sounds so nice. It seems like more than two days since we've been home."

Essie patted the cat. "DirtDoug thinks it was a very successful trip."

"Yes, it was . . . thanks to the very convincing performance of Estelle Cinnia Bowers."

"You and Dougie did pretty good too," Essie offered.

"Why, thank you. It's wonderful that Leppy is out. Now we have a mystery to solve about the Avery twins."

"If the evil Avery sold us the place, does that mean it's not ours?" Essie asked.

"The evil Avery?"

"That's what I decided to call him."

Jolie rubbed her temples and felt dust caked on her face. "We need to get home and wash up and change."

"I reckon we could take a bath in the barn like we did the time our roof fell in," Essie remarked.

"Yes. I'm actually looking forward to getting home, even if we aren't allowed in the house for a few more days."

"Hey, there's the sheriff at the doctor's office. Maybe he'll give us a ride over to Scottsbluff."

Jolie waved at the lawman, and he drove toward them. "You're just the one I need to talk to," the sheriff called out. "I got a telegram to be on the lookout for an escaped prisoner named Lefty Purdue. I presume you two were successful?"

"It was quite exciting," Essie blurted out.

"It ain't exactly been boring here. Do you have time to stop in and try to talk to Mrs. Mitchell?" the sheriff asked.

"She's in the hospital?" Jolie quizzed.

"Rev. and Mrs. Leyland agreed to transport her to Lincoln for me. While they were waiting at the depot, she up and breaks a window and slashes her wrist with a glass shard," the sheriff reported.

"Oh, no!" Jolie gasped.

"I don't know what to do with her, Miss Jolie. That woman is determined to take her life or someone else's. The doc has the bleeding stopped and had her bound to the bed. Dix is in there now. I've got to keep a deputy with her. Meanwhile we need to follow up some tracks of Mysterious Dave Mather east of town."

"Maybe he's all the way to Kansas by now," Essie suggested.

"I certainly hope so. Life is complicated enough as it is."

"I'll check on Mrs. Mitchell," Jolie said.

"Thank you. Mrs. Leyland was quite upset, and the reverend took her home. As soon as she settles down, he's coming back to spell off Dix. Now I'm goin' to get some breakfast."

"Sheriff, can you do me a big favor?" Jolie asked.

"I reckon I owe you plenty, Miss Jolie, for all the help you've been with Mrs. Mitchell."

"Could you give Essie and DirtDoug a lift to the Imperial Café so they can have some breakfast? The stage broke down, and we just arrived in town after an all-night trek."

"DirtDoug?" the sheriff quizzed.

Essie pointed to the cat in the satchel as she climbed up on the sheriff's wagon. "He really prefers fish for breakfast. He says it's easier to digest early in the day."

The sheriff glanced at Jolie, then back at the cat. "If this were any other family, I might think that a strange statement. But comin' from a Bowers . . . it don't even surprise me."

"Have Essie tell you how she dressed little Dougie up as her baby and walked Leppy right out of the Rawlins jail," Jolie called out as the wagon rolled north.

Canvas restraints bound the unconscious woman to the bed. Her face looked frozen in torment. The blond-haired deputy paced the room, hat in hand. His drooping mustache added to his scowl.

"Miss Jolie, I'm glad you're here. I need to get back out there and find Mather."

Jolie gave the deputy a quick hug. "I afraid I'm only here for a few moments,

Max. I promised the sheriff I'd peek in on Mrs. Mitchell."

The deputy took her to the bedside. "There she is."

"She looks twenty years older than she did two days ago," Jolie observed.

"I don't know why life gets so desperate that slittin' your wrist is your best option," Dix said.

"Satan comes to steal, kill, and destroy," Jolie mumbled. "Poor lady. I thought perhaps things would be different now."

Jolie sat in a chair by the woman's bed and stroked her arm.

Maxwell Dix paused behind her chair. "I heard that two dance hall darlin's marched into Rawlins with double-barreled shotguns blastin' and broke Leppy out of jail and shot up the town."

Jolie glanced back over her shoulder. "Where did you hear that?"

"At the Imperial Saloon. What really happened?"

"I think that's the best story." Jolie grinned.

"I know better than that."

"But most don't," Jolie told him. "Maybe that's a better story to circulate."

"You might be right about that. No reason to have 'em show up at *your* doorstep. I take it Leppy's okay?"

"He's on his way to Denver. He knows a lawyer by the name of Wade Eagleman that he wants to talk to."

Dix stared down at the woman on the bed. "Miss Jolie, what happens to a person who kills herself? My mama's faith says they're condemned by God and sent to hell. Or at least to that place in between."

"I don't know for sure, Max. You need to ask the reverend when he returns. I know the Lord is just. He will treat all people fairly. Suicide is certainly a sin, but all of us are sinners. That's why Jesus came." She clutched the woman's hand. "I just don't know." *Give her peace, Lord. I've never known anyone so tormented.*

Jolie stood and walked to the window. "I just can't look at her. It so distresses me. So . . ." She sighed deeply. "Did you and the sheriff find any signs of Mysterious Dave Mather."

Dix slapped his hat on. "Yes, as a matter of fact, but you ain't goin' to like it."

"What're you talking about?"

He pushed back the thin gauze curtains and stared out at the street. "Someone broke into the schoolhouse, Miss Jolie. We think it was him."

"*My* schoolhouse?"

"Yep. Mr. and Mrs. Vockney noticed it when they drove over to visit your mama. Now don't worry. Can't see that anything was taken or destroyed. He built a fire in the stove to keep warm and slept the night. Mrs. Vockney thought you had a pumpkin decorating your desk. That was gone."

"My pumpkin? Are you sure it wasn't Bullet Wells who broke in? He's been acting a little strange lately. Actually he acts a little strange all the time."

"The muddy footprints were man-sized," Dix reported.

Jolie clasped her hands and gripped tightly. "Then he's close to home . . . to Strath and Landen . . . the Wellses. I trust you warned them all."

"Yep, but if he wanted to break into a house, he would have done it by now. Anyway, I want to get back out and search the draws and gullies from the schoolhouse all the way to the bridge."

"If he destroyed any of the students' work . . ." Jolie fumed as she paced across the room.

"If he put himself under the wrath of Miss Jolie Bowers, he has no idea how easy hangin' would be in comparison."

"Did you talk to Daddy and Mama?"

"I was there yesterday afternoon."

286

"How's Mama doing? I felt bad going off and leaving her."

"I didn't get to visit with her much, of course. But she did come out to the door and said howdy. I'm not sure she knew it was me until your daddy told her."

"Wasn't she seeing well?"

"I think she just got up from a nap or something. Your little brother is itchin'."

"I trust he isn't scratching too much."

"I meant he's itchin' to get out and help me track down Mather."

"Gibs has wanted to capture Mysterious Dave Mather ever since we moved to Nebraska," Jolie said.

"Little brother is a trooper, you know. He's never afraid."

"He has this idea that if you're on the right side, there's nothing to be afraid of."

"In the long run of things, I reckon he's right," Maxwell said. "Your daddy said that once the quarantine is lifted, Gibs could ride out with me and the sheriff."

"Gibs will be in heaven if he gets to do that."

"Your daddy and me visited quite a spell out in that new house."

"Daddy likes to sit on that foundation and dream about how to design the house."

The deputy stopped in front of the mirror and brushed his yellow hair back over his ears with his fingers. "He surely likes to talk about that house."

"I think he'd like to get it finished before Grandma and Grandpa come out to visit."

"Yes, that's what he said. I can't imagine two more Bowerses around here."

"They're my mama's parents. Judge and Mrs. Pritchett. And I can assure you, they're nothing like Mama and Daddy," Jolie grinned. "Except for their loyalty to the Lord. You've never met anyone less like her parents than my mother. Grandma and Grandfather have never known what to do with her. She used to tease them by saying that she was adopted."

"As soon as the Mather thing gets settled, I told your daddy that I'd round up a few of the boys, and we'd help him raise the walls and roof of that house whenever he's ready. I lost my roofin' partner when Shakey Torrington moved back to Missouri. But Chug will help, and Leppy if he's back in town."

"I'm sure Daddy would appreciate the help. I know he wanted to get the walls up and roof on before the heavy snow. But Daddy's kind of a dreamer."

Dix retrieved a blue tin cup from the

dresser. "You want a sip of my cold coffee?"

Jolie grinned. "No, thank you."

He took a sip and grimaced. "Your daddy is dreamin' even better than that now."

"What do you mean?"

"Like I said, he wants that new house livable before the wedding."

"But my wedding is not until June 14. That's when Grandma and Grandpa are coming to see us. He's got time to build the house by then."

Dix meandered across the room to the window that faced the street. "I reckon them plans got changed. He said your grandparents are comin' in by Christmas."

"No, not Christmas. Mama and Daddy said they decided to wait and invite them to my wedding."

Dix spun around and faced Jolie. "Oh, no, not your wedding. Your brother's wedding."

Jolie's heart sank to her shoes. "What? What did you say?"

Matthew Dix waved his hand as he spoke. "Your daddy wants that house built before your brother's wedding on Christmas Eve."

She croaked the words out as if she were

lost at sea and going under for the last time. "Lawson is getting married?"

Blond eyebrows raised. "I take it you didn't know."

"But — but — but I've only been gone for forty-eight hours."

Dix rammed his hands in the back pockets of his brown canvas duckings. "Lawson and Miss April are smilin' like a barn cat with a mouse."

"Getting married? They can't . . . I didn't . . . Nobody asked me . . . I . . . But they're so young. Lawson's only sixteen!" Jolie fumed.

"I heard he'll be seventeen before Christmas."

"And April . . . she's only —"

"She'll be sixteen by then," Dix informed her.

"Sixteen is much too young to get married."

"My mama was sixteen when I was born. I never regretted that."

Jolie's arms were folded across her chest. "I don't believe this."

"You think I'm lyin' to you?"

"No . . . it's just . . . Well, it's like they sent me away so they could make these plans," Jolie complained.

Dix pulled off his dark blue bandanna

and wiped his neck. "You're happy for your brother, aren't you?"

"He doesn't know anything about marriage."

"Shoot, Miss Jolie, I'm almost twenty-seven, and I don't know anything about marriage either."

"How can he support a wife? Tell me that, Max."

The deputy parked in front of the mirror, folded his bandanna, and tied it back around his neck. "I was told that Strath Yarrow hired him on shares to do the farming out there and that your mama and daddy are goin' to let him and April live in the sod house after the new one's built. Mr. Vockney said he wanted to hire Lawson some too. That brother of yours is a hard worker, Miss Jolie. I don't think you ever have to worry about that."

Jolie plopped down in the chair next to the unconscious woman. "I just can't believe it! This is too bizarre." She leaned forward, elbows on her knees, face on her palms.

"What are you upset about? That your brother is happy or that you weren't asked permission?"

"That's not the point," she pouted.

"What is the point, Jolie? You want him

to waste ten years like I have? I was such a fool. It's only by the Lord's mercy that I'm even alive. I'd give anything to have met Miss Celia ten years ago and have our own place by now."

"I think it was a conspiracy — hatched out while I was gone."

"It probably was. Nobody chooses to face the wrath of Jolie Bowers. Not even your brother . . . and especially not some shy thing like Miss April."

"I'm not angry!" she snapped, stomping her foot.

Dr. Arbuckle Fix stuck her head into the room. "Is everything all right in here?"

"Yes, ma'am." Dix grinned. "Miss Jolie was just showin' me that she isn't angry."

"Good." The doctor nodded. "Mr. Yarrow is out in the front room. He wants to talk to you, Jolie."

Jolie felt dirty, wrinkled, and sloppy next to Strath Yarrow in his crisply starched white shirt and three-piece suit. He walked with her out to the sidewalk. "I saw Essie at the café and thought I'd see if you wanted a ride over to Scottsbluff to meet Tanner."

"I would appreciate that." He helped her up into the buggy. "Strath, did you hear a rumor that my brother and . . ."

"It's not a rumor. He and Miss April are getting married on Christmas Eve."

She shook her head. "I just can't believe it."

"Little sis was thrilled," Yarrow reported.

"You told her?"

"Yes, and she said that meant the new house would be finished by Christmas and that the cat could stay in her room and not have to bunk with the pig."

"Yes, life is simple when you're twelve."

"You don't approve of Lawson getting married?"

"My approval was not sought," she grumbled.

"Jolie Lorita Bowers, pouting is not becoming to you."

"You offend me, Mr. Yarrow."

"The truth has a way of doing that, doesn't it? Shall we change subjects?"

She watched the road as they approached the bridge across the North Platte River. "By all means. Why did you come pick me up anyway?"

"To tell you I've done some investigation of Mr. Avery," Yarrow announced.

"Oh, yes. . . . What did you find?"

"The original deed is not in the Gering bank safe like Avery said. They say he took it out. He said he didn't. Your deed might be the original."

"Oh . . . I almost forgot." She turned and grabbed his arm. "You need to talk to a Mr. Walther. He's a government authenticator. He said he could tell originals from copies, and he knows both of the Avery twins."

"What?"

"Identical twins."

Yarrow stared down at the river as they crossed over. "They don't see eye to eye, I take it?"

"That's my impression."

Strath rubbed his freshly shaven chin. "I think I need to go visit with Mr. Joseph Avery."

When Strath Yarrow drove up in front of the Imperial Café, Essie jumped up from the bench and ran out to greet them.

"Jolie, isn't the news about Lawson and April the most wonderful thing you've ever heard?"

Jolie stared at the joy in her sister's brown eyes. She took a big, deep breath and let it out slowly. *Lord, You shamed me. She's right.*

"Yes, you're right, Estelle Cinnia. It is wonderful news. We'll need to make ourselves some new dresses for the wedding.

Mama can use the material we bought in Cheyenne. I have a wonderful recipe for a wedding cake with roses in the icing. I wonder how expensive it would be to have Chinese fireworks? There will not be fresh flowers in December, but perhaps we can decorate with pine bows and holly and . . ."

Jolie noticed both Essie and Strath Yarrow staring at her.

"I know," she murmured. "It's April's wedding, isn't it?"

Nine

Lawson was the first to meet them when Tanner drove Jolie and Essie into the yard. He sprinted after the wagon. His long-sleeved white shirt was buttoned at the collar; his suspenders hung loose at his waist. "Jolie! Essie! Did you hear the good news?"

Jolie brushed back her bangs. "Yes, and congratulations."

He was out of breath when he reached the wagon. "It was Mama and Daddy who get the credit."

"They do?" Jolie untied her hat ribbon.

"Others said it couldn't be done, but she said we could do it."

"She did?"

"Don't you remember? Daddy figured out the details and made it work."

"I don't remember that."

"Remember all those nights me and him was drawin' it out on the table?"

"All I remember is the plans for levees and irrigating the corn."

"Yeah, that's what I mean."

"Wait a minute — what're you talking about?"

"Corn."

"Corn? Corn?" Jolie glanced at Essie. "Corn is the good news you wanted to talk about."

Lawson brushed his blond bangs off his eyes. "Yes, did you hear —"

"We heard that you're getting married," Essie blurted out.

"Oh, yeah." Lawson blushed. "Isn't that a fine shinley?"

"A fine shinley indeed!" Jolie puffed. "Lawson Pritchett Bowers, it was the shock of my life."

He scratched his head. "But you knew I love April."

"Yes, but I didn't know you were planning such quick action."

He held out his hand to help his sister down. "It sort of happened all at once. April takin' care of the house, me gettin' the job with Strath, the sod house bein' available. I just couldn't figure out why we should wait any longer. You aren't angry at me, are you?"

"No." She glanced at Essie. "I was upset for a moment because I would have loved to have been here and have you tell me face to face. But that passed quickly. You're right. I can't think of any reason for you to wait."

Tanner helped Essie off the wagon and strolled up to Jolie's side. "What about us? Is there any reason for us to wait?"

"Yes. It has to be when school is out. I have dresses to make. We have to get the house completed. And ever since I was nine, I've wanted a June wedding."

Tanner glanced over at Lawson. "You know, you Bowers boys are lucky."

"Why's that?" Lawson asked.

"You don't have to marry Bowers girls!"

Jolie slugged him in the arm, then pulled her hand back and held her knuckles.

"I'm goin' to check on my folks and Theo," Tanner said.

"Aren't you goin' to kiss your sweetie good-bye?" Essie prodded.

"Sure, darlin'," Tanner laughed. "Come here and give me a big smooch."

Essie stuck out her tongue. "Ahhh! Not me! Her."

"Oh, yeah," Tanner said. "I knew it was one of you cuties."

He slipped his arms around Jolie's waist. His lips were warm, firm, and slightly chapped. Jolie sighed and wrapped her arms around his neck.

"Are you sure you don't want to change the date?" He winked.

"No, how about you, Tanner Wells?"

"Darlin', you're only goin' to get one wedding in your life. I want to do it Jolie Bowers's way."

"It would be easier if we just up and got married."

"Jolie Bowers, since when did you ever choose the easy way over the best way?"

She kissed him lightly on the lips. "I love you, Tanner Wells."

"And I love you, Jolie Lorita Bowers."

"Hey . . . you aren't married yet," Essie called out.

When Tanner pulled out of the yard, Jolie turned to Lawson. "What was all that about the corn?"

"Mr. Armour bought the whole crop, and he'll pay shipping to Omaha," Lawson reported. "His rep was out here yesterday. They had a drought over in the east and in Iowa, and they're goin' to pay twice what we figured."

"Really?"

"I thought Daddy was goin' to cry when he heard that. I don't reckon he's used to succeeding at anything," Lawson said.

Jolie picked up the satchel. "I can't believe so much has happened in forty-eight hours."

Lawson turned toward his younger sister. "I heard Leppy Verdue was rescued by fourteen Shoshone maidens and a civil war cannon."

"You heard what?" Essie giggled.

"That's what Bullet Wells said."

"We should have known," Jolie said. "Where's Daddy?"

"Harvestin' corn."

"How's Mama?"

Lawson glanced toward the door of the sod house. "She's about the same, Jolie. She's sleepin' right now."

"Then let's go out where I can tell you and Daddy everything."

"I'm goin' to put DirtDoug in the barn. He doesn't feel like going out there. He's very grumpy when he wakes up from a nap," Essie said.

"He's done nothing but sleep for two days," Jolie reminded her.

"I think maybe he ate too much at the Imperial Café."

"What did you feed him?" Jolie asked.

"Scrambled eggs with onions. They didn't have any fish."

After they caught up Lawson and Mr. Bowers on their trip, Jolie and Essie hiked back to the barn. "Can we talk to Mama?" Essie asked.

Jolie studied the front of the plain two-room sod house, now dwarfed by the partially completed foundation of the new house. "I hate to holler at the house if Mama's sleeping. I thought I'd wait for someone to come out."

"It seems funny to come home and not get to see Mama," Essie said.

"Yes, it does. Let's build a fire near the barn and warm up some bath water."

Jolie had a large kettle full of well water swinging over a fire when Essie ran to the barn with DirtDoug in her arms. "Dr. Fix is here!"

Jolie met the doctor at the corrals.

Dr. Fix wore a black dress, black coat, and black straw hat. "Jolie, how is your mother?"

"She was sleeping. We haven't seen her yet. Lawson said she's the same."

The doctor stepped down from the buggy. "It'll take a while for her hearing to return."

"I suppose her sight worries me more than her hearing," Jolie admitted.

"Let's go check on her," Dr. Fix suggested.

Jolie took a deep breath. "You mean, we can go into the house now?"

"Yes, I'm lifting Gibson's quarantine."

"Lawson said he still has funny pock

marks," Essie declared.

"Yes, but they'll be all dried up. I was out here yesterday. I haven't had a new case reported in seventy-two hours."

As they strolled around the rock and concrete foundation, Lissa Bowers stepped to the doorway of the sod house. She wore a long brown cotton dress, and her auburn hair hung in a waist-length braid.

"Hi,-Mama!" Essie called out.

Lissa Bowers smiled. "Hi, baby." She looked at Jolie. "Hi, darlin'."

"Hi, Mama. Look-who-came-to-see-you."

"Afternoon, Dr. Fix," Lissa Bowers called out. "I appreciate this everyday care."

The doctor stopped twenty-five feet short of the door and held up two fingers. "Melissa,-how-many-fingers-am-I-holding-up?"

"Two. Why do you ask?"

Dr. Fix hugged Jolie's shoulder. "Her sight is going to recover."

Jolie stared at the doctor's narrow face. "Just like that, you know?"

"Yes."

Jolie clapped her hands. "Oh, that's wonderful!"

"Now let's go check on her hearing."

Essie wandered up next to Jolie. "Can DirtDoug come in the house now too? He isn't feeling well."

Dr. Fix bent over and looked at DirtDoug's eyes. "My, that's a strange name for her."

Essie grinned. "DirtDoug is a boy cat."

"Oh, no." Dr. Fix shook her head. "That's where you're wrong. I can tell when a mama is about to have some babies."

"No, no," Essie called out. "He's a boy. Really."

Dr. Fix pushed Jolie toward the door. "You go on in and visit with your mother. Estelle and I are going to give this cat a careful examination."

"We are?" Essie gulped.

Jolie scampered toward her mother, who waited at the doorway.

"No-more-quarantine,-Mama."

She towered over her mother as they clutched each other.

Jolie wiped her tears and pulled back so her mother could read her lips. "Mama,-Dr. Fix-says-your-sight-is-going-to-be-all right."

"Darlin', the Lord's been good to me."

"But,-Mama,-you-still-can't-hear."

"Can't hear? That doesn't change the

Lord's goodness, does it? Come tell me how you rescued Leppy."

"Did-someone-tell-you?"

"No, darlin'. But there's no way even the gates of Hades could stand against my Jolie Lorita."

"Mama,-I-think-I-faced-the-gates-of-Hades-too. But-I'm-not-sure-I-won."

"Come comb out my hair and tell me all."

"But-you-won't-be-able-to-read-my-lips."

Lissa Bowers gripped her daughter's hand. "If I can feel your touch, it will be enough."

"I-love-you,-Mama."

Lissa Bowers bit her lower lip. Tears streamed down her cheeks, and she nodded her head. She opened her mouth but didn't speak.

April Vockney stood near the stove, wearing Jolie's pink apron as the women entered the front room. April's chin rested on her chest. "Hi, Miss Jolie. Are you mad at me for marrying Lawson on Christmas Eve?"

Jolie swooped over and hugged the startled blonde. "April, it's wonderful. I look forward to you being my sister-in-law. Oh, that sounds nice. I've never said that before."

"You mean, you're not mad that we have our wedding before yours?" April sniffed. "I was scared to death you would be mad at me."

Jolie stepped back and shook her head. "There was never any doubt that we would be sisters-in-law. I must admit I was shocked at first at the timing. I just didn't have any idea that it would be so soon. A Christmas Eve wedding sounds wonderful and romantic."

April leaned closer as if Mrs. Bowers were listening. "Miss Jolie, I'm not strong like you. I don't think I could wait much past Christmas. Sometimes I want Lawson to hold me so bad, my bones hurt. Do you know what I mean?"

"Yes, I do. And I think Lawson Pritchett Bowers is one lucky young man."

April threw her arms around Jolie. "That's the most wonderful thing I've ever heard. When I think of how perfect you are, it shames me. Lawson said he doesn't expect me to be like you."

Jolie loosened her hug and then picked a blue string off the pink apron. "That's good because Lawson knows how imperfect I really am."

The front door banged open. "Well, isn't this a fine shinley!" Essie blurted out. She carried the big cat on its back, cradled in her arms. "Out of the way. I have to put the mother-great-with-kitties on our bed."

"She really is a female?" Jolie strolled over to them.

"Yes, Dr. Fix showed me her . . . never mind!" Essie blushed. "DirtDinah needs her rest."

Dr. Fix came into the house behind Essie and went immediately to examine Lissa Bowers. Jolie stepped into the backroom. Gibs was on his hands and knees with gun parts strewn across the floor.

"Jolie! Can you come in the house now?"

"Yes, Dr. Fix is here and says the quarantine is lifted."

Gibs jumped to his feet. "Oh, wow . . . now I can go hunt Mysterious Dave Mather."

"You might want to wait until you put your Henry back together. I believe Deputy Dix was headed out this way. You'll want to be ready for him."

"I think I'll have this Henry working. Tanner sent me a new mainspring." Gibs held out a little, flat, strap-like piece. "See?"

Jolie nodded. *How does a fourteen-year-old know how to assemble a gun from a pile of parts? He has such a wonderful mind and such a pure heart.*

Gibs chewed on his tongue. "Say, is Miss Candace still at Mrs. Fleister's?"

Perhaps not completely pure. "I'm not sure about that, Gibson Hunter. Would you like to go to town with me sometime and check that out?"

Gibs rubbed his cheek with the palms of his hands. "Not until these pox on my face disappear."

Jolie stepped a little closer. "They do make you look rather rugged."

"Really?" he grinned.

"Yes."

"I reckon I could ride along. We could scout for signs of Mysterious Dave Mather along the way."

After they took hot baths and changed their clothes, Jolie and Essie drove to the schoolhouse. Jolie couldn't find anything stolen except her pumpkin. She decided to mop the floor and scrub the desks. It was after 3:00 p.m. when Essie jumped out of the swing and sprinted to the door. "Maxwell Dix is riding in here!"

Jolie hung her apron on a nail in the girls' closet and strolled out to the steps.

"What a surprise!" she called out. "Are you on the trail of Mysterious Dave?"

"I'm headin' out to the Meekers'," Dix called from the saddle. "Got word they had a pie stolen."

"A pie?"

"That's what I was told. If Mather's still around, he'll be hungry."

"If he gets his Henry assembled, young Deputy Bowers would love to join you soon."

"I'll look forward to it." Dix took a deep sigh and let it out slowly. "But that's not why I came out here."

"Oh?" Jolie shaded her eyes with her hand. "Don't tell me you and Miss Celia have decided to elope this Saturday?"

Dix pulled off his hat. He didn't smile.

"What is it, Max? I take it that it's not good news."

"She died, Miss Jolie," he murmured.

Jolie crossed her arms on her chest. "Mrs. Mitchell?"

"Yes, ma'am. She never came to. When Dr. Fix got back from your place, she checked on the Mitchell woman, but it was too late. The doc said she had just lost too much blood."

"Oh, no . . . no." Jolie felt tears trickle down her cheeks. "Poor lady. Poor lady."

He pulled off his hat. His blond hair curled out over his ears. "I reckon she chose to live that kind of life."

"Yes, but . . . oh . . . Max . . . how tragic that a life should end like that."

"Rev. and Mrs. Leyland said they never could get her to commit herself to the Lord. Mrs. Leyland took it hard. She was with her when she slashed herself."

Jolie sat down on the step and held her head in her hands.

"Miss Jolie, I surely am sorry to have to tell you all of this."

She looked up. "I'm glad you did, Max. I like hearing it from a friend."

"The reverend asked if you want to help plan the graveside service, bein' that you arranged the one for the boy."

"I'll do what I can. Right now my heart is so heavy. I wonder if there are others around that are tormented and burdened like this, and we never know. This world is not our home, Maxwell Dix."

He tipped his hat and turned his horse back toward the road. "No, ma'am. There surely has to be something better."

Matthew Bowers sat on the front room bed. Lissa Bowers was stretched out fast asleep with her head on his lap. Lawson had not returned from taking April Vockney home. Gibs stared at the one small metal part he had left over when the Henry rifle was reassembled. Essie sat in the chair near the fireplace with the purring black-and-white cat in her lap.

Jolie hovered over the stove. "Daddy, you don't know how wonderful it is to have a bath and a clean dress and to get back to cooking for my family."

"There is something peaceful about getting us all back together under one roof."

"Lawson isn't back yet," Essie reminded them. "You would think he'd be back by now."

"He probably wanted to visit with Mr. and Mrs. Vockney," Jolie suggested.

"Why?" Essie asked.

"They'll be his relatives soon."

"Will they be my relatives?" Essie asked. "Will Mary and me be sort of like cousins?"

"Not that close, but when April and Lawson have children, their daughter will be your niece and Mary's niece."

"Children?" Essie gagged. "They're going to have children?"

"Children aren't limited to cats," Mr. Bowers laughed.

"But they won't, you know, have them right away, will they?" Essie probed.

"I'm sure they'll wait . . ." Matthew

Bowers began but was interrupted by Jolie's cough. "Oh?"

Jolie wiped her hands on a tea towel. "It's my prediction that you'll be a grandpa before next Christmas."

"Oh?" Mr. Bowers ran his fingers through his sleeping wife's long auburn hair. "Yes, well, there you have it." He shook his head as he stared at his wife's face. "Grandma and Grandpa? Jolie, your mama doesn't look a day over sixteen herself, does she?"

"Not in your eyes, Daddy. She will always be your young bride." Jolie peeked into the oven. "If this pie doesn't hurry up, it will never cool for supper."

"What kind of a pie, Jolie?" Gibs asked.

"It's called a Savannah pie. I got the recipe from a magazine. It has apples, pecans, and Fresno raisins."

"How can it be a Savannah pie if the raisins come from California?" he quizzed. "I wonder if this is a gun part or just something I found under my bed?"

"Perhaps the lady who first baked it was named Savannah," Jolie suggested.

Essie stroked the cat. "I like that name. When DirtDinah has her babies, I'll call one of them Savannah. And another Baltimore, and one Raleigh, and one Atlanta,

311

and one . . . I wonder how many she'll have?"

"You're going to name one Dougie, aren't you?" Jolie challenged.

"Oh, yes! I love it."

Plates were scraped clean when Jolie poured coffee for her father, mother, and herself and then sat back down at the table. "Daddy, did you want some more potatoes?"

"Darlin', you feed me until I'm stuffed."

"Do you want some pie now?" she pressed.

"Let's just relax and sip our coffee."

"Are we really going to get the new house built by Christmas?" Jolie asked.

"That's my goal. With help and a little good weather, we might." He sighed and shook his head.

"What's the matter, Daddy?"

"I was just thinkin' about the house. Do you know, that corn crop is the first thing since your mama and I married that I actually succeeded at? We will have enough money to build most of the house, and we have a contract for next year's corn, which means the bank will probably lend us enough to finish the house."

"How much more do you think you'll

need, Daddy?" Jolie asked.

"According to my calculations, seven hundred more dollars. Maybe a thousand if we bought furniture."

"I'm so happy for you, Daddy," Jolie said.

"Yet here we sit, and Avery's in town trying to take this away from us. It doesn't seem fair to lose the only thing I ever did right."

"Daddy, we aren't going to lose it. Strath is working on the case."

"Do you think he can do it for us?"

"Daddy, I think Strath Yarrow is the kind of lawyer I would be if they let women into law school."

"He's a bulldog, eh?"

"Yes, he is. And a good friend of ours."

Mr. Bowers turned his wife's head toward his. "Let's-all-go-to-town-tomorrow."

"Do I get to drive?" Lissa Bowers asked.

"Of-course." He winked.

"What about the corn crop?" Lawson asked.

"I don't think it would hurt if we waited one day."

"Good," Lawson grinned. "I want to look at buyin' Miss April a ring."

Jolie glanced down at her ringless finger. *Lord, I'm not going to be jealous. I'm not going to be jealous.* "I need to check on arrangements for poor Mrs. Mitchell."

"I'd like some pie now," Lissa Bowers requested.

Everyone jumped.

"I was too loud, wasn't I?" she whispered.

"It's-okay,-Mama," Jolie replied. "I'll get the plates. Gibs, fetch the pie. I put it on the window sill."

"Oh, no!" Gibs cried out. "I forgot."

Jolie glanced around the room. "What did you forget?"

He stared down at his scruffy brown boots. "You said you wanted to cool the pie, and I figured it would cool better outside."

She marched over to him. "Where's my pie, Gibson Hunter?"

"On top of the well house. I'll be right back."

"What's it doing there?" Essie called out.

"It's a long story." He blushed.

"And?" Mr. Bowers pressured.

"See, when I went to the privy, I took my Henry and the pie."

"To the privy?" Essie asked.

"I set the pie on the well house and was peeking out the privy door with my Henry just in case he snuck in." Gibs waved his

314

hands as he spoke.

"Who?" Lawson questioned.

"Mysterious Dave Mather. Jolie said he stole a pie from Mrs. Meeker. But if he knows anything, he would rather steal one of Jolie's pies."

Jolie shook her head. "You used my pie as bait?"

"Yeah, but it didn't work. I don't reckon the same bait catches the fish twice."

"And then you forgot my pie on the well house?"

"I'll be right back." Gibs dashed out of the house.

Jolie cleared the table. "Daddy, did you really say he could go with the sheriff and Max to look for Mather?"

"It means the world to him, Jolie. I think he'll be safe enough. The sheriff won't let him get in too tough a spot. He can tend the horses and things like that."

The front door banged open. "I forgot my Henry!"

"If you have to shoot the pie," Lawson laughed, "aim for the raisins."

Gibs ran back into the yard. This time he left the front door open.

Jolie tugged on her mother's arm. "Mama,-I-bought-you-some-beautiful-material-in-Cheyenne-City. I'll-make-you-a-dress-for-Lawson's-wedding."

"He'll make a wonderful husband," Lissa Bowers whispered.

Jolie continued to clear the table. "Daddy, did you write to Grandma and Grandpa yet?"

Matthew Bowers sipped on his coffee. "Mama wants you to write the letter."

"I'll be glad to see them." Jolie carried six small plates to the table.

"I'll feel much better if I can get the house finished enough to be useful," Mr. Bowers said.

"Max said he and the boys will help." Jolie glanced over at her sister. "What're you doing?"

"I'm going to tie this ribbon in DirtDinah's hair. She said she likes ribbons."

"Did she ever mention why it was she didn't tell you about being great with kitties?"

"She's a little shy about such delicate matters." Essie shrugged.

"Delicate?"

"The daddy cat ran off," Essie announced.

"Oh, poor dear." Jolie glanced at her father, who was shaking his head.

A rifle shot brought them all to their

feet. Lawson was the first one out of the house.

Jolie was the second.

Matthew Bowers scrambled behind her, his shotgun in his hand.

A dirty, unshaven man danced around the woodpile. He clutched a bloody hand. Standing about ten feet away, Gibs kept the Henry rifle pointed at the man's head.

"Get that gun away from the kid. He's crazy!" the man screamed.

"That's Mysterious Dave Mather," Gibs reported.

"The kid's crazy. I ain't Mather. I'm just a thirsty man who wanted to drink some clean water. That North Platte is just too muddy. You cain't shoot a man for getting a drink."

Gibs didn't lower his gun. "He was eatin' the pie with his fingers."

"I'll admit to givin' in to temptation, but I've never seen a pie abandoned by a well before."

"He's got a boot gun. He started to go for it when I checked the lever," Gibs announced.

"Mister, raise your hands up high," Matthew Bowers commanded.

"What kind of family are you? You shoot a man for getting a drink of water or a taste of pie. Where is your Christian charity? The kid shot the dadgum pie right out of my hand."

Savannah pie was splattered like a buffalo chip in the dirt.

"Gibs, I've got him covered. Hand Jolie your Henry and disarm him," Mr. Bowers commanded.

Gibs handed her the gun, whispering, "Don't pull the trigger. The gun's jammed. It was a lucky shot. I aimed over his head just to stop him."

Jolie pointed the gun at the man. "Gibs, did you ever fix the hair trigger on this gun?"

He glanced back. "No, be careful. Don't even touch that trigger unless he tries to run."

Gibson pulled one revolver from the man's belt, another from a holster. He found a pocket pistol in his right boot and a Bowie knife with a twelve-inch blade in his left boot.

"Mather, you travel well armed," Matthew Bowers stated.

"I told you I ain't Mather."

"Just a pie-stealin' vagrant who carries three revolvers and a knife. You could have sold a couple of those and had yourself a fine meal," Matthew Bowers remarked.

"Do you think anyone as smart and cunning as Mather would be livin' in a cave along the river and stealin' food?" the man fumed.

"Gibs, are you positive this is Mysterious Dave Mather?" Mr. Bowers asked.

"Yep."

"That kid doesn't know anything," the man groused.

Matthew Bowers moved in closer to the man, the shotgun still at his shoulder. "That's where you're wrong, Mather. There aren't two men in Nebraska who know outlaws better than Gibson Hunter Bowers."

The man's hand wound bled down his shirt sleeve. "You believe him?"

"I can take his word to the bank," Mr. Bowers insisted.

"I'll go get some ropes to tie him up," Gibs reported.

"But I'm injured."

"You're in luck. Jolie knows a little about doctoring. She'll clean you up and sew you up," Mr. Bowers told him.

Mather shook his head. "I'm hungry," he mumbled.

"We have roast pork, black beans, and sourdough bread in the house," Jolie offered.

"You got any coffee?" he asked as Gibs tied his hands behind his back. "I haven't had a good cup of coffee in two weeks."

"I'll go fetch you a cup right now," Jolie offered. "Mr. Mather, would you like sugar in your coffee?"

"Yes, ma'am," he murmured.

She glanced at her father and saw him wink.

Then Jolie turned back. "If I can find some clean Savannah pie in that pan, would you like some of it?"

The gunman stared down at the ground. "Eh, yes, ma'am. I reckon I have a weakness for pie."

Jolie had on her flannel nightgown and was combing her wavy auburn hair when Mr. Bowers came back into the house.

"How's Deputy Bowers and his prisoner?" she asked.

"They're both sleeping."

"Is that safe?"

"I'll go back out in a minute. Gibs had us wrap and tie Mather in a tarp, and we used the chain hobble and fastened one end to his ankle and the other to Pullman's fetlock."

Jolie continued to comb her hair. "Pullman?"

"I told Mather that if he laid still, the horse wouldn't stomp him or drag him across the prairie."

"But, Daddy, Pullman wouldn't wake up if you blew a trumpet in his ear. There's never been a horse that can sleep like him."

"I know that . . . but Mather doesn't." Matthew Bowers grinned.

Jolie woke up before daylight, but she could hear a fire pop in the fireplace. She slipped out of bed slowly, knowing Essie and DirtDinah were still asleep next to her. The wooden floor felt a little dusty and very cold. She fumbled for her stockings and carried them with her as she ducked through the blanket divider that separated the girls' side of the room from the boys' side. Then she slipped into the front room.

Matthew Bowers sat in a homemade chair by the fireplace. He glanced up from a book. "Morning, darlin'. Lawson came out to relieve me with guard duty in the barn; so I got the coffee boiling. It should be ready by now."

"Making coffee is my job, Daddy," she whispered.

"No reason to whisper. Mama can't hear. The boys are in the barn, and little sis wakes for no one."

Jolie poured two cups of coffee and set them on the hearth. She pulled a wooden chair up beside her father's and sat down and tugged on her socks.

"What're you reading, Daddy?"

"How to run wires through the house so you can have electric lights."

"But we don't have electricity out here."

"I know, but we will someday. If I can afford it, I'm going to put wires and lamp sockets in the new house. Then when we do get electricity, I'll be ready."

"Gibs said there would be a reward for Mather. If there is, he thinks we should use it to help get the house built by Christmas."

"We don't have to be paid for what we're supposed to do," Mr. Bowers declared. "We're not bounty hunters."

Jolie sipped her coffee. "I have a theological question for you, Daddy."

He rubbed his thick, graying mustache. "Does it involve suicide?"

"That's my second question. But here's my first question: If I pray for a certain thing . . . is the Lord limited as to how He answers that prayer?"

"Limited?"

"For instance, let's say I wanted guidance, and I prayed, 'Lord, show me what to do next.' Is He limited to an audible reply? Or to writing on the wall? Or to guiding me to a specific Bible verse?"

"I reckon He can answer you just about any way He wants. But it will be legal, biblical, and moral. Now what is the subject we're really talking about?"

"Daddy, I've been praying since last summer that the Lord would provide us some extra funds so you could build Mama her house. Now perhaps with the reward money, He's done just that. There's nothing illegal, unbiblical, or immoral about a reward. What if that is the way the Lord wants to answer my prayers?"

Matthew Bowers grinned and shook his head. "You got it in your mind we should accept that reward, don't you?"

"Daddy, you could wire up the house for electricity and do a whole lot more. You could buy Mama a new bed and some furniture."

He folded the book and traded it for a coffee cup. "You are a persuasive woman, Jolie Bowers."

"I don't think you ever called me a woman before, Daddy."

"Jolie Lorita, you are a woman, and I'll never get used to that fact. . . . Are you sure Gibson wants to use it all for the house?"

"All Deputy Bowers wants to do is drive up to the sheriff's office and turn in Mysterious Dave Mather. That will be the thrill of his life."

"Let's take both wagons," Matthew Bowers suggested. "We'll all go in the big wagon."

"And let Gibs drive the other wagon with Mather?"

"What do you think?"

Jolie clapped her hands. "Oh, yes, Daddy. Let's do it!"

Mr. Bowers stared at the flames. "Jolie, in a few weeks Lawson will be gone."

Jolie reached over and rubbed her father's shoulders. "He and April will be next door to us."

"You know what I mean. Things will forever be different. And then in a few more months, my Jolie Lorita will be gone. It'll be a new chapter in your life and in ours."

"What're you trying to say, Daddy?"

"What I mean is, you have completely grown up, and I never could provide you with the life I wanted to."

"Daddy, don't you start talking that way."

"Let me finish, darlin'. I'm not nearly as

melancholy as you think I am. My point is, I couldn't give you stability. We've lived in a dozen houses since you were born. And you surely didn't get financial security. You've had to work outside to put groceries on the table for months now."

"But I'm not complaining, Daddy."

"Shhh. Let me finish. But I have provided you with three things. You know what it's like to love another and to love your family. You know what it's like to trust the Lord for your daily provisions. And you know how to live a life that's not boring. Every day is exciting around here. Now that's the best I can do for you. I would have liked to have done more. But it's not too bad, is it?"

Jolie threw her arms around her father's neck. "It's wonderful, Daddy. I only pray I can do that much for my family someday." She kissed her father's cheek. "I love you, Daddy."

"I didn't do so bad, did I?"

"You did wonderful, Daddy." Jolie kissed his cheek again.

"Jolie Lorita, are you kissing on my man?"

Jolie stood and faced the front room bed. "Morning,-Mama. Yes,-I-was-kissing-your-man. He-just-happens-to-be-the-best-daddy-in-the-world."

"Matthew, when is that girl going to get married and move out on her own anyway?" Lissa Bowers laughed.

"It-won't-be-all-that-long,-Mama," he replied.

"I need one of you to help me get up. I've got a team to drive today," Lissa called out.

"I'm-goin'-to-put-on-my-shoes-and-go-milk-Margaret," Jolie said. "Your-man-will-have-to-help-you-get-around."

"Oh . . . I like that," Lissa replied.

"Yes,-Mama,-I-thought-you-would."

Ten

Gibson Hunter Bowers drove the smallest of the farm wagons north toward the railroad tracks. His slouch hat was pulled low across his tanned face. His dusty white shirt was buttoned at the top. A brown wool vest sported a deputy badge and covered his leather suspenders. His ducking trousers had been brushed and his worn brown boots polished. He held his head high. His old beat-up Henry rifle was on his lap. A bright yellow Nebraska sun illuminated the outlaw, still rolled and tied in canvas, tossed in the back of the wagon.

Jolie sat beside her father in the bigger wagon. Lissa Bowers drove. Essie and Lawson sat behind them.

"Daddy, doesn't Gibs look good up there?" Jolie asked.

Matthew Bowers wore his brown suit, vest, dark brown tie, and spice tonic water. "He was born for that role, Jolie. I don't think I've ever known a more focused kid in all my life. I don't imagine Mysterious Dave Mather will be the last outlaw he brings in."

Jolie clutched her father's strong right arm as they bounced down the dusty road. "Daddy, do you think there has ever been a family like ours?"

He patted her hand, then winked. "You mean in the States or in all of North America?"

"How about in the entire world?" She grinned.

"Are you limiting that to the nineteenth century?" he teased.

"Daddy, ever since Adam, Eve, Cain, Abel, Seth, and those girls . . . do you think there ever has been a family like this one?"

"No." He smiled and gave her a hug.

"Me either," she replied.

When they reached the corner by Strath and Landen Yarrow's house, Lissa Bowers pulled her wagon alongside Gibs.

"Little brother," she called out, "is everything all right?"

"Yeah, Mama," he yelled.

"I'm going to let the big horses run. We'll meet you in town," she called out.

He tipped his hat.

Matthew Bowers pulled his wife's chin around so she could read his lips. "My-word,-Melissa . . . do-you-think-that's-safe?"

"Which?" she laughed. "Me racing to

town or leaving Gibs with the outlaw?"

"Both," he mumbled as the lead lines slapped the horse's rump.

Jolie almost tumbled into the back of the wagon as Stranger and Pilgrim bolted west.

Lissa Bowers handed her straw hat to her husband and then stood up in the wagon. Her auburn hair hung in a thick braid down the back of the charcoal gray dress with white lace on the cuffs and collar. Her narrow face was bronzed. The normal creases around her eyes melted away with the wind plastering her face. Her white teeth beamed through her smile as she slapped the lines and rocked up and down on bent knees.

"Yes," Lissa called out. "Yes . . . yes . . . yes . . . yes. Thank You, Jesus!"

Mr. Bowers glanced at Jolie, shook his head, and grinned.

Lissa Bowers didn't sit down until they came to Bobcat Gulch, and she didn't slow the team until they roared into Scottsbluff.

"Too bad we didn't have Mysterious Dave with us," Lawson called out. "That would have put the fear of the Lord in him."

"I'm glad DirtDinah was too tired to come with us. I would have had grandkitties by now," Essie commented

"I'm feeling very good, Matthew. Did the boys' hooves thunder?"

"Mama,-I-think-you-woke-up-some-residents-of-China!" Jolie replied.

"I like that . . . but I miss the noise. At least I have my wind. Where are we going now?"

"I want to go to the land office," Matthew Bowers replied. "We can't invest one more penny in that new house until we're sure the title really is clear."

"Mama,-take-me-by-Tanner's,-and-then-I'll-wait-for-Gibs-at-the-sheriff's-office," Jolie mouthed.

Jolie found the Platte River Armory closed. She sauntered around to the alley and beat on the backdoor, but there was no answer.

I could take a quick peek at the oak wardrobe closet. He would never know.

Her hand was on the cold, round brass door handle. She pulled it back.

No, Jolie Lorita, you do not have to know everything. You do not have to control everything. Lord, this is hard for me. Really, really hard.

She backed away from the alley door, meandered back to the street, and strolled toward the sheriff's office.

Mr. Tanner Wells, it's 10 a.m. on a Monday. Your hours say 8 a.m. until 6 p.m., Monday through Saturday. You should be at work. How are you going to make a living and support a wife if you don't show up for work? I can't understand how you could desert your place of business. Was there an emergency? Are you injured? Did you go to the hardware store for a tool? Did the sheriff need some help? Did some lady need some help?

"Stop it." Jolie was surprised to hear herself speak aloud. "There's a perfectly reasonable explanation."

"Are you talkin' to yourself?"

She looked up to see Luke and Raymond sitting on the bench in front of Saddler's Grocery store.

"Oh, yes, I am. I'm giving myself a lecture."

"I was trapped in a cabin with Two-Tone Tony Gee all one winter, and from Christmas until the thaw all he did was talk to himself all day long. He didn't say one dadgum word to me except Merry Christmas, and then in April he said, 'See you next fall,'" Luke reported. "Much to my happiness, I ain't seen him since."

"Did the sheriff ever find Mysterious

Dave Mather?" Luke asked. "I heard he was out at your schoolhouse."

Jolie brushed dust off the sleeve of her dress. "Someone broke into the school, but I have no idea who it was."

Luke pulled out a square of tobacco and offered it to Raymond and Jolie.

Both declined.

He bit off a chaw and shoved the plug back into his pocket. "I'd like to be there when the sheriff arrests old Mather. Yes, sir. I was in Chadron right after he robbed the bank. At least they said it was him. You can't always tell. He can fool ya. Why, he's . . . he's . . ."

"Mysterious?" Jolie supplied.

"Downright mystifying," Raymond added.

"Why don't you boys walk over to the sheriff's office with me?" she suggested.

"You need some help, Miss Jolie?" Luke asked.

"I want you to see something. I know you aren't busy." She slipped in between them, took their arms, and led them along the sidewalk.

"Shoot, Miss Jolie," Raymond drawled, "me and Luke learned the first day we met you that something excitin' happens ever' time you come to town."

"I think that's an exaggeration. Some trips to town are quite boring and routine."

"Name one," Luke challenged.

"I can't think of one," Jolie laughed. "But there must be one."

A buggy rattled up and parked alongside them.

Jolie released the men's arms and stepped to the curb. "Good morning, Candace. I'm surprised Mrs. Fleister let you out of her sight."

"Yes, Aunty Mildred can be quite possessive. I think she means well." Candace toted a yellow parasol over her shoulder. "In a smothering sort of way."

"What brings you downtown?" Jolie asked.

Candace's dark black hair made her white face glow. "I'm going to the bank. What time does it open?"

When Luke pulled off his hat, his gray hair flopped over his ears. "Mr. Meynarde opens it at 8:00 a.m."

"He opens it? I thought perhaps the bank guard opens it," she murmured.

Jolie's green eyes widened. "You need to see Chug?"

"I told Charles I would stop by and see him at work."

"Charles?" Raymond quizzed.

"Charles Quintin LaPage," Jolie explained.

"Mrs. Meynarde reports that he's extremely effective at his vocation," Candace said.

"Ol' Chug's got sand," Luke blurted out. "He'll stand and fight."

"Miss Jolie is the only one to ever chase him out of town with a gun," Raymond added.

"She did?" Candace gasped.

"Me and Luke was standin' right there."

"That was my first day in town," Jolie tried to explain. "Chug has been a good friend ever since."

Raymond spat in the dirt and then wiped his mouth on his sleeve. "He ought to go out with Dix and find that Dave Mather."

"Is there really a man named Mysterious Dave?" Candace asked.

"Yes, there is. You might enjoy coming over to the sheriff's office with us. It's not every day you'll see such an adventure," Jolie suggested. "This is something you won't see back east."

"Oh, my." Candace smiled. "I get a front row seat on one of Jolie Bowers's legendary adventures."

"I'll just be watching with the rest of you," Jolie informed her.

Candace Clevenger drove the buggy alongside the pedestrians as they proceeded east. Nadella Ripon and Pearl Anderson stepped out of the meat market as they passed by.

Jolie paused, and so did Luke, Raymond, and Candace, who was still driving the buggy.

"Jolie, dear, did you hear about poor Mrs. Mitchell?" Nadella asked.

"Yes, it's so sad."

"I heard you were making arrangements for the service."

Jolie took a deep breath and loosened her hat ribbon. "I'll check with Mr. Mendez and Rev. Leyland. This is not a role I want to repeat often."

"Are you going to mention the cause of death?" Pearl Anderson quizzed.

Jolie tried to study the thin woman's deep-set eyes. "Eh, well . . . I'll leave that up to Rev. Leyland."

"Yes, of course. We should talk to him. She died of an apparent heart attack, you know," Pearl declared.

"I hear she —," Luke began.

Jolie poked him in the ribs.

"Yes, it seems her heart just stopped beating. Probably died of a broken heart," Nadella added.

Jolie nodded.

"If the sheriff watched his prisoners more closely," Nadella complained, "perhaps we would have fewer heart attacks in our jails. He and the deputy are wasting their time trying to catch Mysterious Dave Mather. The man is much too smart to be captured. Why, I'd like to see the person who could bring in that outlaw."

"I'd like to see that outlaw," Pearl murmured.

"If you ladies would come with me, I think you'd enjoy witnessing something," Jolie invited.

Sheriff Riley and Deputy Maxwell Dix stood on the porch in front of the jail as they approached.

"Miss Jolie, if you're leading a riot, I'll resign," the sheriff laughed.

She glanced at the crowd following her. "No riot."

"Miss Jolie promised us a show," Raymond explained.

"A show?" Max inquired.

"Just wait a minute or two," she advised.

Sheriff Riley rested his hands on his hips. "I was just telling Dix that I got a telegram from North Platte that Mather was seen spyin' out a bank there. So I guess we're done with him around here."

"You can telegraph them back and tell them they were wrong," Jolie said.

"What do you mean?" the sheriff pressed.

"Ask your deputy," she replied.

The sheriff turned to Dix, who pulled off his hat and shrugged.

"Your other deputy." Jolie pointed to a farm wagon rattling down the street toward the sheriff's office.

They all stared as Gibs circled the wagon in the middle of the wide dirt street and pulled up in front of the sheriff's office. He tied the lead lines to the hand brake and jumped down on the boardwalk, his Henry rifle still in his hand.

Gibs tipped his hat to the young woman in the buggy. "Mornin', Miss Clevenger, you surely look handsome today."

"Why, thank you, Gibson. You look quite mature with a gun and a badge," she replied with a wide, easy smile.

Sheriff Riley stepped over to him. "Son, I told you only to wear that badge when you're actually doing deputy work."

While only fourteen, Gibs was almost as tall as the sheriff. "Yes, sir. I know."

"Gibs, do you know where Mysterious Dave Mather is?" Maxwell Dix asked.

Gibs glanced at Jolie and grinned. "Yep."

"Where?" the sheriff asked.

"He's in the back of the wagon, Sheriff." Gibs pointed. "I've been doin' deputy work, like I said."

"What?" the sheriff exclaimed. He led the whole procession to the back of the wagon.

"Well, I'll swan," Luke drawled. "He's got him hogtied."

"But . . . Mather is in North Platte," the sheriff mumbled.

"Are you sure you got Mather?" the sheriff quizzed.

"Oh, that's Mysterious Dave," Pearl gushed. "I never forget an outlaw!"

When the excitement died, and Mather was safely locked in a cell, Jolie and Gibs crawled back into the wagon.

She held on to his arm. "You were wonderful, Gibs. I'm so proud of you."

"Thanks for getting Miss Candace there," he said.

"She just happened to drive up."

"Some things are just meant to be." He smiled.

Lord, I can't tell him she has her sights set on Chug. "It's a wise person who can accept the Lord's leading in his life."

"Do you think I impressed her?"

"I think you impressed the entire state of Nebraska," Jolie declared.

"Didn't know there was a thousand dollar reward. It went up since last month. I thought it was only seven hundred dollars. That should help with building our new house, shouldn't it?"

Jolie tied on her hat as her brother drove back out into the street. "Yes, but I don't know if Daddy will let you do that."

"Nothin' he can do about it," Gibs grinned. "I told the sheriff I wanted the entire sum placed in the Bowerses' account at the lumberyard."

Jolie clapped her hands, then hugged her brother. "Oh, that's wonderful! What made you think to do that?"

"I was ponderin' it all the way to town."

Jolie shook her head. "Some days, Gibson Hunter, I feel like I'm the youngest of the Bowers kids. Are you really only fourteen?"

"I'm fourteen and a half," he corrected her. "Hey, there's Lawson. I think he's waving at us."

Gibson stopped in the middle of the street. Lawson ran out to them. "Jolie, come help me pick out a ring for Miss April. I can't decide which one to buy."

"Go on," Gibs told her. "I'll find a place to park the rig."

Jolie climbed down from the wagon and scurried with her oldest brother to Brownberg's Jewelry and Watch Repair. Lawson led her over to the case of gold rings.

"How much did you want to spend?" she asked him.

Lawson swallowed hard. "Twenty dollars."

"Oh, my!"

"I've been savin' up for years."

"Yes, well . . ." Jolie's eyes searched the case. "I know the exact ring you should buy. It's my favorite, and I'm sure April will love it."

She studied the case. "It's, eh . . . engraved with . . . oh . . . oh!" she gasped. "It's sold!"

"I like this one." Lawson pointed to the case.

"But — but that was my ring." She scooted to another glass case. "It's got to be here."

Lawson pointed to the case. "What do you think, Jolie?"

"But I wanted that one," Jolie sniffed.

Lawson sauntered over to his sister and pointed at the case. "Maybe I should buy this one over here."

"I don't want any other ring," Jolie said.

"I'm not buying it for you, Jolie. I'm buying it for Miss April."

She took a deep breath. *Lord, it isn't fair. You know I wanted that ring. I've looked at it for months. I should have bought it for myself.*

"If it isn't Miss Jolie Bowers."

She spun around. Tanner Wells stood on the other side of the small store.

"Why aren't you at work?" she blurted out. "Your hours state 8 to 6, and I just went by, and you weren't there."

"Did you sneak in the backdoor?"

"No, I did not!" she snapped.

"Whoa. Miss Jolie is having a bad day, I take it." He strolled across the hard wooden floor. "Now what is it that made you so animated?"

"Someone bought her ring," Lawson explained.

"Oh?"

"It was just that there was a ring I liked. I'd been looking at it for months."

"And you never mentioned it to me?"

"You needed to save money. I knew that. It's not important," she sniffed.

"Was it the one with rubies and diamonds?" Tanner pressed.

"No, it was plain gold and engraved with clusters and leaves — simple elegance. I've never seen one like it in my life. It was a silly girl's dream. Really, it's okay."

Tanner hugged her shoulders. "Sounds like you had your sweet heart set on that one ring."

"Yes, and I know better than to covet the things of this world. The Lord is teaching me a much deserved lesson."

"Yes, He is," Tanner agreed. "But not the lesson you think."

Jolie's eyes widened. "Oh? Just what lesson do you think He's teaching me?"

"That Jolie Lorita Bowers does not know everything and can still be totally surprised."

"What are you saying?"

He pulled something out of his pocket. "I'm saying that I bought you a ring." He held it out in the palm of his big, callused hand.

Jolie covered her mouth with her hands. "You . . . you . . ."

"It better fit since I just paid twenty bucks for it." He slipped it on her finger. "What do you think?"

"I think it's wonderful!" she sobbed.

"What's wrong?" Lawson asked.

"Nothing," she wept, staring at the ring on her finger.

"But you're crying."

"I've never been happier in my life," she sobbed. She threw her arms around Tanner's neck and kissed his lips.

Essie burst in through the door of the jewelry store. "Are you kissin' him again? You're as pathetic as Mama. Come on, Daddy wants us to meet them at the courthouse."

Jolie pulled back. "Lawson has to buy a ring."

"I already bought a ring, Jolie. I was just sayin' that to get you in the store so Tanner could surprise you," Lawson admitted.

"You ganged up on me?"

"Get used to it, darlin'." Tanner smiled. "Now I'll go open up the shop. You'll stop and see me before you head home, won't you?"

"You're supposed to eat supper with us at the hotel."

"Which hotel?" he asked.

"That depends on how things go at the courthouse," she answered. "Tanner Wells, you're the sweetest man alive."

"No. But as long as you think so . . . I'm a lucky man."

"I'll come by a little later," she promised

as she followed Essie and Lawson out to the wagon.

They climbed up into it, and Gibs drove toward the courthouse.

"What's all this about?" Jolie asked.

"We spied Strath Yarrow on our way to the land office, and he told us to go to the courthouse. Judge Whiting is going to rule on our deed and Avery's claims."

"Who's Judge Whiting?" Jolie asked.

"Strath called him in from Lincoln," Lawson announced. "The other judge is on vacation."

"He can do that?" Jolie asked.

"Strath knows a lot of judges."

Joseph Avery stood in front of the judge's desk as they entered the court-house. He held his hat in his hand; his nose was red and crooked. Strath Yarrow stood to the left.

Strath looked up and motioned for them to come over to the desk. "You're just in time. Judge Whiting has the ruling."

Avery waved his finger at Matthew Bowers. "Yes, and I demand protection from that man. He broke my nose." He scooted behind the judge.

"Good thing we have a deputy." The judge nodded at the badge on Gibs's vest.

"What?" Avery gasped. "He's one of them."

The judge motioned for Avery to go around in front of the desk. "Do you want my ruling or not?"

Avery nodded and shuffled around next to Strath Yarrow.

The judge cleared his throat. "According to the expert testimony of Mr. Walther, a government-employed authenticator, the Bowerses possess the original deed to the contested property. It has been determined that they purchased it in good faith. However, evidence leads to the conclusion that it was Mr. Avery's twin brother Jacob who sold it to them. In other words, it was a stolen document and should revert back to the original owner."

"Oh, no," Jolie gasped. When she looked up, only her mother, who had heard nothing, was smiling.

"However, if Mr. Joseph Avery presses the claim, he will owe the Bowerses for all the improvements made to the place, which include rebuilding the roof of the house, construction of irrigating levees, and a foundation for a new home, among other expenses. The total will exceed the original purchase price. In addition, Mr. Yarrow has collected nine false claims on the place, with five more to follow where others have been deceived into buying it. If Mr. Avery chooses to reclaim the property, I am told that he will be sued by these claimants. If they win the case, he will need to make full restitution of each other claim plus legal costs."

"What? You can't do that. That was my brother who kept selling the place."

The judge turned to the legal clerk. "So ordered."

"But — but —"

"What is your choice, Mr. Avery?" the judge asked.

"They are trying to steal my valuable property!"

"I have written testimony of a witness who states that when you left town 370 days ago, you told him the property was worthless because it flooded every year, and you never wanted to see it again." Strath Yarrow held up a handwritten document.

"Who made up those lies?" Avery shouted.

Strath Yarrow handed the sheet of paper to the judge. "Sheriff Riley. Shall I call him in so you may call him a liar to his face?"

"You may sign a quit claim," the judge announced, "or you may pay them what is due."

"Pay them? It was my brother who cheated them," Avery whined. "Am I my brother's keeper?"

"I think the book of Genesis sufficiently answers that question," the judge mumbled. "You pay them and then collect from your brother."

"Collect from that crook? I don't even know where he is."

"Excuse me." The legal clerk cleared his throat. "I moved here recently from Lake City, Colorado. There is a Jacob P. Avery who has a one-third interest in the Honeywell Mine there. If that's your brother, he has the funds to repay you. The man looks identical to you except that he has a mole on his left cheek, instead of his right cheek."

"He's got a gold mine?" Avery mumbled.

"I believe it's only a third of a gold mine," the clerk corrected.

"My dear, sweet twin brother?" Avery mumbled.

"What is your decision?" the judge asked him.

"About what?" Avery stammered.

"The homestead."

"Oh . . . well . . . I have other pressing matters. I don't have time to sort this out."

Avery headed toward the courthouse door.

"Mr. Avery, I've prepared a quit claim for you to sign," Strath Yarrow said.

"I really don't have time. I need to go to Colorado."

Strath Yarrow followed him to the door. "Mr. Avery, if this quit claim isn't signed, I'll file suit on behalf of nine claimants that your agent knowingly and maliciously defrauded these people."

"My agent?"

"You'll have to prove in a court of law that your twin brother was not your agent. You can imagine what a Nebraska jury of homesteaders will think of that," Yarrow maintained.

"Are you blackmailing me?" Avery huffed.

"In front of a judge?" Yarrow asked. "Not at all. I'm just helping you understand the implications of your actions so that you might act with wisdom."

Judge Whiting stood. "Mr. Avery, may I ask why you abandoned your place?"

"Because it's worthless and floods every year!" he blurted out.

"Then why did you return?" Jolie asked him.

"I heard that . . ." Avery paused. "Never mind. It's not totally worthless."

Strath Yarrow shoved the legal document at him. "If you legally sold the place to the Bowerses on this date, then you are cut free from litigation stemming after that point."

"No one can sue me?" Avery pressed.

"No," the judge assured him.

Joseph Avery glanced at his gold pocket watch. "I need to catch the stage down to Kimball."

"Yes, I imagine you do." Yarrow blocked the door. "Just step over to the judge's desk and sign this paper."

Avery stalked back to the desk and dipped the quill into the bottle of black India ink. "I should never have come back here," he mumbled as he rubbed his still swollen nose.

"How would you have learned of your brother's gold mine?" Jolie asked.

A slight smile broke across Avery's face as he signed his name. "That's true. Very true." He marched to the door, and Matthew Bowers blocked his path.

"My word, you aren't going to strike me again, are you?" Avery said.

"Mr. Avery, your obstinacy has caused my wife to lose her hearing. I'm having a very difficult time with that. However, I want to apologize for flattening your nose.

That was wrong, and I regret it. My wife is the sweetest woman the Lord ever created, and I lost control." He held out his hand. "But there's no excuse for my failure to behave as a Christian."

Avery hesitated. His back was toward all in the room except Matthew. "I'm sorry about your wife's hearing," he murmured. "I lost my wife six years ago. In the quiet of a dark night, I can still hear her sweet voice." He reached out and shook Matthew Bowers's hand, then shuffled out the door.

For several moments there was silence in the room.

"Does this mean the homestead is ours?" Essie whispered.

"It's yours, and no one can contest it again," Strath assured her.

Jolie strolled up beside her father. "I'm proud of you, Daddy."

"People are real, Jolie Lorita. We err greatly when we think of them as objects instead of living, breathing, hurting people. There was sadness in his eyes."

"And there's hunger in my stomach," Essie called out. "Can we go eat now?"

"I think we'll go celebrate at the Nebraska Hotel Restaurant," Mr. Bowers announced.

"Daddy, that's very expensive," Jolie cautioned.

"My family deserves it," Matthew Bowers insisted. "Strath, would you like to join us?"

Strath gathered up his papers. "Any other day I'd love to, but I have to meet with Mr. Fleister. I'm thinking of renting a room above his hardware store for an office."

Jolie bounced on her toes. "That's wonderful! 'Strath Yarrow, Attorney' painted right on the window."

"Strathmore Yarrow," he corrected her. "I figure I need an office just to keep up with all the work I do for the Bowerses."

"You'll go broke if you have to survive on what we pay you," Matthew Bowers laughed.

Strathmore Yarrow, Esq., loosened his black tie. "Being an attorney is not about money; it's about justice. It's a sad day when anyone forgets that."

"Your real name is Strathmore?" Essie asked.

"Yes. Quite ostentatious sounding, isn't it? Mother had a flair for names. I will never tell you my middle name."

"Jolie will find out," Essie promised.

"I already know." Jolie smiled. "And

your secret is secure. It's quite an unusual name."

"There you have it, Estelle Cinnia," Strath laughed. "It's impossible to keep a secret from her royal highness."

"That's not true," Lawson piped up. "Tanner just did it."

"He's a better man than I then."

"Of course he is," Essie agreed. "He's got Jolie."

Mr. Bowers sat at the end of the long linen-covered table, his back to the window that faced the street. Crystal goblets, gold-rimmed china plates, and silver utensils lay in front of each one. To Matthew's right sat Lissa, Jolie, and an empty oak chair. Across from them Lawson, Gibs, and Essie completed the seating.

"This is like Thanksgiving," Essie exulted.

"You're right, little sis," Matthew pronounced. "We're celebrating the first corn crop in western Nebraska."

"Plus having a quit claim on the homestead," Lawson added. "When I thought of losing all our levees and ditches, I about cried."

"And Gibs's capturing Mysterious Dave Mather," Essie added. "With the reward money, we'll have our house built quicker. DirtDinah is very excited about staying in my second-story room. Pigs can't climb stairs, can they?"

"That hog is not getting in the house," Jolie insisted. "And we certainly are thankful for Lawson and April's engagement. That's worth celebrating."

"I'm glad Essie and Jolie got Leppy out of jail without being arrested," Gibs reported, sporting scattered remnants of facial pock marks.

They all turned to Lissa Bowers, who sat sipping her coffee and staring across the room.

"What-do-you-say,-Mama?" Jolie asked.

"I've never seen anything like it," Lissa Bowers whispered.

"We-are-celebrating-some-wonderful-things, -aren't-we?" Jolie replied.

"No, I mean the lady over at the table by the door." Lissa nodded. "I've never seen anything quite like that. She's one well-dressed woman."

Holding a white linen napkin in front of his mouth, Matthew Bowers whispered, "That's one large woman."

Jolie glanced up to spy a gray-haired woman who looked about sixty years old sitting by herself in front of a table overflowing with rich food. "Oh, my," Jolie gasped. The woman, who Jolie guessed weighed a good 250 pounds, slowly dipped green grapes in what looked like chocolate gravy.

She wore a round skirt of pleated white gauze with little embroidered gauze ruffles and a diamond-shaped mesh scarf. The dress had a tablier front and a pouf in the back held up on the side by three huge bunches of hyacinths. A diamante white gauze corsage adorned her fichu neckline above a vestee simulated by a garniture of the same embroidered gauze as the skirt. A three-strand diamond necklace draped down across her ample bosom. Dangling diamond earrings seemed to catch every sunbeam in Nebraska. Rouge colored her cheeks and drew one's eyes away from her full, unpainted lips. Her hat was white straw, with a wide ribbon around the crown and rosettes and plumes on the raised part of the brim in electric blue velvet.

Jolie was still staring when Tanner strolled into the restaurant and sauntered over to the large woman's table. After a brief conversation, he came over to the Bowerses' table.

"Hi, darlin'. Is this chair for me?" He

slipped in beside Jolie.

"We already ordered for you," Essie announced.

"Tanner, do you know the lady by the door?" Jolie asked.

"Yes. She seems quite nice. She came in and ordered two ivory-handled Colt pocket pistols. She's going to South America soon."

"Who is she? I don't think I've ever seen her before," Jolie remarked.

"She used to live around here, but she has lived in Paris the last few years. She's on her way to San Francisco and will take a ship to Chile from there."

"Why did she come here?" Essie asked.

"To visit a few old friends," Tanner explained.

"What's her name?" Jolie inquired.

"Don't you know?" Tanner grinned. "That's Mrs. Shinley."

"Shinley?" Jolie gasped.

"Mrs. LaFina Shinley," Tanner announced.

"She's. . . . she's the original 'fine shinley'?" Essie asked.

"Apparently." Tanner grinned.

Jolie held her chest and tried to catch her breath. She leaned over and tugged her mother's chin around so that she could see

Jolie's lips. "Mama,-that-lady-is —"

Her mother patted Jolie's arm. "Shhh, darlin'. Not so loud. You wouldn't want Mrs. Shinley to hear you."

"Mama!" Jolie cried. "You can —"

Lissa Bowers placed her finger on her eldest daughter's lips and whispered, "Yes, Jolie Lorita. The Lord has been quite good to me. Poor Mrs. Shinley."

About the Author

Stephen Bly has written more than 80 books for adults and kids, including 11 series for Crossway. Besides writing, he serves as pastor of the Winchester (Idaho) Community Church and is the town's mayor.